Good

by Peter J Larrivee

Other Books by Peter J Larrivee
(In no particular order)

Revenant

Legend Haunted

Icon

No man is an island

Entire of itself

Every man is a piece of the continent

A part of the main

- John Donne

Foreword

This book has been a long time coming, started initially over 5 years ago, and has been a quiet little pot on my back burner ever since. The last year of work was spent in fits and starts, trying to not only finish it, but actually complete it, edit it, polish it until it was ready for the light of day.

Initially inspired by a graveyard hidden in the woods behind the apartment where I live with my family, this book took on a life of its own as I spun the characters into existence, raised the story from an ash heap multiple times and incorporated some ideas experienced while house hunting.

Please note that none of these events are actually real, but drawn from imagination and stories, or echoes of things that have happened to others, appropriately changed, amplified or exaggerated for effect. Except for the bit about the insects not chasing me past the gate of the graveyard. That was pretty weird. I literally tested it and every time I stepped past the bars, the bugs came back. Step back within, they back off. Maybe there were some anti-bug herbs there or something. Yeah, let's go with that.

I guess we'll never know now, though. A developer bulldozed the land and put up half-million dollar homes. So, whoever winds up in that particular house, best of luck, my friend.

And now, the *trigger warning*.

This book is a work of horror, and before we even get to the spooky things, there's a lot that happens to the characters that involve a lot of cruelty. Some truly terrible treatment of children by terrible parents and the resulting psychological damage that haunts them later in life. Please be aware of this and make your decisions on reading it accordingly. I'm not looking to hurt anyone with this book, and in fact, this is very much about thriving and being a better person *despite* terrible past trauma, or even because of it.

In that way, I hope this can be a little bit healing for people, but I also understand that it's a difficult and personal journey not everyone is ready for.

But if you're going to move ahead anyway, then thanks for taking the chance. I love and appreciate you. I'll see you on the other side.

Prologue
1805

Beneath a frosted night sky, glowing with cold radiance, the wind swept a brisk, hateful gale through flesh and bone. Among the darkened pines that stabbed into the New England night sky, a pair of figures stood on a muddy bank. With grim, wary eyes they gazed into the calm waters before them.

The echoes of stars shone back at them, dancing on the subtle waves. In the air, a sickening smoke still lingered, mingling with a mournful mist that crawled along the dark water, roiling and seeking, like ashen tendrils. A mournful sigh slipped from one silhouette, a taller man who wore a wide-brimmed hat that collected stray pine needles when they fell. His face was leathery and lean from sun and age, and the white collar around his neck felt especially tight this evening. He turned to his companion, who shared the somber sentiment of the evening, but hid it beneath a perfectly calm, neutral face, as he was used to doing. The eyes of that stoic man hid a kind of darkness, one the preacher was reluctant to even contemplate for long. Yet he could not keep his peace. He spoke.

"This will weigh upon my soul," said the preacher.

A noncommittal grunt followed from his companion.

In the distance, that crawling mist rolled across the water, something ethereal and haunting. It glided over the surface, settling upon lily pad and driftwood.

"My friend," said the Magistrate, putting a heavy hand upon his shoulder, "We did what we had to. There can be nothing left. The Earth had to be salted that nothing else could grow."

"God forgive us," said the Preacher.

"He will," said the Magistrate, "For we have done his work and banished the evil to the depths."

The Preacher turned, walking away from the ponderous dark waters. His mind was as clouded as the mired waters behind him. For he knew the deed had to be done, but to watch all those souls perish for the madness of just one twisted man, taxed him too heavily. The punishment was severe, nay, biblical. His brow furrowed as he walked back up the hill. The stench of burning wood, crops... flesh... still lingered in the air.

The Magistrate remained at the water's edge, and looked out on the gentle ripples with some satisfaction. It would be short lived, though. Odd shapes began to appear in the glittering murk, and soon, the lumpy, bloated backs and faces began to pierce the surface, their horrified eyes glinting in the scant starlight, locked into horrified rictus at the apathetic night. Gentle ripples swept away from the bodies. The mist settled over them like a shroud and the Magistrate wiped away his own tears as the thick, damp air filled his sorrowful lungs.

His heart would carry this guilt, and he would happily bear that cross so that something worse could not be loosed upon an unsuspecting world. Only he and his God-fearing friend saw the horror within that barn. They did what needed to be done. An evil like that cannot be suffered to live, nor mar the Earth with its vile filth.

Chapter One

Tommy crooned along to *'Sweet Home Alabama,'* as the F250 bounced along the rutted dirt road, kicking up a train of dancing dust in his wake. It was one of the first warm days of the year, and the sun that poured in through the windshield gently baked the 24 year old man, and his 2 year old canine companion. The jet black mutt sat next to him and attempted to croon along to the dulcet tones of Skynard. Outside, the sun cooked away the morning dew and released a choking moisture into the already muggy air.

By the diminishing presence of power lines and street lights on his long drive, he knew that he was nearly there. Signs of civilization, or more to the point, people, dwindled to the occasional power line above, or the reinforced mailboxes that stood sentinel at the ends of driveways. Each one had its own particular fortification against bored teenagers with cars and baseball bats. One was surrounded by thick metal pipes. One was literally half-encased in concrete. His favorite was a flat, wide box with what looked like a large wasp's nest slowly enveloping it. That one might not have been intentional, but he was sure nobody went playing mailbox baseball around here. The Skynard came to an abrupt end, cut down by an obnoxious radio ad three seconds early. The nasal, jabbering voice promised a ludicrously low down-payment on a new car, a promise surely placed atop a column of tiny print. Tommy cringed and turned the sound all the way down. That kind of shrill voice carried dark familiarity.

The dog looked at him for a moment. The gigantic, jet-black husky mutt seemed briefly confused as to why they'd stopped their howling, but was soon distracted by something else out the window. He let out a little woof and pawed at the door.

"Easy, buddy, easy..." Tommy said with a smile, "You can chase all the squirrels you want when we get there."

Then dog seemed appeased by this, and let its tongue loll out as he panted happiness.

Tommy didn't see the huge rut in the road, and the entire vehicle bounced wildly, tossing some loose papers and pens around the cab, and causing the pooch to almost tumble, scrabbling with his paws to stay upright.

The truck skidded a little and the drag from their cargo hitting the rut almost made Tommy lose control of the vehicle. He slowed down and glanced in the side-view mirror. The camper seemed to still be attached, and with any luck, nothing inside was broken. But he'd have to do something about that rut. Was that even on his actual property? He'd have to check. Not that it actually mattered, since if he was driving over it every day, he was going to fill it in somehow. Tommy didn't like living with easily fixable problems that were left unfixed. Little items like that annoyed him. It was an unfinished job, the worst kind.

Up ahead he could see the break in the tree line, and the point where the old power lines ended. He smiled and reached out to ruffle the fur of his excitable companion.

"Here we are, Mac," said Tommy, "We're home."

He pulled the gleaming truck up the long dirt driveway. Ahead of him squatted the massive rotting hulk of an old manor, a blend of Victorian and Gothic architecture currently home to only rats, termites, and the stench of decay. A single turret rose above the flaking rooftop, with one glass eye that looked over the field of dry weeds like a cyclops, standing sentinel over long years. Everything about it was gray with age, flaking, drying up, like a long dead corpse. Even the sloping roof of the porch looked like a jaw hanging open, with just a few rotted teeth left.

Sitting there, coated in wild dust and yellow pollen, was the little red Honda. He'd hoped she'd be here first. He felt a little guilty now, making her take this rutted old road out here again in a vehicle designed for zipping about city streets, but he wanted to get started as soon as possible, and it was faster to just meet her here. He even had the paperwork for the work permits half-filled out, and some already approved. Not that he expected anyone way out here in the thick sticks to care even a little what he did to gut and rebuild the ancient house. This place was so distant from civilization that there would probably be trouble getting his mail delivered. He still made sure he had all the necessary paperwork signed and stamped, but that was for him. There would be no Homeowners association, no nosy gossipy neighbors, no cul-de-sac concentrations of pasty people with more free time than sense.

His truck came to a stop, and a small cloud of dry dust from the road wafted around the sides. Mac started barking and bouncing around the cab, desperate to be released into the wild. His claws scraped gently at Tommy's thighs as he barreled over towards the driver's side door. Tommy obliged him and opened the door. The black furry missile fired out onto the dusty driveway and bounded off towards the tree line. So many trees to sniff and mark, Tommy thought, that dog would have a lot to do. He was used to a small city apartment and daily walks to the median of grass between shopping plazas. It was hardly enough for an energetic pup. The endless trees and weeds were a feast for his canine soul. And he didn't need a leash. Out here, no semi carrying sugary liquors threatened to slam into the overexcited pup. No speeding Hondas with badly-modded spoilers, or motorcycles with careless riders would threaten him. Tommy almost wished he could live here himself, but that wasn't the plan.

Tommy slid out of the truck right after Mac had zoomed off into the foliage. He closed the door with a solid thunk. He took a brief pause to check the camper, making sure nothing was broken or out of place after the rough jostling. The right rear wheel looked a little askew, and Tommy was both irritated and relieved. It could have been worse. It looked like just some rim damage. If it had happened further out from the house, he'd have had to turn back or figure out how to fix it on the side of the road. He did not want to try to figure out how to load it onto a tow truck. For the next six months, this was going to be his home while he made the property habitable for humans instead of termites.

His feet crunched on some rough grit as he approached the manor. The ground of dried, dead grass and gravelly earth that might have, at some point, been a paved path crunched underfoot. Although with the age of this property, maybe it was cobblestone he trod upon. Tommy turned his attention from the brittle dry ground to the looming gray behemoth:

Three stories of old world architecture, plus the attic, a tall spire with a big iron spike at the top, and a stone foundation right out of the 1800's. It looked like hell, but it was his vision of heaven. The front porch had a leaning roof over it, and there were some rusted old gutters that hung down from the sides. The shingles were flaking away and sun-bleached from time. The windows were almost all broken, with the exception of the one at the top of the hexagonal spire. There, a small window looked out over the property, coated in grimy cataracts. One could probably see all the way to the lake in the back from up there.

He heard footsteps, and turned towards the little red Honda. Linda was clearly not dressed for the terrain just as her car was unfit for the roads. She was in professional garb, and the lines in her 50-something face were wrinkled in worry as she approached Tommy. They rearranged into a professional smile when their eyes met, and she seemed to stride with more confidence, despite her modest heels almost causing her to stumble on the patches of weeds and rough, pitted ground.

Tommy extended a coarse, calloused hand, which she took gently.

"Well, Tommy, it's all yours," she said. She handed over a Manila envelope with a small set of old wrought-iron keys taped to the corner. "Are you really sure about this?" she asked.

Not that it mattered now. It was too late to back out. Tommy would lose a hefty deposit and a *lot* of buying power if he backed out now. But even then, if you went by the numbers, it was a gamble to keep it.

"Absolutely," said Tommy. The woman shrugged.

"Okay. But if you ask me, what this place needs is a pack of matches."

Tommy laughed. It was true, the old manor was pretty much uninhabitable, and buying it even for as little as he paid for it was borderline crazy. But Tommy had a vision, a plan. He just shrugged.

"Okay," she said skeptically, "But even if you do manage to flip this old place, I don't know if it will be worth it."

"It will," said Tommy. He smiled at her and took the envelope. The keys taped to it were ancient, toothed things, except for a single modern key that looked completely out of place with the old forged iron.

"Well, I wish you luck. Let me know if and when you're ready to sell," she said, "But this place has scared off a dozen investors before you."

"I'm looking forward to this. This right here, this is my early retirement."

She just shook her head. She couldn't understand. The housing market was a strange economy all of its own, and so many people looked at properties like this and thought they were best demolished. Tommy personally knew people who would level all of this land and put up a condo complex, or build cookie-cutter cul-de-sacs with crisp, sharp houses on perfectly manicured lawns and pristine, modern, white fences. Nothing made Tommy shudder more than the thought of destroying all of this. But more to the point, even if he built a dozen homes on this property, who would live in them?

No one could afford those sharp-edged homes anymore.

More to the point, no one wanted them. People who could afford them could afford better. And the people who could afford better than that, well... They would salivate at the chance to own a genuine historical home, with plenty of open land. They'd pay their grandchildren's inheritance, and a couple of their own limbs for something like that. True earthen beauty beat glistening plastic every time. One bored Newport yacht club member would fork over millions for land like this with a genuine manor.

Tommy smiled, remembering the night he'd found this little gem. He'd left a rough job site after a *long* day of being hassled with inspectors and town officials over the damage done by downed trees in the freak storm, one that still hadn't finished unleashing its fury. The winds were still gusting wildly, and as Tommy climbed into the truck to get out of the downpour, he saw a text from his boss that he could finally leave and let the bureaucrats sort out the mess.

He was happy to leave that madness behind, but then he had to find his way out of the labyrinthine woods. Twice he had to stop and get out his chainsaw to cut through downed trees, and he still hadn't found the main road yet after half an hour of twisting dark country roads. The sky darkened to near black, and soon he was rumbling on pebbled dirt with no GPS signal, poor visibility, and the only illumination from the rare branches of lightning that struck the forest around him.

He'd mistaken the driveway for another road, and soon found himself pulled up next to the gothic monster of a long-abandoned manor, illuminated by a furious sky of fire and a torturous downpour. Tommy very slowly, carefully, backed out and tried to navigate away. Somehow he kept taking wrong turns and passing the house over and over again. But between the familiar downed trees and this house, he was able to eventually get his bearings. It became his North star, and then he found his way back to the main road, the highway, and then home. But the image of that house was burned into his mind, like some strange fever dream. For weeks he tried to find it on a map, first checking the obvious places online, but it was oddly elusive even there.

He had to find it again, see if it was real or if he was losing his mind. He googled the area, and located a satellite view of the old home with no context for property or value. He needed to know more. He was endlessly fascinated.

The property wasn't listed online, or in the paper, or even on most property sites. It was perfectly hidden, viewable only on satellite maps and in some obscure records. The old Worthington manor was almost an urban legend, and even when he called the town hall, those who knew the legend didn't think it was still standing. Rumor had it that the place had burned to the ground in a freak thunderstorm years ago, but it was still standing... mostly. Only the realtors had any solid, reliable info on it, and getting them to part with that took the better part of a month of playing phone tag.

The first time he viewed it during the day, it looked as if a stiff breeze would send it tumbling into a pile of rotting timber and mossy stone, but Tommy didn't see a worm-eaten corpse... He saw a mansion. Tommy saw the kind of upscale, wealthy home that the rich, reclusive people in Newport and Martha's Vineyard shell out ungodly amounts of money for. It was miles from any other house, and had vast yard space, deep woods, and a great big pond. It was unclaimed, untouched, and slightly wild. By the time Tommy was done, it would be worth a fortune.

He knew just what he wanted to do, too. After touring the place with Linda, he set the layout to memory and sketched everything out on graph paper. He calculated the square footage of wood he'd need to completely re-do the hardwood floors. He felt that the load-bearing walls and posts were mostly good, that the foundation was solid, and the land itself was worth at least as much as the house, if not more. If he went to the extra trouble to plant some feature plants, like grapevines and throw together some inexpensive trellises for them to wind around, he'd make money just renting it out for soap operas to shoot there.

But the work it would take, the investment of time, the paperwork to either show it met code or was exempt from code, to say nothing of the physical labor and the structural engineering... The details and logistics were staggering.

Its price was so low because those who had tried to flip it before him never made it very far, and would sell it off again. But Tommy was certain he could do it *and* turn a profit. Despite being the sole laborer for most of it, Tommy knew enough about construction work to outline what he could do, and what he couldn't do. He had an entire plan mapped out on paper for the interior and exterior. The lumber was being delivered according to very specific orders.

He was a carpenter by trade, and dabbled in plumbing and wiring. He picked up tips and skills from other people he met on job sites. He had learned a whole new way to look at how a house was built, and during other rehabs he'd worked on, he would watch would-be flippers absolutely blow up at his boss over the cost of a project jumping up because of cracks in a foundation, old pipes from a town water supply still connected and dripping behind the walls, or finding cat pee soaked into the subfloor and needing to toss almost everything down to the joists. He knew the ways an old home like this could become a financial nightmare.

And if he was going to sweat and put in long hours, it might as well be on his own flip. He'd be spending a fraction of what professional flippers spend just to buy a property, and he'd get ten times his investment, if not more.

He'd accumulated a ton of overtime pay by agreeing to work insane hours, and he had a side job for the state that filled up his evenings and his bank account. That, plus the little Christmas gift from his father allowed him to offer a large amount of cash up front, which was another prerequisite these days. But shockingly, the bank that held the property seemed unconcerned about the form of payment. They were eager to get it off their books, and somewhere, one of their underwriters must have been happy to sign off on the sale.

But they didn't realize what a gold mine this could be. It would take a lot of time, but by the time he was thirty-two, he'd be sitting on a three or four million dollar property that he bought for 100k. Thinking of all this, he felt a smile touch his lips. It would be the last time he worked himself to the bone for someone else to be rich. Now it was his turn. One last, big job. One great big investment. He'd retire on the money from this flip. He'd retire young, and laugh at everyone in his life that ever told him he'd never amount to anything. He'd find whichever prison, rehab facility, or asylum his mother was in and rub her face in his success.

He'd send pictures of his life of luxury to his stepmother, and stepbrother, and let them stew in their fury.

"I hope you're right," said Linda, shattering his train of thought, "If you can flip this for what you think you can... yeah, maybe we'll both retire early."

She gave Tommy a look. There was a lot of skepticism in those eyes.

"It doesn't look like much, but this house has good bones," he said.

She laughed. "Yeah, but the flesh is rotting off."

Linda had always been straight with him. True, she was desperate to unload this horrible property, but she'd also told Tommy right from the start that she didn't think it was worth his time and money.

But Tommy was adamant. More importantly, he wasn't going to take 'no' for an answer. He had a plan, and he wasn't going to let go of it.

She didn't argue. But she did tell Tommy every grimy detail, every failed sale, every foreclosure.

Tommy wasn't the first person to want to flip it. It had changed hands several times over the years. It seemed like everyone who got in there to start never got past some light demo or surveying. She said it was probably full of mold and rats, and fleas because of the rats. She didn't even know the property existed until Tommy showed up with maps and bank records to her office, and said he wanted it, and needed someone who could facilitate the sale. Even back then, she assumed he was either crazy or ignorant, which he proved incorrect at every turn. Tommy was thorough, determined, and stubborn. And every time they met to sign documents or go over details, she still tried to talk him out of it.

Tommy actually appreciated that. He wanted someone to challenge him. Almost like he needed it. Like he had to have someone tell him 'no,' so he could then spit in their face in defiance. But at the end of the ordeal, she ran out of arguments and he put his signature on the bottom of the page, the same page stuck in a manila envelope now his most cherished possession.

Tommy walked the property for a little while after she left, exploring the vast space. Weeds and grass rose as high as his knee, bordered by bare dirt paths not yet totally reclaimed by flora. A huge boulder sat in the center of the sea of drying greenery. Tommy climbed up onto the top. The stone was warm beneath his hands. He took in a breath as he stood a little taller, looking over the land.

From up there, he could see the water from the pond in the woods a few hundred feet back. He knew there were some old stone steps down there that led to a crumbling dock, and a rotted old gazebo set over the calm waters. His minds eye saw it as it could be, fully restored and gleaming, a little shed by the water's edge with a rack for rowboats, or maybe kayaks.

A great swath of tangled weeds to his right would be the perfect spot for a big old barn, or maybe a guest house if he had sufficient time and an unexpected windfall.

From the back, Tommy could see the great stone chimneys that rose up nearly as high as the spire. The house seemed more flat from this angle, cobblestone foundation peeking up from the ground beneath the wooden shingled exterior. The wood was grayed from alternating wet and hot dry weather, sun bleached with old paint peeling in volute curls.

The back door was a windowless, thick old hunk of oak, as weathered as the rest, but holding its own against time. The grain was worn, and parts scratched as if randomly assailed by wildlife. Some of the finer details of the hand-carved wood were worn away, turning gray like the stone beneath. Tommy approached this back door. He unlocked it with one of the old iron keys and stepped inside. It took a moment for his eyes to adjust to the sudden gloom, as only hazy light came through old grime-covered windows. He stood in the mostly brick kitchen, with some half-assed tile work from whenever the last renovation was attempted. A small stack of old linoleum was left in the corner. God, linoleum! In a place like this!

But the gold mine was the big fireplace oven, the bricks a bit worn and stained by time, but replaceable, or repairable. There was enough room for one of those old-style witch cauldrons above a real fire if someone was so inclined.

Some of the walls were bare to the studs, but Tommy didn't mind, it was easier that way. He considered those areas his blank slate, and he had the most fun sketching various uses for the space on graph paper..

He could see through to a little pantry area, and next to that was a big white-painted door that led to the basement.

The basement was dry and cool, but significantly darker. Several configurations of sticks and grass spoke of some kind of animal nests that were now long since vacated and dusted over with gray. The cellar windows were mostly broken, but a few remained intact with the same screen of old grime upon them. There were a few different rooms down here, separated by stone archways in the foot-thick cemented cobblestone. But the foundation, support beams, everything was made of solid, strong material that resisted the age that had ravaged the rest of the house.

Tommy climbed back up, and passed through the kitchen to the dining room, probably the room that would need the least work. The hardwoods were in great shape, needing only a sanding and refinishing, and the walls were actually finished drywall, just waiting for some paint. Clearly the last flippers were competent at this, but for some reason didn't go much further.

Next came the living room area, with its huge stone fireplace, complete with a cast iron grate. They had apparently used this room as their staging area on prior remodel attempts. There were still some old tools, a hammer here, a tape measure there, and a small scattering of beer cans with labels Tommy hadn't seen since he was a teenager. One old brown bottle had mold-coated cigarette butts and dark brown water inside. Had these been the contractors, or bored teenagers that found a secret place to drink cheap booze?

He climbed the staircase to the upstairs. There, a long hallway stretched in both directions, with a half-dozen rooms abutting it. One of these rooms was probably intended to be a bathroom at some point, but was currently just sub flooring and bare walls, with some exposed pipes gaping at him.

Each little room was bare, and apparently hadn't been changed much over the years. They had been painted at some point, possibly back when Disco was in fashion, as they had a distinct 70's vibe, vivid orange and greens. The closets were seemingly crammed into corners at haphazard angles when the house was first built. At the end of the hall were two offshoots, with a set of stairs going to the right, and a set of stairs going to the left. Tommy climbed the left stairs, and found himself in the master bedroom, which took up most of the top floor of the house. It was a mess, with boards over the windows, and lit only by shafts of renegade sunlight casting beams over the dust. It was roomy, with space for almost anything, and Tommy could even see putting a full bathroom up here without much loss to the square footage, and depending on time and materials, a balcony overlooking the property.

The other set of stairs led to a locked door, which Tommy had assumed was the top of the spire, and possibly another bedroom, but to his annoyance, it was locked. They had tried every key on walk-throughs before, but none of them caused the old metal to budge. He could always break it down, but just for fun, he tried one of the old iron keys in this lock again. Nothing inside would move.

He grunted with half-hearted annoyance. It irked him that he couldn't get in, but he didn't feel invested in the feeling. He could take his time. He had plenty of work ahead of him, this room could keep its secrets for a little while longer.

Back down to the ground floor, Tommy concluded his tour by walking through what might have been some kind of den at one point, and then to a final room with built-in shelves on the walls, like an old study. The old woodwork was painted over with some insane orange color that Tommy intended to strip away at the first opportunity. It was clearly once that same vibrant 70's color, but time had eroded it into a faded yellow where it hadn't been covered by spare lumber, old tarps or layers of dust.

Outside, Mac was barking. He'd finished with his own tour of the property and its various trees and wildlife, and now looked for his best friend. Tommy smiled and stepped out the front door, where he saw Mac circling the truck and looking around with confusion.

As soon as he saw Tommy, the pup bounded over in glee, almost jumping into Tommy's chest.

"Okay, buddy, okay," said Tommy, "Time for supper."

Tommy went to set up the camper. Mac followed, showing off all the mud and grass in his fur with a big sloppy grin on his face. At some point he'd gotten his paws wet, so he likely had been down by the water. The poor puppy had a massive sensory overload, and Tommy was certain he would not be able to bring him back to the tiny apartment after this.

"Come on, boy," Tommy said, "Want some meat?"

Mac knew what that word meant. He hopped excitedly in a circle and his tail fanned back and forth in a blur, shedding twigs and pine needles.

A half-hour later, Tommy had a small circle of rocks and the beginnings of a nice campfire. He removed a big cooler from the camper and started roasting hot dogs while Mac paced back and forth hungrily. He didn't seem interested in the kibble in his dish. He wanted the tiny tubes of pork meat and salt. Tommy knew he shouldn't indulge him so much, but this was a special day, a day to celebrate.

Tommy sipped a beer and looked at his prize as the sun drifted down into the tree line, bathing the scene in long, intricate shadows. First thing in the morning, he was going to go through the house with a fine-toothed-comb, make sure he had everything on his list for the first phase of the renovation.

Mac paused to chew at a phantom itch, and Tommy waited for him to finish before tossing a hot dog at him. The beast caught it in the air and bit it in half. He gulped down one half, while the other fell to the dirt. Mac went in search of his dusty prize. Tommy chuckled and sat back, feeling the warmth of the fire clash against the chill night air creeping up on his back. It would get cold tonight, and the cool breeze coming off the lake would carry with it the moisture and scent of wet pine.

He could imagine living here. He could imagine rising with the sun, strolling through lush fields of green. He could imagine the smell of breakfast cooked on a wood stove floating on the soft breeze.

Though this home was far more lavish than he needed, he could see the appeal. Country-cooked meals, fresh eggs and meat lingering in the air on a crisp morning... He could almost taste the smoky bacon in the air. Or maybe that was just the fire.

He reclined back in his folding chair and looked up as the first few white pinpricks of stars appeared in the growing ebony sky.

Five years of work, and he would be a millionaire. He would have a modest home, he would have freedom from the grind, and he would have respect. He could do whatever he wanted, and never spend another day working to make someone *else* rich.

Chapter Two

Many tears had landed on the hard stone floor, disappearing into the damp, mossy masonry. The only noise was the beating of her heavy heart and her desperate tiny whines as she tried not to make any noise.

Children are meant to be seen, not heard.

With both hands clamped over her face, almost suffocating herself for fear of making noise, she whimpered quietly and shivered in the cold. Her back burned from the sting of the lashings, the cold air taking some of the pain away. Her skin had been turning cold and clammy for hours, making her shiver and shudder. Still, she was desperate not to cry out even when the cold became an aching agony. The only light came from the floorboards above, the only noise the creaking of the heavy wood as *he* stepped to and fro upstairs.

He would pass the cellar door now and then, and her heart would leap in dread, her body flinching from the expectation of new, fresh pain. But then he would step past, and she would relax slightly into her more comfortable, anxious misery.

He said she deserved it. He said it was because she was filthy, she was unclean, and God was punishing her. He said he would continue to bleed her dry as long as she was dirty, and only then would she be pure. Only then would he, and God, accept her.

He said this every time it happened. She'd taken to using rags and scraps of cotton to try and stop up the bleeding every month, then burning the remains, but he somehow always found out. He always knew.

She could hear the distant muttering of tiny, quiet voices. Her younger brother and sisters sitting in prayer, begging for God to keep them clean and pure so they would never be unclean like she was.

Little Peter was crying. He was the youngest, and understood the least. And she knew, not far away, the others would be locked up in prayer as well, some literally. She prayed to God... Prayed for her mother to come back. Her mother had shown her warmth, shown them all warmth, and always had been able to soothe the fury of her father, like calm waters. Those arms that would hold her, that gentle voice that would sing in the mornings, the soft woman of mercy who was faithful and kind... She longed for that tender touch again.

The footsteps approached the trap door. Her heart leapt in terror.

The horrible creak rang like a peal of thunder in the dark silence. Dim firelight cascaded down through a haze of dust, illuminating her pale, marred skin and emaciated face. The light, dim as it was, hurt her eyes.

"You will come upstairs now," he said, his silhouette somehow darker than the blackness of her prison. "You will be cleansed."

She rose, numb, climbing the stairs on bare, calloused feet. As her naked form emerged from the cellar, she heard the cries of anguish from her siblings who were sneaking peeks at the long red gashes on her back.

The tall, imposing man who was her father grabbed her by her long, muddy brown hair and dragged her towards the door. It hurt, yanking on her scalp, threatening to pull off of her skull. She screamed, which earned her a hard slap across the face from a large, rough hand.

Her siblings wept uncontrollably, which seemed to only fuel his ire.

"*Return to prayer*!" he barked.

The front door opened, and she was hurled out into frigid cold. Icy rain assaulted her thin body, relieving the burning of her wounds, but sapping the life from her bones.

"You shall baptize in the tears of God until you are clean!" he shouted in his shrill voice. She turned to look at him, and in the dim orange haze from the firelight, she could see the madness in his eyes, the burning hatred for her.

"Hateful harlot!" he shrieked, "Whore of Babylon! Clean thyself and return only when you are pure!"

Wracked with sobs, she shivered in the freezing cold. Through the tears she saw the light disappear with the heavy slam of a hard wooden door, and a thick clunk of an iron lock.

She wept in the rain, bleeding from between her legs, as she did from the wounds on her back. But the cold was making her numb, and slowly taking away the pain. She looked back at the house, illuminated from within by the various stone fireplaces and lanterns. Far in the back, the barn sat in terrifying shadows. She could find refuge there, hide among the others, the foundlings that father had taken in and held in his house of God until they were deemed worthy and pure...

She tried to run for the barn, but her legs stumbled, too numb and weak, and she collapsed into cold mud. Her naked body went white with cold, frozen pain. She couldn't go on, she'd never make it to the barn.

She rolled onto her side, curling up into a ball, trying to hold whatever heat was left in her body.

She thought of her siblings within the house. She would be free soon, but they would be trapped for their entire lives within the home of her father, trapped with his hatred and rage. They would suffer the love of a God that existed only in words. In her sobbing gasps, she choked slightly, as the bark of harsh laughter forced its way out, into the night. Her breath fled her mouth like a wraith. She wondered if that was her soul, flying away to Heaven, but knew deep down, that was not where she would go when the cold took her.

Millions of tiny icy daggers from heaven struck her limbs. She prayed to God to send her to the fires of Hell that maybe, just maybe, she might know warmth again. But God did not answer. Something else did. A warm embrace did take her, and she rode into safe, black dreams.

• • • •

The morning came with an unexpected heat, damp and heavy, it woke Tommy early. The typical New England weather shifted from one pole to the next, bringing a swampy punishment from the weather gods. He was sweating profusely, and Mac wasn't helping any by being curled up next to him, the thick fur insulating Tommy and compounding the overheating problem. Tommy rolled out of bed, but Mac remained sleeping peacefully. With a grumble, Tommy went to the bathroom and started washing himself off. He would need to examine the well, see if he could use it, or if he'd have to dig another. Running water was going to be a priority. Bathing himself with rags and bottled water was going to get old very fast. He'd budgeted for well re-drilling, if he had to, but the plumbing inside had worked when he checked it. It just wasn't hooked up to anything useful, yet. And who knew what kind of water quality, since the pipes going to the well could be lead for all he knew. It might be safer just to dig a new well.

After a good wipe-down, Tommy pulled on his jeans and a Metallica tee shirt. It was time to survey the mess.

Mac padded over after a good stretch and started whining for food. Tommy rubbed his back and nodded.

"Yeah, yeah, I know," he said, "Gimme a minute."

Outside, the ashes from last night's fire were dead cold, but Tommy soon had a new fire roaring in its place. He set up a tripod with a pot to heat up water, then dumped some kibble into a dish for Mac.

He watched the sun creep up towards the treetops, casting shafts of light down on the whole world. It was a damned muggy day. Working would be agony. He'd be sweating bullets from light work.

But he was determined not to waste a single day. He had a plan, a timeline, and he was not going to pass up the chance to get an early start.

Once the water was heated up, he used it to make some coffee and instant oatmeal. He ate quickly, his mind always on the job ahead of him while Mac quietly licked his bowl clean.

Tommy picked up his toolbox and sledgehammer, then headed towards the looming house. So much was going to need to be torn apart, and it was going to be brutal.

On his walkthroughs before, he'd noticed the damage done by father time and mother neglect.

He unlocked the padlock on the front door, then watched the ancient, worm-eaten portal slowly swing inward, creaking ominously the entire time. He stepped into the shadowy hallway. On his right was a large archway leading into what he thought of as a dining room, and on the left was a similar archway for a living room. The floor creaked heavily with every slight movement. Tommy thought he could hear scurrying from inside the walls. He stepped into the dining room, then through an empty door frame into a kitchen from the early 1900's. There was a big brick fireplace for cooking, with a lower and upper tier. The sink was ancient and covered in grime, a rotted out old porcelain basin, cracked halfway to hell and with a drain so rusted that the pipes underneath had to be utterly worthless even as scrap metal. The cabinets and cupboards were all moldy and crumbling old wood. The various metal handles and knobs were all rusted half to oblivion. Even the window, lazily boarded up with a piece of rotted plywood, was unsalvageable. This was where so much had to be torn, smashed, pulled, with violence if necessary. Tommy slid a pair of safety goggles on over his face.

He put the toolbox down, then hefted the sledgehammer. The sink would be the first thing to go. He raised the hammer and swung down at the old ceramic. It smashed with a satisfying sound, the hammer's head plowing through the material like it was glass, tossing shards into the air, covering Tommy with a piercing snow.

Another swing at the sink, and every stroke felt gratifying. Each time he hefted the hammer, he thought about his father, his step-family, his worthless drunk of a mother, and the strange gift that brought him here.

It was last Christmas, and out of the blue, a card in a seasonal red envelope arrived. It bore his name, and the return address had been the one he put in his rearview mirror over a decade ago. It had been forwarded a couple of times, frankly it was surprising it even made its way to him, but beyond the USPS stickers, he could feel a weight in the cheap cardboard stock. He was sure his father never wanted to see him again, but the little card had his father's handwriting, and the words weren't what he had come to expect from that man.

The old man had never been one for sentimentality, but there it was, in his signature scrawl:

"Tommy,
We'd love for you to join us for Christmas Dinner.
"Love, Dad."

He used the word 'love.' Twice. The word appeared on the card two more times than Tommy had ever heard it from this man. He almost tore the damned thing up on the spot.

His first instinct was to snub it, let the old bastard sit and stew for the whole holiday with his *new* family, the wife that secretly hated him, Tommy's half-sister that they all treated like a maid, and his half-brother that served as the receptacle for all of the old bastard's love. Even the little photo on the card told the tale, mother and daughter wearing forced smiles, the Old man grinning behind his thick glasses, and his teenage son, smirking like an imp.

Tommy drank three beers in an hour while he tried to parse out his emotions and his decision. The whole time, the phrase *"Just like your mother,"* drifted through his head. A phrase that came up every time he so much as sneezed wrong. He would get a scolding, four inches from his face, complete with yellow-brown, tobacco-tinted teeth and breath, for any infraction, no matter how minor. The ache for even the smallest amount of acceptance tugged him backwards, and his rage and defiance propelled him on.

No. He pushed it back. He felt ashamed at his own cowardice, like less of a man for shying away from the old bastard. He should face him, head-on, and confront him with all the horrible things he had to say.

And yet... those few moments where the Old Man would take him into the workshop and show him how to use a drill press, or a belt sander, usually a few hours after smacking him across the lip for calling his wife a dingbat, twisted his mind and heart. It was as if the old man were attempting to absolve himself of guilt, atoning for that sin against his own flesh and blood, but prisoner to his short temper. Tommy had more than his fair share of sucker-punches and backhands to return to the bitter old bastard. Maybe it was unkind, maybe it was even a crime, but his beer-battered brain was relishing the thought of returning that abuse with interest.

He was set to do just that, driving his truck through the thick wet rain of a typical gray Connecticut Christmas. He pulled up to the idyllic gingerbread house, nestled within the manufactured cul-de-sacs in the picturesque little town. Even from the highway, there was a sickening 'Hallmark' quality to the wholesome and artificial homes.

Across the freshly paved road, his truck idled. He sat there for ten minutes screwing up the courage to walk into the house. He had a bottle of cheap whiskey still in the paper bag, a little cheap bow around the neck. It was the old man's brand, and he wasn't sure if he wanted to give it to him, or pop the top in front of him and down the entire thing out of spite. He didn't even like whiskey, but he liked the idea of pissing him off. Tommy had grown a foot taller and gained a lot of muscle mass since he ran away.

His indecision made him feel more anxious. He stared at the bottle with fury, and the thought occurred that he could always smash it to pieces on the floor. That had a certain satisfaction to it. Ruin that finish with this one-degree-off of paint-thinner amber garbage booze, that would really infuriate him. Let him try to take a swing at Tommy NOW.

He ascended the steps to the front porch where he once started a small fire by playing with a lantern battery. There was still a slight wilt in the vinyl siding from the heat of the flames, covered over by an ornate sun decoration. It was a perfect metaphor for what he was walking into. He knocked on the door.

His heart fluttered, his rage faltered and he almost turned back, almost ran... But running wasn't an option anymore.

The doorknob squealed, then the door was pulled inward, slowly. He was greeted with the smell of cinnamon and pine, as a real tree stood in the corner of the hallway, decorated in bright glistening LED lights and shining silver bells. A rail-thin, wrinkled and stringy-haired woman appeared, her fake nails raking on the door frame, her tobacco-stained teeth exposed in a smile that was reserved for people she truly loved. His step-mother's bright face visibly fell when she realized who he was. She strained herself to put on a polite smile, but her eyes burned with cold fury. The message was clear: *"Go away, you are not welcome."* That had been the message since he was 6.

"Hi, Margot," he said. Her eye twitched. He couldn't help but feel a perverse pleasure in irritating her. She was the second mother in his life, and only slightly better than the first by the extremely low bar she set.

"Tommy," she said, "Well... Why, I didn't expect you."

He heard the footsteps rushing up to the door. He chose not to respond, not until...

"Tommy! My boy!" said the gruff old voice. The door was pulled all the way open, and his father smiled with genuine warmth.

It was... odd.

"Dad," he said, "I got your invitation."

Margot swung her head around to glare with the fire of Hell behind her eyes, but the old man didn't even glance at her. He stepped out into the cold with his illegitimate son and shook his hand.

"Tommy, I'm so glad you could come," he said, "Please, come on in. God, you got tall. You hit Six-oh?"

Tommy followed inside while he felt two burning holes of hate being drilled into the back of his head from his step-mother. He wasn't prepared for the smile, for the handshake, for the true and deep emotion emanating off of the man. This was maybe a slice of the old man like he'd been when Tommy was young, before the custody hearings, before his other children by his new wife...

The old man took them into the living room, where the half-siblings sat and held awkward conversation. Tommy's sister was the only other person who gave him a genuine smile, the portly girl of 19 wore a tie-dye sweatshirt and grungy jeans. His half-brother, though, sat in military fatigues and at Tommy's appearance, started standing up with rage burning his face red.

"Tim, Jamie," said the old man, "Look who it is."

"What the fuck is *he* doing here?!" demanded Tim.

The tone stung more than the words, but Tommy knew he deserved it. He hadn't been kind to his little brother, but then, nobody had been very kind to Tommy as a child, either. Tommy had been a baby in a house of cigarettes and needles. He didn't know what caring felt like until he was six, and that caring always came with a complicated emotional price tag.

Jamie stood, then crossed the room to hug him warmly. He could smell some kind of earthy herbs on her, and he realized how much he missed her. She had always cared, and how she had such an open heart living in this house he could never fathom. She broke the embrace quickly, and her eyes darted to the Old Man, as if expecting some kind of explanation, or perhaps a scolding. Meanwhile, Tim's fingers twitched.

"I invited him," said the old man as Jamie drew slowly back.

He looked back at Jamie, and they shared a moment of wordless connection, both survivors of a deep darkness. They were both puzzled, but enjoying the discomfort of the rest. Yet they knew such joy was shallow, short, and often ended with a storm of violence. Whatever the old man had on his mind, he hadn't shared it, and all of them were nervous.

"You *did*?!" demanded Tim, fury burning within his crimson face.

"I did," said the old man, "You got a problem with that, *boy*?"

At the word 'boy,' Tim seemed to settle, though slowly, reluctantly returning to his seat and simmering in his anger. His fingers tapped an uneven beat on the arm of the chair.

"Have a seat, Tommy, my boy," said the old man, clapping him on the shoulder.

My boy? Tommy slid uncomfortably into an easy chair next to his sister while the old man took a glass decanter full of brown liquid from a high shelf. He poured a little into small round glasses, then returned, presenting one to everyone, even Jamie and Tim, which shocked them both. Jamie was only 20, and Tim was still 19. But they took the glasses because it was their father, and you never disobeyed him. The strange jovial look on his face was baffling. This was a man who would bloody your nose for spilling cereal on the kitchen floor, or tracking mud in the house. Here he was pouring liquor for his underage kids. Tommy looked into the glass. The smell wasn't his normal cheap bottom-shelf, plastic-bottle swill. It didn't smell like paint thinner. It actually had a smoky aroma, and Tommy was surprised to realize it was some form of scotch. Good scotch, too.

"I wanted all you kids together for this," he said. From the doorway to the kitchen, Tommy could feel the haunting, eavesdropping Margot hovering and waiting to strike, fearful of her husband, but not of the bastard child that got a portion of his love. Whatever his change in attitude was about, she was as clueless as the rest of them. The old man smiled like the proverbial cat sitting next to an empty canary cage.

"Dad, what's going on?" asked Tim.

"Well," said the old man, "First we need to catch Tommy up on current events."

Tommy frowned and turned to Jamie. She smiled, but with slightly sad eyes.

"Dad... Well, Dad's been fighting cancer," she said.

Tommy didn't even have time to react. The old man laughed and slapped the arm of his chair. The sound resonated in the otherwise quiet room.

"Fighting nothing," he said, "I won! Full remission!"

"Cancer?!" Tommy spat.

"Relax, Tommy-boy," he said, raising his glass, "Because I have good news. The best news I could ever have. The doc's say I'll live another twenty or thirty years."

Tommy raised the glass, though he usually shied away from the hard stuff, he numbly sipped the sweet, burning liquor and looked at his siblings, who both had strange, puzzled looks on their faces. The mystery lurked behind that mischievous gleam in his eyes. The distant scent of Margot's nervous cigarette lingered in the air, the smoke performing a languid dance in the low lights of the tree. The silence was punctuated by crackling and popping fire logs.

He put his glass down on the coffee table and clicked his tongue. It seemed like he didn't put much thought into his big proclamation, but decided to forge ahead.

"Now, I know we ain't always been a picture perfect family. But I love you kids, all of you. And I wanted to tell you... Well, I had a chance to do a lot of thinking. See, when I was in the hospital, all hooked up to them machines and watching that little beeping line tell me I was still barely alive... Well, I'm man enough to admit, it really shook me up. I started to kinda... Kinda see things more clearly. Tommy, your Mom used to talk about that, what was it... A moment of clearness? Between bein' on one thing or another, anyway. Never lasted long. Well, that's kinda what I had, I think. Clarity, that was it."

Margot came into the room, carrying a plate of little round pastries crowned with frosting, and seemed desperate to try to change the topic of conversation. Perhaps she had an inkling of what was on his mind, or maybe she just wanted to distract attention away from the old man long enough to needle Tommy a little bit.

"Anyone want a puff pastry? I made them with real butter and even-"

"Can it, Margie," said the old man, eliciting a shocked gasp from the woman, and a cascade of fallen jaws from the kids. "I'm trying to make an important announcement. Take a seat, this is about you, too."

Margot's face went ashen, and she numbly settled onto the couch next to Tim. Tim's fingers were still beating that arrhythmic pattern until Margot put her hand over his and held them still. She was breathless, terrified...

She knew something. Or she suspected.

The Old Man nodded in approval, then chewed his lip for a moment before continuing.

"Kids, Margie... I spent ten years building this house. I spent twenty raising you two, and I've spent a quarter-century with you, Margie. And when I was lying there seeing my life laid out in front of me... Well, it made me realize something. This house... This ain't my house. I put in this floor, built those steps, put up that drywall," he said, pointing to the various parts of the living room. "I threw up from heat over there and had to replace the sub-floor."

"But this house ain't mine. I worked at the base for twenty years after spending ten in the army, and none of that stuff I did was for me. I did it for God and country, I did it for Margie, and I did it for everyone else. Well... I'm done doing that. I'm sixty-two years old, and I just had cancer scraped out of my lungs. I ain't never really thought about what makes *me* happy. But... Well, I sure know what don't make me happy. This house, my job, working hard so my money can all go flyin' out the door for Margie to spend... and Margie, who ain't done nothing but bitch at me for things not being perfect for twenty-five years. Well, I'm done with it all."

Margot dropped the tray. Pastry rolled across the floor as Tim sank back in horror. Jamie's eyes went wide, starting to tear up. And Tommy... Tommy was too stunned to say or think anything as his father closed with:

"I'm leaving you, Margie. The kids are grown, you can keep the house I built, and I'm gonna go do what I always wanted to do. I'm gonna live by the ocean, I'm gonna paint, and I'm gonna enjoy my retirement. And you can have everything I built for you... But not me."

The next hour was chaos. Margot threw a complete fit bouncing from sobs to furious rage, and when none of that moved the Old Man an inch, she tried to be flirtatious, even outright lewd, which devolved into desperately pleading on her hands and knees. And the Old man had none of it. He told her to act her age, have some dignity, and stop acting like a weak little girl when she was a "grown-ass woman." He admonished her with the kind of stern discipline he'd used on the kids, but instead of violence, it was just words, powerful words that inspired the kind of shame she was desperate to avoid facing.

Tim was ready to punch the old man, and spent five minutes screaming in his face, spit landing on those thick glasses. Jamie just sat in the corner, quietly watching and smiling a strange smile. Tommy suspected she had known for a long time how unhappy he was. Maybe that was why he always made them miserable, for the company.

Tommy felt a strange sympathy for his step-mother that he never expected. He'd hated the woman for years, receiving her scorn for the crime of not coming out of *her* womb. But now... Now Tommy watched the only family he'd ever really known completely self-destruct and implode on itself. Words with vicious edge were flung from person to person, and the whole while, Tommy watched in silence, too stunned to make a single sound. His glass of scotch never touched his lips.

At some point, the claustrophobia made him get up and walk outside, onto the huge wrap-around porch. He closed the door on the chaos within, taking a deep breath of cold air. Wet snow melted irregularly all over the lawn. Cars whispered past on the road while he gripped the railing, his mind utterly frozen.

He stood there, staring out into the neighborhood of picture perfect houses while Margot's muffled wails shook the glass in the windows.

The last thing in the world he expected was to feel the heavy clap on his shoulder as the Old man joined him in leaning against the railing. He hadn't even heard the door open, he was too busy staring out at a still, quiet world, mentally retracing his steps from the last time he fled this home.

"She took it better than I thought," he said with his characteristic "shit-eating grin." Tommy felt a smile touch the corners of his lips. His pity well for Margot had hit bottom already, and now the childish delight was pulling the corners of his mouth up. He shouldn't take such delight in what was happening to Margot, but there it was, and it was keeping him warm for the moment.

"Dad-" Tommy started.

"Yeah, I know," he said, "Seriously, though... that woman has been the bane of my existence since ten seconds after I said 'I do.'"

"Yeah, well," said Tommy with a small grin, "You sure can pick 'em."

That made him laugh, a full, light, hearty laugh that startled Tommy. He'd never heard his father laugh like that. It was wild, free, and bouncing off the houses all around the picturesque winter scene. Snow tumbled off a roof across the street with the force of the guffaw. The old man took a prescription bottle out of the pocket of his flannel shirt and started fumbling with the lid.

"Ain't it the truth, Tommy?" he said, "Ain't it just the truth. But you three... Shit, especially you, I never did right by. Turned out just like my old man, and his before 'em. I ain't never reckoned with that, but I kinda always knew. Felt like shit to think about, so I didn't. And so I just lived like that." Here, he shook his head slowly, as if it might dislodge the right words.

"Well, I am gonna change that. I got a pretty penny saved away from my pension and some cash I been squirrelin' away so Margot can't get at it. Told her we spent it on hospital bills when insurance paid the most of it. I wrote you back into my will when I thought the big guy was callin' me home. But hell... I'm thinking I'll just give you the money now."

He lifted a cigarette to his lips, but Tommy didn't realize for the longest time that it wasn't a cigarette. From the little pill bottle, he'd pulled a rolled joint. Now, as he lit it on the cold winter night, taking a long drag and holding it, Tommy couldn't help but gape in absolute shock. Who the *hell* was this man?

"Dad... Is that..."

"Yep," he said with a barely-held voice. He waited a beat, then let the smoke escape his lungs so he could speak. "What do you think put my cancer in remission? Stuff's great. Helps with my arthritis, too. And Margie, now that I think of it. Way easier to put up with her."

"But... and money... ?"

"Only way to keep Margot from getting her hands on it and spending it on porcelain dust catchers. I shit you not, I had to talk that woman out of buying a fake dalmatian statue last month, cost $400. So take it, do something great with it. I'll get by just fine, I always do. I don't need a half-million dollar house and crystal glassware to be happy. I need some paint, the seaside, and quiet. Took me more than half my life to figure that out, son. If I never teach you anything else... Just don't spend your life working to make *someone else* happy at your expense. I did, and it's left me all twisted up and full of regret. So you, Tim, Jamie... You're all getting a piece of my savings. Margot, too, I guess, but she's gonna have to fight me for every penny. Got me a mean ass lawyer already. Splitting up the cash was his idea, you know."

He chuckled and took another toke.

"Jesus, Dad... I don't even know who you are right now."

He paused for a long moment, his eyes reflecting strange thoughts and silent struggles he could only barely comprehend. The man's chest was puffed out with some mix of pride and marijuana. Then he exhaled. "Neither do I," he said, "But it's high time I found out. Oh, hey, high time..." He laughed, and Tommy's mind twisted yet again to fit this scene in his head.

Two cold winter weeks went by before Tommy found a check in his mailbox for $150,000, with the note "Merry Christmas," and a card with some exotic shoreline on it, palm trees shading white sand.

A few months after that, Tommy figured out what he wanted to do with the money. What the old man had said about building the house... If he didn't have to give it to Margot, it was worth a good amount. He'd turned that home from a raw, small one-bedroom to a spacious 3 bedroom home over the course of a decade. Tommy could do the same, but better. He was younger, more focused, and the market right now was absolutely bananas. He just needed to find the right property.

Of course, the Old Man would think he was a fool, but this was the same old man that taught Tommy to work with his hands. So that's what Tommy was going to do. He was going to build something, something he could be proud of, and fund his own retirement on. And this ancient estate was the perfect blank canvass to work with. When he was finished, it would be a work of art.

Chapter Three

The porcelain shattered away with a satisfying crash, a cloud of tiny mold-tipped shards flew everywhere, and Mac barreled away from the big noise. Tommy hefted the sledge again, and swung at the ancient, worm-ridden woodwork around the sink. The hammer crashed through like it was Styrofoam. More splinters and shards rained down. Tommy continued swinging and crashing until most of the kitchen was a ruined heap of old wood and jagged shards of porcelain. Every swing came on the echo of a memory, and every impact was a satisfying blow to the madness of his youth.

Dust stuck to his sweaty brow, and all around him worm-eaten and time-ravaged splinters littered the floor. The old cabinets were little more than heaps of sawdust and jagged shards.

Tommy let out a satisfied sigh. The rotted old wood had fallen before him, and now he could tear back the walls and see what he had to work with. The wiring, if any, the plumbing, what remained, and whatever dead rodents lingered in the structure of the home, he would find them. But it had taken the better part of the morning already to demo the kitchen mess, and he was coated in grime from sweat and heat and rot.

The shower was cold, running off limited reserves in the trailer, as he hadn't gotten a propane tank yet, but it cleared the grime away and left a mess of mushy sawdust, mud and splinters around the drain. It mixed in with his dark hair and general body grease to form a hideous, congealed mess. He picked it up and flung it out the window into the woods.

He dressed again, having tossed his dirty clothes into a trash bag, and soon stood outside the house once again, staring up at the turret.

Smashing the kitchen was catharsis. Now he had to buckle down and really start checking over the house. Besides wiring, plumbing, and pests, he had to find a way into that turret.

A sudden weariness washed over him. Perhaps he over-exerted himself. He could feel where some back muscles were complaining a little. He didn't often get to fling around a hammer with such free abandon. He decided to switch tasks. It made more sense for him to head into town to pick up supplies than to fumble around that old place later, battling an aching back at the same time he fought decay in old oak.

He looked back into the camper, where Mac was napping happily on the floor. He smiled and carefully propped open door a half inch. He'd only be gone an hour, and Mac was very well behaved. Worst thing he might do is go chase more squirrels into the pond.

Tommy climbed into the truck. He had a notebook, and flipped through to a page that listed everything he still needed for phase one.

There wasn't much to the 'town' of Ingham, but for endless swaths of pine and maple trees, old dusty roads, and houses that looked in almost as much disrepair as his estate. The woods grew wildly tangled in some places, where root and vine even threatened to annex the paved roads themselves. Telephone poles curved from age and weather warping. Road signs marred by the sun and occasional pellet gun told him the Hub of civilization was near. Past a trailer park and a few cul-de-sacs sat juxtaposed from each other, across a busy road from a golf course. If there was such a thing as town pride here, it wasn't on display. The place was a mish-mash of old rural and new suburban. Housing boom snap-together neighborhoods sprang up almost as quickly as the wild weeds.

He drove down one long stretch of poorly-patched and bumpy road, lined on each side by what passed for local amenities: a McDonald's, supermarket, two liquor stores, a pizza place, a Chinese restaurant, two local bars, and two gas stations with wildly different prices. A few second-hand clothing stores and a small town hardware store completed the strip's main attractions. No movie theater, no office buildings, no fancy expensive chain restaurants, no car dealerships, no signs of urbanization at all.

That would change.

He looped back to the hardware store, pulling into the lot beside two other Ford F-series. He snatched up his notebook, mentally reviewing what he needed.

It only took a few minutes to fill the back of the truck with the various and specific bits of lumber, additional tools, extension cords, and several tarps. Then Tommy looked across the plaza, where a red neon dragon beckoned him. His stomach growled at the promise of something deep-fried.

The place was a study in mediocre atmosphere. Dollar store paper lanterns hung over the bar, and the waitresses were all noticeably local farm girls of the pale persuasion dressed in plain black. The bar was linoleum-topped, about eight feet long, and dull with the spilled remnants of generations of sugary rum concoctions and cheap beer.

It was mid-day on a Monday, and the place was packed to the gills.

Tommy could barely fight his way to the cheap bar, dodging unpleasantly aromatic men in various states of daytime intoxication. Under the vaguely red lantern light, Tommy found an empty stool and slid into it. To his right was a tiny, sad looking woman with fake eyebrows staring at the bartender with bleary eyes containing the sparkle of unrequited affection. To his left was a boisterous older man with a mangled avocado of a nose and carefully waxed little mustache. He wore denim and flannel with suspenders that just barely held his old beer gut in check while he sipped straw-yellow liquid from a Samuel Adams glass and laughed at some probably crude joke that Tommy had missed the punchline of.

As Tommy settled on the puffed vinyl cushion of the bar stool, the bartender came over. He was the only Asian human being in the building, and looked young enough that Tommy felt he should card him before he served any more drinks. He smiled with a friendly smile, and reached for a menu beneath the counter.

"Good Noon," he said, "Here for some lunch?"

"Yeah," said Tommy, "Is it this busy every day?"

The kid laughed. "Only the ones that end in 'Y.' Can I get you something to drink to start off with?"

Tommy looked at the tall ceramic tiki cup grasped by his stool neighbor. A drink was appealing. But the words came back to him, "*Just like your mother.*"

"Just an iced tea," Tommy said, "And a General Tso's combo?"

"Sure thing," said the kid. He looked like he wanted to keep talking, but he clearly needed to get things moving along, as someone down the other end of the bar was waving to get his attention.

He nodded to them, then went to pour Tommy's Iced tea. Tommy turned to look around the restaurant again.

The bar area was packed, but now that he could see beyond, the restaurant section was almost abandoned. A couple of teenagers were sharing a pu-pu platter, but besides that, it seemed pretty desolate. Tommy was debating moving over to the restaurant section when a glass was plopped down in front of him. As he turned to seize it, he caught the eye of the avocado-nosed man, who only just now noticed him. He eyed Tommy up and down, taking stock of his dirty jeans, boots, tee shirt, and rough hands. This seemed enough to win his instant approval.

"Say there, you new in town?" he asked.

Tommy nodded. "Yeah," he said, extending a hand, "Tommy."

"George Englehart," he said, taking Tommy's hand, "I heard somebody bought the old Worthington house, was that you?" His smile had a secret inside it, and the gleam in his eye threatened

Tommy with another bout of mocking, boisterous beer-perfumed laughter.

"Yeah, that was me," said Tommy.

On cue, George erupted in guffaws and slapped Tommy on the back.

"Son, you better be packin' a Uhaul fulla priests for that place," he said, "'Cause the last young buck tried to flip that ol' pile of rat-shit gave up and headed home after a week."

Tommy raised an eyebrow. "Priests?"

"Well, doncha-know?!" bellowed George, just loud enough to attract attention from the rest of the room. "That ol' place is haunted up the ass."

The woman with no eyebrows was now looking at Tommy, as was the young bartender and a dozen other people. Tommy felt his face burn.

"I don't believe in ghosts," Tommy said. So far, he wasn't enjoying the town's welcome wagon.

"Ah, I'm just messin' with ya," said George a little more quietly, "So serious. You're a young guy, you gotta relax. Lemme tell ya, I don't buy into that hoo-ha about ghosts either, but that place has got some nasty stories. Scuttlebutt is that there were fires, hangin's, an' some evil hocus pocus from old man Worthington."

Tommy cracked a small smile. This guy came on pretty strong, but he reminded Tommy of his own Dad, way back in the day. It was almost like a version of his father that had never undergone any growth, just an old man telling old jokes to his friends in the old VFW hall, drinking stale cheap beer and remembering a different world. He could understand that, even if this man was far less reserved than his father had been. There was a familiarity to the personality Tommy could wrap his head around.

"Yeah, well, there are stories like that everywhere," Tommy said, "I worked on a house one time up in Gardner, and this old lady who lived there kept going on about her dead husband visiting her. Creepy stuff, but just some old senile lady. It happens."

George smiled and gave Tommy a nod of approval.

"Well, just the same, I'll put my Ford up against there being somethin' buried up there you don't wanna find. Somethin' been scarin' off developers, but probably more that the place is a money pit."

Tommy chuckled along as the plate of General Tso's was slid in front of him. He nodded in thanks to the busy bartender. As he turned to his food, he saw Miss Eyebrows staring at him with wide eyes.

"You're... You're buying the Worthington place?" she asked.

Tommy felt uncomfortable enough with the attention from George, but now this woman was staring at him with an intensity that bordered on mania. He tried not to visibly shudder.

"Uh, already did," he replied sheepishly.

She grabbed his hand from the bar, and pulled it into a strong grip between her hands. She was stronger than she looked, an itty bitty slip of a thing with worry lines invading her overly-made-up face. Her grip was surprisingly strong, and her fingers had a bony quality to them.

"I'll pray for you," she said, her words deep, breathy, terrifying in their hushed intensity. She slipped off the bar stool and almost stumbled as she went towards the door.

Tommy shuddered and turned back around. George was shaking his head.

"Aw, don't pay attention to her. She's a few cuckoo's short of a clock. I'd say she's the town drunk, but we got a hundred town drunks. She's just the town drunk we all wish would get sober and employed."

Tommy turned to George's hideous nose and tried to keep a straight face.

"Well," he said slowly, "If she's the spookiest thing I have to deal with, I think I'll be okay."

George guffawed and slapped Tommy on the back again. He turned to the others at the bar and jabbed a thumb back in Tommy's direction.

"This kid's all right!" he declared, and with the respect of the avocado-nosed man, apparently, Tommy became the most popular man in town, as everyone raised their drinks and let out a half-hearted, half-drunk cheer.

Tommy picked at his lunch while George introduced him to a handful of the self-proclaimed 'town elders.' There was Mitch Rogan, a thin old man with neat rectangular glasses, a goatee, and sparse hair on top of his head left to fly wild in the breeze. He owned the antique store down the way, and judging from Mitch's glassy eyes, he would likely not remember the meeting.

He met Sarah Levesque, a very tall older woman who owned the local liquor store along with her wife of fifteen years. She was not shy about hurling dirty jokes right along with the old men, and despite the conservative vibe from these people, she seemed perfectly at ease, just another one of the guys.

Then there was Charlie Wong, who came out of the kitchen, and spoke with an accent. Despite the fact that they called him Charlie Wong, he told Tommy his name was Chen, and telling these gentlemen any different was like pushing a boulder uphill.

It was a whirlwind after that, and Tommy lost track of time. He needed to pack up and get back to the house. Mac would be expecting him, and he was already keeping the pup waiting too long.

As Tommy dropped his cash on the counter, George piped up one last time.

"Oh, hey, one more thing, kid," he said, "You got a gun?"

Tommy blinked for a second, but nodded.

"Good, you're gonna need it. It may not be haunted out there, but we can hear them coyotes all the way from the river." He pronounced the word 'Kai-yote's.' Tommy was now more worried than before. He shook George's hand and headed out the door, happy to smell the fresh, piney air instead of the stale reek of old beer.

When he returned, Mac was bounding around the camper. When he saw the truck, he ran right up, and escorted Tommy to the parking spot by running alongside the vehicle. When Tommy got out, the pup jumped up all over him.

Tommy felt guilty for leaving him alone this long already, and given what he'd been told about coyotes, he didn't want Mac out for too long by himself. He'd rather clean up doggy pee in the trailer than lose his best friend.

For the next few hours, Tommy unloaded the truck and started setting up his work stations. The logistics alone for this project were staggering, but Tommy could see each step in his mind. It was his nature, his experience, his meticulous attention to mental detail that formed the plan way back when he first walked through the old house.

A portion of his mind ticked over the local legend George had laid on him. Creepy stories grew around old houses like mold. He didn't take it very seriously. The kook that said she'd pray for him, though... That creeped him out. He was not a religious man, and anyone who had eyes that wild and starry, drunk or not, was worrying. His sister had gotten into some of that voodoo, but Tommy didn't believe in it. Reality could be held in your hands. Witchcraft couldn't. Ghosts couldn't appear and bite. Coyotes could. Luckily, he had Mac, and he was armed, so if coyotes and crazy kooks were all he had to deal with, he could deal with it. But to be safe, he took his rifle out from its case stashed under the tool box and checked it over. He wondered if it should stay in the camper with him for a little while.

Chapter Four

Tommy had just finished getting everything in place when the raindrops began tapping against his head. He'd barely taken note of the clouds creeping over the horizon, but now the dark gray masses were threatening to unleash torrents upon him. Tommy called Mac in, and they curled up for leftover Chinese and an old pulp novel about gangsters.

Outside, the rain assaulted the roof of the trailer. Thunder rumbled in the distance, but it was an impotent threat. No lightning struck nearby as the summer storm rolled past and drenched the land with fertile fury. Tommy fell asleep to the sound of the rain.

Day two saw another delay as the storm from the previous night had done nothing helpful. The mud was slick and goopy, so moving any heavy machinery around would be trouble. The house itself was damp and dank inside now, and Tommy did wonder whether or not he should just torch the place and start from scratch, if the old mold would even ignite. There didn't seem to be any major holes in the roof, but every broken window allowed in moisture from diagonal rain.

Once again, he carefully inspected the rock-wall foundation in the basement. Surprisingly, the basement was perfectly sealed, and the foundation solidly intact. In fact, the major support beams seemed to have resisted the rot and ruin that had befallen the rest of the house, and showed no signs of the moisture damage present elsewhere. This was a good sign, and meant that Tommy really had a shot to build something here. The old basement was huge, but low, and had several chambers leading off from the main entrance. One area looked like it had once been a wine cellar, but nothing remained but for old rotted racks. Likely the previous developers had taken the rare vintages and sold them to recoup their losses. In the back was a very old furnace, absolutely rusted through. He'd need to tear it out and install a new one, but the scrap iron might help bring that cost down. Finally he came to an alcove where huge old barrels sat, and here is where he found his first indication of a problem.

The stone foundation did worry him a little, so he spent a lot of time checking it over for cracks or loose stones on the initial walkthroughs right up to the sale. But with these old stone and mortar foundations, you could never be too sure. He was diligent in checking each stone. He was fairly confident the old stones would hold.

Except one...

It was approaching lunchtime when Tommy found the big loose rock in the bottom of the foundation. It was in the deep back of the house, through some tomb-like chambers, beneath where he was fairly certain the old kitchen was. He tapped it with his foot and felt it shift. The big brown stone was almost as big as the tires on his truck, smooth, rounded, but shaped with a kind of peak or arch at the top. Tommy found that if he worked at it, he could slide it around. That would need to get fixed.

Tommy knelt down and took a screwdriver off his tool belt. He wedged the flat-head into the stone wall and carefully jiggled it. There was some give, so he put more pressure on it, and the stone slid out of the wall some more. Now able to grip it with his fingers, Tommy put the screwdriver away and pulled, almost falling backwards with the effort.

The big stone ground against the rocky floor, squealing as it went. Behind the rock was pure darkness. Tommy pulled a keychain LED light out of his tool belt.

He turned his light towards the hole. The darkness ate the light up and gave nothing back. Frowning, Tommy extended his hand into the hole. Warm, dry air greeted his fingers. He found he could touch the edges of the archway the stone had left behind, but beyond that was nothing...

He was suddenly aware of the barking. Mac was yapping away, but this wasn't simple excited dog barking. He was scared. Tommy knew that sound all too well. He jumped up from the floor and headed up the old stairs. Dust fell with every heavy footfall.

His gun was in the truck, but he had the screwdriver and a hammer, and if some coyote was going after Mac, that wild beast was about to have a really bad day.

Reaching the front door, Tommy saw Mac with his head low, growling and gnashing his teeth towards the house. He seemed to be looking at the ground itself, but the dog was all teeth and menace.

"Mac? Buddy, what is it?!"

Mac looked at Tommy quickly with a quiet whine, then turned his head back towards the patch of dirty ground in front of the house.

"It was probably a vole or something, buddy," said Tommy, approaching Mac cautiously. As soon as he was close enough, Mac bound up to Tommy, and then turned around again, putting himself between Tommy and the house.

"What the hell?" Tommy said out loud. Mac looked at him and whined again. He stroked the pup for a few minutes to soothe him, and brought him back towards the trailer. He didn't want to bottle him up, so to speak, but he couldn't worry about Mac and a foundation at the same time like this. He started up the generator and turned on the trailer's meager air conditioning. It would keep Mac cool and safe for the time being. He made a mental note to park the trailer in the shade later.

Tommy led his old friend back to the trailer and let him inside. Mac seemed uneasy, but curled up on the floor and stared at Tommy with frightened eyes. Tommy hadn't seen the mutt this scared since the day he picked him up off the streets as a puppy. He turned to leave, but then stopped. He went to one of the cupboards and removed a big spotlight. He checked it by clicking it on once and almost blinded himself. The LED assault stung his eyes. He sighed at his own mistake and shut the door. Then he turned back for the house.

Tommy descended once again into the dark, dusty basement. Once there, he found the hole gaping at him. He shone the spotlight on it, and illuminated rough-hewn stone and the small crawlspace within. In that crawlspace was a skeletal hand reaching out for him, and just a hint of a staring skull lurking behind it.

Tommy dropped the spotlight and fell backwards onto the cold stone. The darkness in that hole seemed infinite and gaping, beckoning him to stare at its secret. His heart pounded, and his hand trembled when he went to grab the light. That couldn't have been what he saw. This was just the town gossip getting to him.

Sitting in the dark, panting, Tommy found a powerful urge to take off running. But instead, he picked up the spotlight and aimed it at the darkness once more.

The body inside wore very old tatters, there were wispy remnants of hair, and clutched in the other hand was a small leather rectangle. It was completely dusty, very old, and if the placement of this stone was any indication, placed there deliberately. But this person couldn't have been dead when they were entombed... Not with their arm reached out at the stone seal like that, and as Tommy looked more closely, he could see long scratch-marks... No, not scratch marks... Trails of ancient, dried blood stains from the desperate scrabblings of fingers, trying to escape before the air ran out. Tommy shuddered and backed up even more, allowing the shadows to swallow up those reaching bones.

A few hours later, Tommy was sitting on the steps of the trailer while a Dodge Charger decked out in blue and white rolled up his driveway. The phone call had been awkward enough, and terrifying. Even though Tommy was new in town, and this body had to have been there for at least decades, Tommy felt certain the police would somehow pin this on him. He never liked police. As a child, everyone told him the police were there to protect him, but all they ever did was show up to arrest his mother's boyfriends, who would inevitably return and with a temper. Then he'd get the back of the hand, a cigarette butt in the ear, or worse. Police always meant pain, always meant the discovery of some horrible secret that would cause suffering. Police meant consequences that were not his to bear. He had locked away all his beer and changed into a cleaner shirt. But still the fear sat and roiled in the pit of his stomach.

But what else could he do? He sure as hell wasn't going to touch a dead body.

Nothing the police said on the phone indicated he might be in trouble. They were very professional and calmly took all of his information before promising that someone would be out there soon.

Soon was a relative term. The town couldn't have a very large police force, but surely they wouldn't linger when an actual body was discovered. Yet still, the sun was high in the afternoon sky when the shiny cruiser rolled up to the house.

The cruiser came to a stop just behind Tommy's truck. He remained seated until the officer opened the door and stepped out.

The man was almost Tommy's height, but all lean muscle, short-cropped hair, and a crisp uniform. He wondered if the guy might be ex-military. He seemed to take notice of the gun rack on Tommy's truck before stepping up towards Tommy. Tommy stood slowly, approaching with open arms. His terror screamed at him to look normal, to appear non-threatening, don't even meet his eyes. Avert your gaze. His insides were cold and trembling.

"Afternoon," Tommy said, a little nervous.

"Hello," said the man in return, "Corporal Miles."

"Tommy Walker," said Tommy, offering his hand. The corporal shook it firmly, formally, looking Tommy in the eye. Tommy's gaze shied away.

"So what do you have to show me?"

Tommy bit his lip and nodded towards the house. "It's in there," he said, "In the basement."

The corporal nodded and gestured towards the house.

"Lead the way," he said.

They didn't share any other words as Tommy entered the house first, the corporal a few feet behind him. He had this odd paranoia that the cop was going to shoot him in the back if he so much as sneezed. Police brought pain. But he guided the corporal to the gap in the stonework.

"I was checking the foundation for weakness," said Tommy, "And this stone was loose. I pull it out, and well... There it is."

The corporal took a few discrete steps away from Tommy and shone his light into the hole. It fell on the skeletal hand first. The corporal stared for a moment, then turned back to Tommy.

"Looks as old as this house," he said.

Tommy nodded. "Yeah," he said, "I called right after I found it."

The corporal knelt down and crawled a little closer, turning his back to Tommy for the first time. He peered into the hole for a few minutes, then turned back to Tommy, taking a seat on the floor.

"Looks like a woman," said the corporal, "Did you touch anything on this body at all?"

"No way," said Tommy, "You couldn't pay me to touch a dead body."

The corporal eyed Tommy for a moment, his expression neutral, but he seemed to relax a little. He took the radio clipped to his uniform and pressed the button down.

"Hey, Brenda, this is Corporal Miles out at the Worthington place. We've got a body here, very old, might have been a murder like a hundred years ago."

There was a brief hiss of static, and a woman's voice came on the radio.

"Say again, Miles, a murder?"

"Old murder," he said, "Like, a hundred years ago. Better get the chief down here."

"Understood, Corporal. I'll get George to pry him off the bar stool."

Corporal Miles rolled his eyes, then stood up and looked to Tommy again.

"So tell me again how you found this?"

Tommy went through the story twice more with the corporal, and again when the half-drunk Chief showed up. Now that Tommy saw him, he recognized him as one of the barflies at the Chinese place the day before. He was an overweight man, and didn't have a uniform or badge. He approached the house with a swagger, and shook Tommy's hand a little harder than he needed to. His face was wrinkled with sun-leathered skin, big sunglasses rested on his face, and a mustache with yellow staining the very tops scented his every word with old tobacco and beer.

Soon, the tipsy man was down in the basement, looking at the corpse.

"Well fuck all," he said, "Whaddya wanna bet this was Mary?"

Tommy and Corporal Miles exchanged clueless glances before the Chief stood up again and turned to them. Reading their expressions, he just chuckled.

"Mary Worthington," he said, "Only open murder case in the county, from, oh... I wanna say, like 1800. Old man Worthington swore that she ran off in the middle of the night, but nobody ever found hide nor hair of her." He chuckled in what seemed like an inappropriate way and shook his head. "I guess we can close that file now."

"Uhhh," said Tommy.

"Right, you're new," said the chief, "So old man Worthington was an odd duck way back in the day. He was a pastor, ran the local church, but he was a strict son of a bitch. He'd flog people in public for blasphemy and crap like that. Well, one day he quits the church, says he found a new way to God if he's pure enough, and becomes a hermit out here on his plantation. He'd taken in some orphans, tried to raise them as his own. No one knows what exactly happened, but one night there's this fire in the barn, and some kind of big ruckus. People died. Place has been abandoned ever since."

"Jesus," said Corporal Miles.

"I wouldn't worry," said the Chief, "We'll bag and tag everything, send what we got to the historical society. They're gonna love this."

"So how is this gonna affect me? Do I have to file more paperwork and crap?" Tommy asked. He knew from experience historical buildings could be tricky, but that didn't even factor in murders and police investigations.

"Aw, I wouldn't worry. I ain't gonna stick you for some paperwork shit. You got no trouble from me. You might get some kids coming around to see the haunted house come Halloween, but it's pretty clear you ain't a suspect, and the guy who did it went to dust a long time ago. But I'll tell ya, this is gonna be the talk of the town for months."

Tommy rolled his eyes. His rapidly growing fame was exactly the opposite of what he wanted, and the discovery of a body was probably going to bring the property value down.

The Chief guffawed and muttered something to himself as he headed back up the old steps. Corporal Miles sighed and shook his head. He seemed to almost be disappointed. He gave Tommy a silent shrug with his eyes, as if to say *"He's just like that."*

"Wait," said Tommy, just then picking up on something the Chief said, "What was that about a barn?"

Hidden in the waist-high brush behind the house, recessed slightly into the woods, Tommy found the rubble and remains. It swam with greenery and buzzing insects, small crawling things, and probably unseen rodents. It was exactly where Tommy thought to build a barn of his own, or a guest house. There was even a hint of a path to it through the dirt you could just make out if you were looking for it.

Miles and the Chief watched as Tommy reached into the tangled mass and removed a rotted old plank of wood, still charred at the edges, but spongy now, infested with mold. He dropped it back into the mess.

"Shit," said Miles, cringing at the wet thud of the sodden relic.

"There's a foundation here," said Tommy, prodding at the ground with his foot. That changed things. An outbuilding or garage was an added bonus. It maybe even saved his entire investment.

"Better not be no bodies in here, either," said the Chief.

"I agree," Tommy said, nodding. This elicited another guffaw from the Chief.

"Well, let us know what you find."

Tommy frowned and even Corporal Miles seemed taken aback.

"You're not gonna, I dunno, call in a CSI unit?" Miles asked.

"We ain't even got cable at the station, gotta call Staties for that shit. And I don't think they'd be in a helluva hurry. Then they call feds and it gets all hell and gone with paperwork. I'm certainly not callin' them in. Not on a two century old murder. What they gonna find, anyway? She ain't getting less dead, and ain't nobody alive who needs the ass-whoopin for killin' her."

The Chief gave Miles a look, as if the two had a silent disagreement on the matter, but the Chief had rank. Miles looked away, and the Chief started back for his car, whistling off-key.

Miles gave Tommy a report to fill out, but it was obviously a perfunctory measure. They exchanged masculine nods and Miles went back to his cruiser with the clipboard.

"Hey, wait... Is someone gonna move this body?" Tommy asked. Miles stopped and seemed to think on it briefly before cursing and walking back.

"Yeah, okay," he said, "This is so against procedure it fucking hurts."

Miles took a box of latex gloves from the trunk of the cruiser, handing it to Tommy, who was grateful, but hesitant. He stared at the box for a moment.

"Uh, what are we gonna..."

"Look, I don't know," he said, "We're supposed to have professionals do this. But Chief Firewater has some beef with the Staties, and all we get around here are drunk drivers and kids being kids, so this is probably the only murder this town's ever seen."

"Lucky fucking me," Tommy muttered.

"Yeah, sorry, man. You call the shots on this, I'll file my report, and see what happens, but I wouldn't hold my breath for someone to come and remove that thing."

"God, I don't wanna touch a dead body," Tommy complained.

"You religious?"

"No, man, just... It's a body."

Miles nodded. "Sorry, man. I mean, I'll help ya, but... I'm probably the only help you'll get."

Tommy sighed and half heartedly kicked a stone into the distance. He felt a chill creep up his spine at the thought of handling the old, dry, rotted bones that used to be a person. But what else was there to do? He could leave it and then what, hire someone to move a dead body? Seal it up and hope no one discovered it in the future? Neither idea sat right with him. The only thing that seemed decent was to give the poor thing a proper burial and try to forget about it. It was the decent thing to do, but it still made his skin crawl to think about. At least he would have help, though. Miles seemed to be waiting for him to make a decision.

Tommy sighed and went to his truck, grabbing one of the big plastic contractor bags from the tool box, and after some biting back of his jangled nerves, a shovel.

The bones came apart as soon as they pulled, and Tommy shuddered. Piece by piece, they removed tattered shreds of human. The skull still had crusty bits of substance Tommy tried hard not to think about. Miles grabbed the skull, and wisps of ancient hair fell away as he put it into the bag. Mercifully, the bones were soon collected, but the right hand held a small, leather-bound object, the brittle fingers popping off as the corpse was disturbed.

Eager to look at something besides the bones, Tommy picked it up. The leather was very old, dried, flaking away as he unwrapped it. Inside was a book... The tiny leather-bound journal had an embossed cross upon it, but it was scratched across the surface as if slashed repeatedly.

"Her diary?" Asked Miles.

Tommy opened the book, and the very disciplined scrawl revealed the name of the owner: *Mary.*

Seemed like the rumors were confirmed now. Maybe he could turn this over to some historian. Maybe it would even be valuable to someone, somewhere.

Tommy and Miles dug a hole at the edge of the tree line before placing the bag inside, as respectfully as possible. Miles crossed himself, and Tommy just sighed, unsure what to say or do. The whole ordeal took two hours. Tommy's arms and shoulders ached.

Miles had removed his button-down uniform shirt, and the thin body armor beneath. By the time they were finished, he was obviously angry and constantly checking his watch.

"I'm sorry to keep ya," Tommy said, for what it was worth. It wasn't his fault that there was a body in his house, but he still felt a little guilty for keeping him.

"Not your fault," he said, "My wife's gonna be pissed, though."

Tommy smirked slightly. "At least you're armed," he said. He felt a lot more comfortable around the man now, but then, burying a body with someone is an odd bonding experience. Here was a cop helping him, even though he didn't want to. And through this weird circumstance, they had a strange trust.

"Yeah," he said chuckling, "I've been to Afghanistan, and it's nothing when those hormones hit." He paused briefly, then seemed to realize how that sounded. "She's pregnant."

"Oh, congratulations," Tommy said.

"Thanks. Second kid. My little girl is three, and making her mother crazy. She's gonna bury *me* in the basement for being so late." He collected up his armor and discarded shirt. He tossed them into the cruiser almost spitefully.

Tommy chuckled. "I think finding a dead body is a good excuse for running late."

"You'd think..." he said as he opened the cruiser door. "So hey, I'm not gonna lie... This could get outta hand. If the local rag finds out, we'll probably be up to our asses in trouble. Now, we can pin this on the Chief, I have to follow his orders, but anyone ever asks, I wanted to call State Police. You remember that."

"You got it," said Tommy, extending his hand. They shook, fresh earth falling from between their calloused fingers. "Not like I'm gonna argue with a cop, either. And, well... thanks."

Miles nodded, and they broke eye contact at the same time.

Miles got into the cruiser. Tommy turned to head to his trailer and wash off the grave dirt. Mac sat there, waiting at the door, wagging his fluffy tail. He sniffed Tommy all over with excited vigor while Tommy pushed his way inside.

The rest of the night, Tommy tossed and turned. The thought of the dead body kept rattling around in his head.

"*I just buried a body*," he kept thinking. Over and over, the thought drove away sleep.

Around 2 in the morning, he turned the light on. Mac was fast asleep, so Tommy went looking for his book. Sitting on his bedside table was his cheap paperback, and next to it, still with ancient dust on the flaking leather, sat the dusty leather-bound journal from the basement. Tommy stared at it. He didn't know how it got there. The crumbling thing sat there as if he'd put it nearby when he came home and emptied his pockets... but...

They didn't have it when they buried the bones. They didn't have it when they put her in the plastic bag. How had it gotten there? He picked it up, noticing the dusty fingerprints on the flaked off leather. They were his prints. They matched the size of his fingers, the shape, everything. He'd taken it with him, but had no idea when or why.

He probably should have handed it over to the Corporal, but he didn't. The book was there, in his hands. He unwrapped the brittle leather tie that bound it. He had opened to the first page before he even realized what he was doing.

Today, father brought in a score of foundlings. Without mother, I must take up the duties of cooking, cleaning, and caring. I feel so blessed to have such a loving father. He says we are a chosen family. Though he has been more stern of late, but it is all in the name of the Lord, he says, and spreading the word to new children. He even delivers sermons to the slaves, though they seem less attentive. I think they had their own gods before being taken. I find that fascinating. Other gods? What could that mean?

Tommy closed the book and put it down. He stepped back, unsure if he was really awake. Mac stirred, but the rest of the night was still. Outside, the chirping of crickets and distant call of night hunters seemed muted.

Tommy left the bed compartment and went out to the front of the camper where a tiny living area merged with the kitchen. He opened a cooler and removed a beer. He sat on the plush cushion and popped the top. He took a long pull, then put the can down next to him. He looked at the black emptiness out the window, just behind his translucent reflection.

Tommy took a deep breath, realizing his heart was pounding. He was too young for a heart attack, but there was a tight knot in his chest. His stomach felt cold, and met the incoming beer with an irritated gurgle.

For some reason, Tommy felt like it should be raining. It was an odd thought to have, but something about this nightly chill was seeping into his flesh, down to the marrow. His toes were numb. His hands began to tremble, and something hot began to burn on his back. He leapt to his feet, spinning around, but finding no heat source.

Then it was gone. The floor felt chilly, but had lost the sapping, wet, icy cold drain he'd been feeling.

Mac came padding out of the bedroom now, a tiny whine escaping his throat.

Tommy felt his heart rate slowing, and the tightness in his chest seemed to loosen, as if he were just now able to breathe again.

He grabbed the beer and took another pull. His stomach still gurgled, but his anxiety seemed to pass.

Tommy spent the rest of that night in fitful sleep, his dreams fleeting, but featuring icy rain and the life slipping out of him, soon to be replaced by the sensation of cold stone, and hot blood on his thighs.

Chapter Five

Tommy woke in a cold sweat, his phone chiming his alarm. Mac was whining at him, and the old diary was clutched firmly in his hand. His arm spasmed in revulsion, flinging the thing away from him. Its old pages fluttered in the air, shedding dry dust.

Everything was wrong. It was too bright, the air smelled... late? Like instead of early morning dew and the gently rising temperature, that the ground was well cooked already from the rising sun. The humidity was wrong. His phone alarm kept sounding.

"Fuckfuckfuck!" He said. He grabbed the beeping device and saw the time. 10:37 AM. He was over three hours late for work. A cascade of text messages demanded to know where he was. His alarm had been going off for three hours and he was oblivious to it, lost in his sensate nightmare.

Mac leapt up and licked his face, clearly still worried about his best friend. Tommy quickly rubbed the dog's ears to reassure him, then scrambled for his clean clothes. He'd taken the last two days, but was due back today, and it never looked good to show up late after several days of PTO. He knew he couldn't be fired, but there was a lot that could happen between not-fired and fired. He didn't want to start down that road at all.

The cramped, paneled office let in all of the afternoon sun, gently baking the room and causing Tommy's sweat to turn from cold to tepid. The rotund creature at the desk with a strained button-down shirt, exposing wiry chest hair, and matted black curly hair on its head with a clear indent from the hard hat, gave Tommy the stinkiest of eyes.

"So what happened?" He asked, his voice rough and phlegmy.

"I, uh... Don't know. I had some kind of, uh... episode, last night." Tommy didn't even sound convinced of his own words.

"Kid, if this were anyone else, you'd be getting your ass kicked."

"I'm sorry," said Tommy, "I'm gonna go see a doctor. Get a note."

"That note better say you're fucking dying, kid," he said, but took a breath and softened. "Union rules, I gotta give you a warning. Is this your second?"

Tommy nodded. His first warning came earlier that year, when Mac had thrown up something nasty and needed emergency vet care. The pup had gotten into the garbage and eaten something that poisoned him. Tommy spent a thousand dollars that day keeping his best friend alive, and he'd do it again in a heartbeat.

"Well, you got one more. Save it for a rainy day. I know you ain't the kind to skip work, but this shit don't look good."

"I know," Tommy said, "It won't happen again. I took every step, but something... I don't know, something weird happened. I'm gonna take care of it."

"Take care of it," he echoed, and wrote something on a small pad. He held up to Tommy a pink carbon-copy paper slip, compressed between fat, slug-like fingers. Tommy plucked the slip away.

"You're a good worker, Tommy. You never complain and you're always on time. I'm not gonna fire you. Hell, I wish I had five more guys just like you. But you know how it is. This ain't a Mom and Pop, I got ten bosses, all who wear suits and ties and they don't like when stuff like this happens. And I know you put in for some PTO this month. *I* know this is just one of those things, but one of those Wall Street assholes gets a whiff, they'll start breathing down *my* neck. *Capisce?*"

Tommy nodded. He was practically backing up to the door. He didn't want to push his luck any more. He knew his boss's problem, and it was getting worse everywhere. Investors would start hiring construction companies to build or renovate flip homes and they were impatient, angry, childish taskmasters that would sue at the drop of a hardhat. Petty, angry, and almost universally pasty white-collar types who didn't know a sump pump from their own pecker. Sometimes the contracts were good and sometimes they were very strict. Other times, entire flocks of lawyers had to oversee them. Tommy had seen the boss's job, and he did not want it.

Tommy sulked back out to his truck, his tail between his legs and a quiet, cold terror in his heart. If he lost this job, he'd lose a lot more than just his income. He was counting on that money for the renovations. The entire plan could go up in smoke.

If he lost his union membership to boot, he'd be stuck behind a register or something. He'd be the proud owner of a crumbling estate and nothing else.

He got into the truck and slammed the door behind him. He was infuriated, mostly at himself, but also at the vague nightmares that haunted him last night. Discovering the body must have shaken him up more than he thought. Through the anger, though, was a fire of determination. No goddamned dead body was going to frighten him off. No, that must have been what some of the prior investors ran across. That's why the stone was loose in the first place. Well, the dead posed him no threat. Nightmares were just in the mind.

He started the engine, and pulled up directions to the nearest place he could get checked out. He was going to cross every T and dot every I so that no one could say he didn't do everything he could. He would have doctor's notes, records of his visit, and all held in a neat little file.

The Urgent Care Center reeked of disinfectant and old people. He filled out his info on a little tablet, then sat next to an extremely elderly woman that trembled slightly. He chewed his lip, hoping she wouldn't talk to him. Her figure was nearly skeletal, and it made Tommy think of a walking cadaver, as if he didn't have that image already traipsing through his nightmares.

Her leathery old face wrinkled into a smile. "Is it still raining out?"

"No," he said, his tone curt and impatient. Mercifully, a younger woman walked over from the desk to escort her away to be seen by an available doctor. Tommy suppressed a shudder. Something about her was deeply unsettling. It hadn't rained at all today, not since last night, so maybe she suffered from some kind of dementia.

"What day is it, Tommy?" the voice came from the many years past. He shrugged it off. It was a voice that had came with the stench of cigarettes, and liquor, and rotting teeth from the meth.

The tiny exam room barely had enough room for the exam table and a little rolling stool, let alone a bigger guy like Tommy and the short, petite nurse. Still, he went through the usual procedure, had his temperature taken, and described the strange night he'd had. The nurse was just getting the blood pressure cuff around his arm when she stopped, frowning.

"What's this?" She asked, "It looks like... scabs."

Tommy tried to turn his arm to see, and could just barely make out what looked like some swollen, scabbed tissue on the soft skin beneath his arm. It seemed to lead back up to his shoulder. The nurse traced it in a line with her finger, and he was surprised to find it seemed to burn at her touch.

He removed his shirt, turning around and trying to see his back. The nurse gasped.

"Oh my god..." she said.

Tommy twisted until he could see his back in the mirror on the wall. His back was covered with what looked like dozens of welts and slashes. All were scabbed over, like they were healing, but had been inflicted recently. Tommy turned back and forth, but there seemed to be no angle that didn't reveal his mutilated back.

"What the hell?" He barked out.

"You didn't know you... Those look like they hurt!"

"I don't feel a thing..." Tommy reached back with his hand and gently prodded the marred skin. Tender pain answered, and left a lingering itch. He winced. The welts were painful, and the scabs seemed to just now begin itching and burning. It was as if seeing them somehow made them real, and even putting his shirt back on felt mildly painful.

Nobody had an explanation, but Tommy's strange dream poked at the back of his mind. He felt like the victim of some bizarre, cruel prank. They treated the wounds as best they could, prescribed antibiotics, but by the time that was over, Tommy had forgotten to even mention his sleep problems. He'd been at Urgent Care for two hours now, far longer than he'd expected.

Could Mac have done this? He didn't see how. Tommy would have remembered

that, and the pup never had done anything like that before. Four years ago Tommy had fallen on a job site and landed on some broken timber, but even that hadn't done this kind of damage. Could he have somehow done it to himself? In his sleep?

Tommy barely remembered his journey home. He remembered leaving and driving, but his mind was completely devoted to his injuries, and the insane dream that had taken over his sleep.

He had no explanation that made any sense, and now that he was driving, he could feel the pressure and soreness as his back made contact with his seat. It was distracting, and only helped fracture his attention from the mundane task of the long, winding drive.

He could hear Mac scrabbling to escape when he got back, the echoes of keratin on plastic reaching him from across the short driveway to where he'd parked the camper. The poor pup probably had to pee. Tommy hadn't had time to let him out that morning.

He opened the door and Mac leapt out, scrambling in the dirt to turn around. His whine didn't sound right, it didn't sound like he wanted to be let out, it sounded almost like he was afraid of something. Mac leveled a look back at the trailer. His tail between his legs, he backed away. Tommy frowned, reaching out to the terrified animal.

"What's up, pup?" He asked. Mac whined again and looked towards the open trailer door.

Tommy stepped up and peered inside. Everything seemed normal, but there were scratch marks all over the interior door. Mac never clawed at the door like that. Did he claw at Tommy's back like that to wake him up?

Mac suddenly barked at the trailer, and scrambled aside, as if taking a defensive posture, but his gaze went way out towards the trees. Tommy tried to follow what Mac was tracking, but there was nothing there.

Tommy let out a breath. "What is going on around here, little buddy?"

Mac looked back at him, responded with a strange huff, then bounced back into the trailer. Tommy followed him inside. This was enough for him. He was done. Whatever was going on, Tommy was in no mood to be messed with. He needed time to sort things out, and though he was loathe to do it, he did have a doctor's note that would keep him off of the job site for a few days. That would be enough time for his back to heal up, and next week, his paid time off began.

Tommy moved the trailer into the shade. It would only get sun for a little while in the late afternoon now. He spent the rest of that day resting, reading, and guzzling beer to distract his mind.

It didn't help. But at least his sleep was free from nightmares.

The weekend was spent in quiet planning, and he limited the physical labor as much as he could. But when Monday came, he showed up to the job site with doctors notes, signed forms, and everything kept crisp and pristine in a little folder, as he promised himself. Then, he was clear for the rest of the week.

Tommy had fished through the old keys to figure out which one opened the final locked door in the house. It was this door, he was sure, that led to the spire. He had come to glean that the spire was an addition they had built some years later, with the timber being a little fresher, a little more resilient, and less water damaged. And with needing to take it easy so his back would heal, it was a quick errand to satisfy his curiosity.

He climbed the groaning old wood stairs to the top and tried each old key in the wrought iron lock. Nothing seemed to connect properly with the mechanisms. It was a lot hotter up there than he expected. The house got the full brunt of sunlight from dawn to dusk, and it had already been cooking for several hours. It was sticky and uncomfortable, further adding to the frustration. He tried again, and spun the knob back and forth, feeling the knob itself loosen and come off in his hand, popping free from very light force. He already had stinging sweat dripping down into his eyes. The heat brought his impatience and frustration to a simmer. He wanted to know what was behind this door.

Tommy kicked at the door and wood splintered. The door latch slowly slipped from the frame, and the old door swung lazily inward, spilling muted daylight on the dusty scene within.

Inside was an antique crib with some old, faded stains on the deteriorating sheets and blankets. It sat right in the center, on a circular rug that seemed hand-woven centuries ago, but now crumbled with age.

Tommy had expected many things, but not this. The room was some kind of old nursery, and the rotting crib in the middle of the room was not the only furniture. There were old chairs in the corner, empty bookshelves, and the faded remains of wooden toys from a bygone era. One corner chair seemed to be covered in a pile of old rags and something vaguely oily. The floor had dark spots on the wood that looked like old black mold from some kind of water seepage. And he was unprepared for the sheer number of dead, dessicated flies all over the place. Some were stuck in thick spiderwebs up in the corners of the ceiling. Above him, a huge network of intertwined old webs wafted in the sudden airflow from him opening the door. He could almost feel the crawling legs of tiny arachnids on his skin just from looking at the gauzy cobwebs floating above him.

The stench that came from this room turned his stomach. It was beyond anything he'd known in his life, and carried a pungent sweet rot smell that had a dry, papery feeling when the air touched his tongue.

Tommy had no thoughts. The morbid scene of decay surrounding what was once a room of love seemed unwholesome and corrupted. He approached the crib and saw the old moldy sheets were still perfectly made, as if the only use the cradle had ever received was to farm fungus. Tommy shuddered involuntarily and left the room. Somehow, this made his skin crawl more than the actual dead body. This empty chamber of potential life stared out at the property through the hexagonal eye, now more ominous for the terrifying secret it had held.

Tommy walked back down the stairs and decided to leave that room alone until he could work up the stomach to deal with it. A part of him wondered what other foul things prior flippers had discovered here. Was he the first to find this room? If not, was that why it no longer had a key? Tommy could easily see someone tossing the key to this cursed room into the pond and driving away forever.

He pushed through the clouds of fear and disgust. Maybe this would scare away others, but not Tommy. He would take another day, and maybe another night to think things over. But he would come back, and he would confront this and clean this mess up. If he could survive living in that cramped little apartment with his addict mother, he could deal with this. Tommy was a survivor. He just had to make some adjustments to his plan, and take it one step at a time. Everything in that room could go in a dumpster, and he'd sand and scrub the filth away. Whatever happened in there happened a long time ago, and it was over.

He could rip up the flooring, put down new, make it a little sunroom or reading nook. He would restore it to something wholesome, and more importantly, profitable.

For the next few weeks, Tommy's life fell into a stable, comfortable routine. The ratty old journal sat forgotten in the corner of the bedroom, and Tommy spent his time on planning and some light demolition. The work on the house went surprisingly quickly now, and it wasn't long before he had reinforced the good beams, and replaced the handful of bad ones. He and Mac would enjoy a campfire meal every night, and his sleep was undisturbed by phantom wounds or toxic dreams. On the weekends, Tommy had some of the other guys from work come down to help him with the heavy lifting. Only a month later, just as the mid-June sun began to blaze late into the day, the sub flooring was done, and the power was running through new wiring for the tools.

Tommy paid his friends in hot dogs and beer, laughing, and having a great time. They told filthy jokes, most of them old cliches, and griped about having to pay taxes on their homes, wishing Tommy luck on the tax bill when he was finally finished. These were men who had owned homes for years, had wives, children, things that so many people right now did not have, Tommy included, and he listened to them bellyache about problems he wished he had. Well, he would have them soon. And in a few years, he'd be complaining to them about how much taxes were taken on the multi-million dollar sale, and then he'd laugh all the way to retirement.

Most of the truly difficult work was done by week 5, and Tommy was running low on his beer budget for the crew. Mac had just as much fun, and between snacking on leftovers that weren't properly secured from hungry pups and chasing the small wildlife that lurked far away from the noise of power tools, he was just as busy as his human friend. He often took little swims in the pond, and emerged needing a good hose-down and some doggy shampoo.

Tommy's fears of the plumbing were well-founded, but putting in the well was not nearly as expensive as he had budgeted for. Running the pipe went smoothly, and soon the house had running water, though not all connected at once. He had a specific plan for that to test each segment one at a time to spot leaks and mark them without unleashing gallons of water on an unsuspecting living room.

Tommy's back healed, and to his surprise, seemed to leave very little in the way of scars. It now looked like nothing more than faint scratches and sunburn.

Tommy had the flooring done in the master bedroom and hallways by the time the last of the marks had faded. It was approaching the height of summer when Tommy had permanently set up the basement as the command center of the rehab project. The arched stone had been cemented back in place, which seemed to ease the sense of dread that had lurked in the musty air. The stairs were replaced with fresh, pressure treated wood, and the cool underground stone was a welcomed relief from the hot sun outside.

The master bedroom had a box spring and mattress, boxes set up as a side table, and two working outlets. It was incomplete, but for now, it was home. All Tommy had to do was finish the roof and install the new windows to make the house completely safe from the elements. He still had to get up to that attic, but for now, in the hot summer, his North-facing master bedroom was nicely cool, and when he turned out the light, warm darkness enveloped him and cradled him into a gentle sleep.

Chapter Six

Tommy woke to the sound of chirping birds and Mac's excited scrabbling as he raced back and forth downstairs smelling and chasing the tiny woodland creatures he could hear outside. He stretched, rolling out of bed with a slight groan. He stood, then turned to check his back in the mirror. He was happy to see how far the marks had faded, but less happy as he turned to the side, and the consequence of living for two months on junk food and cheap beer threatened to roll over the waistband of his pants. He grunted and stepped over to the window. He could hear Mac barking at something. He used to run, back before he took on this project, in order to keep in shape. Long hours on job sites and quick fast food meals often led to the perception of contractors as fat and out of shape. He didn't like that image, and he didn't like that the protruding belly would make *him* look fat and lazy.

He decided it was time to start running again. He grabbed a shirt and his sneakers from the corner. He had the land, and there was some kind of trail in the back. He had no good reason not to use it.

Mac bounded happily beside him as Tommy started off at a leisurely run through the field. The sun was already warm and the grass was wet against his ankles, making him choose a small trail that led off into the trees. The shade actually worked against him, chilling him beneath the piney canopy. Old leaves squished and crunched underfoot, fallen trees lined the path as if by design. Mac wound back and forth, literally running circles around Tommy, who already felt the fatigue from his lack of cardio.

In the shafts of light from the sun filtering through the trees, Tommy could see the remains of an old stone wall, some ancient property boundary from New England's remote past.

Tommy slowed up, and as he did, he felt the incessant flicks and impacts of tiny buzzing insects. The whine of tiny wings invaded his ears, and he swatted at the sudden swarm. Mac let out a bark, and it seemed as if the insects were becoming more than just a nuisance, but a full cloud of stinging and biting.

Tommy resumed running, bounding over a small fallen tree and stumbling a little. He almost slid off his feet, but at the last second he caught a thin sapling to steady himself. As soon as he slowed, the swarm returned to its orbit around him. Now they were visible as a whirling, angry tornado. Tommy got going again, his heart pumping in his chest, and now he couldn't tell which way he was going.

He saw a tall stone pillar, some kind of boundary marker he guessed, and stumbled towards it. He didn't notice the dark divide in the ground where the dead leaves turned from brown to black, but he did notice the swarm vanished as soon as he crossed it.

Mac was barking after him, but as Tommy looked around, the furious swarm suddenly gone, he realized now where he was. In the middle of this patch of woods, where the ground was black decomposed leaves and old mossy stones, five flat, jagged slabs of stone jutted from the dark Earth.

Some were cracked in half, others leaned against trees that had sprung up more than three decades ago. The lettering on them was obscured and worn by what looked like the age of centuries. Tommy looked back and forth at all the rubble and rotten overgrowth, the black slime leaking from the old, festering fallen foliage. The squared off edge of the graveyard itself was barely delineated by old, bent, broken iron rails clinging to torn, rusted metal loops from the stone pillars. A wrought iron gate hung by a single rusted hinge, dangled between smaller pillars that formed the official entrance. The rough stone-laden ground seemed uneven, hurled up and tossed by untold years of frost heave. No grass seemed to grow, and the decayed leaves seemed sparse over the ancient ground. Yet the decomposition under his feet was real, and tacky like old tar.

Mac lingered at the edge of the black sludge, whining and letting out worried barks as he paced the line. Tommy took a few steps back towards the frightened pup and found the swarm returning to his face as soon as he crunched a crisp leaf. He stumbled back as some hideous blue horsefly bounced off his eye. He reached out, gripping the edge of the stone pillar that held the gate. It creaked in complaint, and Tommy let go quickly.

The graveyard seemed the only place safe from the swarm. Tommy looked over the stones, straining his eyes to try and see the faded engravings.

He had to step past the gate, and once he did, a chill wind seemed to dance across his sweaty skin. He approached one of the stones, leaning in close to read the inscription. Most of it was faded, but he could easily read the name at the top. *Worthington*, it said, and the faded dates beneath were too vague to decipher. Tommy shuddered. This was the graveyard of the family that lived in his house, whose patriarch had likely murdered the girl they'd found in the basement.

Tommy was finished running for the day. He didn't want to face the wrath of those insects again, so he picked a different section, hopped over the rails and bolted straight back for the property. Maybe he could just start eating more salad.

During the run back, he turned over a lot of the happenings in his head. For a home this old, and for the number of times it changed hands, there had to be more to this. Even the locals knew something was up with the Worthington place, and its passage into local infamy worked to his benefit when buying. But now?

He couldn't help but wonder. He didn't go this far without doing research, but it hadn't mattered much at the time who the people were that had tried to flip it. None of the stories or records he'd looked through mentioned anything like what he'd encountered so far. Had someone else found the body at one point? Or maybe had phantom injuries or something similar? Had someone found that spire room before? Or encountered strange insect swarms? Had they discovered the graveyard, crossed themselves and taken off running?

Tommy had seen enough haunted house movies to accept the possibility, but he didn't personally believe in ghosts. He could definitely be creeped out, as he was, by the many strange things. Normally flipping a house came with problems like plumbing being torn out, or the ground being too soft and the foundation sinking. This house came with literal nightmares and a dead body.

He finished his run by passing the great big pond down the hill, then turned up the hill towards home. He paused for a moment to look back at the water. For some reason, he expected there to be shapes in that placid, glistening surface. Sweat-soaked and suddenly cold, he shivered.

Determined to dig through those records again, Tommy opened the trailer and went into one of the storage compartments. He kept everything about the house in a big accordion folder, separated by dollar-store colored tags with labels. But it was dense with forms and records, histories and transaction records. Some items he'd simply stuffed in after a quick read, but now he began pulling specific files and spreading them out on the kitchen table. He focused on the photocopied files from the records office. There, he might find some answers.

Looking up the most recent owner, it seemed to be some real estate equity firm, and he didn't know what that was, but it certainly didn't seem like they'd done any work to it. Just held onto the deed.

Prior to that, it was owned by a local bank that had foreclosed on it. It took a little more digging to find the person that purchased it before, but Tommy found the name Ianotti & Sons. From there, he looked up the company, but couldn't find a listing. He found the domain name on the website had been for sale since 2019, and the phone number went to an inactive line. But when he tracked down the facebook page, he was able to then locate the contact info of Michael Ianotti, the man who had run the company at the time. But his facebook page listed him as deceased as of 2021.

Tommy picked up all of those files and placed them in the folder. As ominous as that may have been, he didn't think the house gave Mr. Ianotti pancreatic cancer.

Tommy backtracked again, and the prior company to hold the title was a company called One-Eighty LLC. That company seemed to still be operating, but when Tommy called, they said the prior owner, a man named Gregg Samson, had retired. But they were kind enough to locate his phone number.

Tommy took a deep breath before calling. He was afraid to find the answer, even after all the work he'd gone through that afternoon. He needed to at least put his own mind at ease.

He dialed, and after three rings, a voice came on the line, one that was very deep, even gruff, much like his father.

"Hello?"

"Hi, is this Gregg Samson?" Tommy asked.

"Speaking," he said, an edge of impatience in his tone.

"I hope you can help me out. My name is Thomas Walker, and I'm looking for some info on a place your company had the title to a few years back. The old Worthington manor?"

The phone was very quiet. Tommy didn't even hear breathing. It dragged on for several leaden seconds.

"What do you know about that?" he asked.

"Just that it passed through your company's hands, but then wound up sold to a different company. I was wondering if you had any details on that deal."

"Do you own that property now?" he asked, his voice low, almost as if he were angry, or maybe suspicious.

"I do." Tommy decided honest was best.

Another breathless pause. "Well, Walker, I can't talk about that right now. I'm in the middle of something. Are you at that property now?"

"Yeah," said Tommy.

There was a jostling sound, like he was moving the phone around. Then he came back on the line.

"In town, after the boat launch onto the lake, there's a little greasy diner. Meet me there in... two hours."

Tommy frowned. "I guess I can do that. Why there?"

"Because I'm not getting any closer to that place. See you at four."

The line went silent. Tommy felt a creeping sensation along his back, and felt it was time to move on to another task.

His mind kept wandering off the job. He couldn't keep his attention on any single task. His head swam with how the conversation could go, what he would learn, or if maybe the whole thing was an elaborate prank and this was the part where someone showed him the cameras and the whole world got to laugh at him.

He checked and re-checked his batteries and tools, spent a few minutes measuring for the drywall cuts he'd need to make, and then noticed it was almost 3:30.

He sat in his truck for an additional fifteen minutes, and then took the long way into town. He wanted to get this meeting over with, because that information was tantalizing, and at the same time, he was terrified he might actually get some answers.

Most diners have a retro 50's feel, from when roadside diners were everywhere, before the chain restaurants exploded. But this one had almost a lazy 80's vibe, maybe early 90's, with those odd smear wallpapers and muted colors intended to look tasteful, but ultimately just looked like a hangover felt.

Tommy's nose was struck by burned coffee, greasy meat, and something that might have been bacon if it had been removed from heat thirty seconds ago.

He took a seat at a booth, and waited for Gregg Samson. A tense young girl took his order for coffee, then scurried off. An old-style wind-up clock above the main counter ticked with painful monotony. The only other diners were a pair of teenage girls off in the corner, occasionally sharing a not-so-secret giggle at some youthful mischief.

He looked back towards the door, and a man was striding in, clearly recently sunburned. The outline of sunglasses were on his face. He wore khaki's and a polo shirt, slightly worn loafers, and thick rings on his fingers. Class rings, most likely, and a slightly tarnished gold wedding band.

Tommy stood. "Mr. Sams-"

He shushed Tommy and took a seat at the booth across from him.

"God, you're just a kid," he said.

"I'm twenty-seven," said Tommy.

"Whatever," he said, and self-consciously ran a hand through his salt and pepper hair. "You actually bought the place?"

"Yeah," said Tommy, "And so did you at one point?"

"Biggest mistake of my life," he said. He seemed like he wanted to say something, but then just exhaled and looked out the window.

"Why?" asked Tommy.

Samson seemed to chew on his answer for a moment before opening his mouth, and when he did, he shook his head a little as if he were trying to shake loose something he didn't want.

"All right, look, before I say anything, you gotta know. I'm nobody's fool, all right? Like, spirits and spooky stuff, I don't believe in all that. I believe in what I can see and touch, you get me?"

Tommy nodded. The man stared into his eyes with something like fury, but Tommy knew from bitter experience the look of someone hiding fear.

"That house you got is fucking cursed," he said.

Tommy swallowed, and asked the question he didn't want to ask. "Can you tell me what happened?"

He started to, but shut his mouth when the waitress came over with Tommy's coffee.

He waited for her to wander away, clearly not even comfortable talking. Still, that look of fear never left his eyes. The young waitress eventually moved on to another customer.

"Okay, kid... So here's what happened. Me and my guys were checking the place out. It was one of those sight-unseen buys, you know? But I saw those property lines and thought, damn, that's a find, right? Well, we get there, and that house is about as creepy as you're gonna find. But I'm more thinking it's got mold, right?"

"Exactly," said Tommy.

"Okay, so me and my guys start going over it, and it goes to shit real fast. My foundation guy opens the door, and this big goddamned wasp nest falls down in front of him. Those little fuckers stung him like thirty times. He blew up like a balloon and we had to get him to the hospital. He's ok, by the way, wasn't even allergic, but I guess a whole bunch of stings from those things can really mess ya up. So me and my guys go back the next day, with a lot of Raid, and go in the back door. This time, my carpenter is checking out the bedrooms upstairs, and I'm looking the kitchen over. Well he comes downstairs and he's yelling at us. 'Why you slamming doors? It's not funny.' Only three of us were inside there, kid. He was upstairs alone, and we didn't hear shit. My buddy Dave, with me in the kitchen, is checking some closet and lets out this yell. We go look and he's red and sweaty and says he was sure he saw some kind of long pale arm coming out of the dark in there. And this was a guy who was in Iraq, okay? Hardened guy! And then, we go in the basement."

"And what was in the basement?"

At this, he seemed to pause in his story, and sit back a little. He looked Tommy up and down.

"You a city kid or a country boy?"

"A little of both," Tommy said.

"So you know how dark it gets when you got zero light, yeah? Real pitch dark? Like, cloudy night so there ain't any stars even, right?"

"I do."

"And you know that basement has windows, right? And the door down doesn't have a lock, right?"

Tommy nodded, but he didn't like where this story was going.

"We went down there, and when we got to the bottom of the stairs... slam! Door shut behind us, and it got real dark. It got pitch dark. I couldn't see my hand in front of my face. We take out out phones, right? Nothing! No glow from the phones. Now... I was a Marine once upon a time. I don't spook easy. But it was like we all went blind down there. We tried to find the stairs and climb back out, but nobody could get to them. Now, those stairs were right behind us. I backed up like twenty steps, never hit anything. Felt like we were in a goddamned tomb. We must have wandered around down there for at least an hour, trying to find walls, the stairs, windows, anything. A whole hour, just wandering around blind. When I did find the stairs, I must have climbed thirty of them, more than just the ten or whatever to get down. And when I bumped into the door, it was locked. No keyhole. Nowhere light could come in. Just like a solid wall with a doorknob in it. And it didn't budge."

Tommy pushed his coffee away. "How did you get out?"

"I don't even remember," he said, "But I do remember running outside. It was dark by then. I checked my phone, and it was six hours later. I never went back, and I'm never gonna. Sell that shit off, or burn it to the ground. And don't ever bring it up again."

Tommy sat there stunned for a minute. "Is this a prank?"

"I got two ex-wives and three mortgages. I don't got time for pranks, kid. It's a warning, because I'm a nice guy. You either burn that house to the ground, or sell it to the next chump and live in a Condo." Here, he stood, clearly anxious to leave, his eyes glancing to the window as if he could feel the house watching him from five miles away.

"I wish you luck. Get a priest."

He put his sunglasses on his sunburned face, and walked out in six fast, long strides, almost running. Tommy sat there with swirling thoughts. It couldn't be real. This kind of thing wasn't real. This was the twenty-first century, and not one person had actually proven the existence of ghosts. It couldn't be real. If ghosts were real, every house would be haunted. Tommy knew enough history to know that New England, and especially old Europe, was built on bones of civilizations so old that if ghosts were real, there'd be thousands of them on the nightly news.

These were all rational thoughts. They did not quell the cold fear in his stomach. He left some bills on the table, far more than was needed for the coffee.

Outside, Samson's shiny ride bounced out of the parking lot, grinding its engine to pick up speed. Tommy watched him speed off, and had to force his calm so he didn't do the same.

Haunted house stories were just stories. He kept telling himself that the entire drive back, and began repeating it verbally as he came within range of that cyclopean turret. It watched him, but he knew the shifting shadows were just from the shade cast by trees and the passing clouds. The sense of being watched was just imagination.

Ghosts were not real.

Tommy started for the door, and found himself faced with that avocado nose and breath laced with cheap beer and cigarettes. George looked up at him, and without the equalizing effect of the barstool, he saw now the man was a head shorter. But those yellowed teeth caused his odor to project as he spoke.

"Hey! Walker! How's things?"

"Oh, uh, good," Tommy stuttered.

"Drove by that place of yours the other day, damn if you ain't got a project there. Ya know, if you need any help, I know some guys."

Tommy mumbled something like a thank-you. He was eager to get out of that door.

"Wait, Walker... You okay? You're lookin' kinda pale."

Tommy was outside before George could finish the sentence.

He spent that night in the trailer with Mac, and watched cartoons on his phone. He had to shake off the creeps. He knew, *knew* that it was all superstition. What else could it be? But all these little incidents, and Samson's story, were damned convincing. He could almost really believe it, and it certainly made the gothic old spire that much more intimidating. That spire room and the unknown horror within, the body in the basement, he could only wonder what had happened here all those years ago. The answer was probably in that diary. He looked over at it, sitting there beside his bed. He was sure if he read it, it would tell him the whole story. But that would be giving in. He couldn't explain why, but he felt that if he did read that diary, it would just reinforce his fears, not calm them. He didn't need to add gasoline to that emotional fire.

No, whatever happened, it happened two hundred years ago, and it's over. He made himself think this over and over again. But still, as the lights went out and his little bedroom was shrouded in the evening gloom, he felt a tiny pang of fear still running through his heart.

After all, there was a body buried fifty feet away.

He kept trying not to remember the dreams, and forced his imagination to stop conjuring the image of a walking corpse at the window. He desperately clung to rationality, to the real world he could see and touch.

The thought that kept him awake, though, was that something not of the real world had, in fact, actually touched him. He had the doctor's record to prove it. He could still remember that stinging pain, and the strange sensation of cold.

Chapter Seven

Tommy's stepmother, Margie, was always playing mind games. That had to be what this was, he reflected the next morning. He did get sleep, though fitful, and in the light of day he had a better grip on his own mind. Tommy was all too familiar with fear. He knew it came in all kinds of flavors. There was the fear of looking stupid in front of others, the fear of imminent pain, the fear of loss, the fear of change, and the fear that came pre-packaged in every human mind: the absolute dread of the unknown.

His emotions had gotten all worked up, and he started jumping at shadows. It had always been that way. His emotions would always get the better of him when he was young, and the biggest fear attached to that was that someone would use those emotions to punish him. He could often get angry or afraid when he thought he was being manipulated, or when someone was trying to provoke him. He knew the smirks and stares of that kind of sadistic glee.

This house was messing with him. Not literally, it was only a house, not a living thing. It was made of wood and brick, glass and stone. Houses didn't mess with people. No, the idea got planted in his head by the town drunks and now he saw everything as a scary story. These were campfire stories designed to scare children. Samson had spooked him, but with a little rest under his belt, Tommy could see holes in the story.

Three simple men, none of them with more than a high school education, probably brought up with a lot of religion, spooked by darkness in an old house. Some were combat vets, but Tommy knew people who had been to Iraq and Afghanistan that were practically ruled by fear. They would overcompensate, acting big, tough, and angry, but they were the kind to crack easily under pressure. You'd see them, drowning their deepest terrors in alcohol so they couldn't feel them... for a while.

It was easy to get carried away on fear. Tommy worked really hard to conquer his fears, but his coping skills were no better. From when he was little, when he would get too angry and lash out at people when he was afraid, even poor little Tim. He still shuddered at the pain he inflicted on that boy, and felt guilty for what he'd turned that kid into. But he didn't really hold all of the blame. That entire household was broken before he arrived, but his presence just proved to be a catalyst for everything bad. Sometimes, that's all you needed. Some new element, something to throw off the normal flow of things. People would get scared. Scared people start believing dumb things. That's all this was. Tommy's life and fortune was tied up in this house. That's what he was afraid to lose. And he angry that some other flipper with Bond-Villain foresight was just trying to scare him off. This was, of course, irrational. But that's how fear works. In the light of day, he could be rational.

The body he'd discovered was the reason for the legend. The legend was the reason for the fear. The fear was misplaced. He could mentally grapple with this. He could ease the coldness in his belly, refocus his mind and see the house as the challenge it was, not some ominous force out to get him.

Over a plate of fire-roasted sausage, Tommy began making the necessary calls.

Mr. Samson maybe would get spooked by the lights going out. But Tommy wasn't going to let a ghost story manipulate him. He was now more determined to get this house finished. He'd show everyone how wrong they were. He'd turn this from a haunted nightmare, into a luxury dream, and everyone would forget the superstitions.

He needed to tackle the installation of the new boiler, and oil tank. He was dreading this step, because it was beyond his experience. This meant hiring contractors. Tommy was a contractor, and he knew how something like this could go from a straightforward job to a complete mess in almost no time at all.

But he also knew if he didn't get this done now, it would hold up seven other things at least, and he did not want this to hang over his head any longer than the contractors likely would take.

It was a necessary evil. He had to get someone out here to dig.

Tommy worked up the nerve to call. He knew some people in the business, so he knew who was the most reliable, but 'most reliable' was a relative term. Tommy had padded the budget for this by an extra 20%, and hoped it wouldn't go more. No matter the nature of the cost, everything ate into the profit of the eventual sale.

Alberti and Sons was run by a man named Adam Morgan. He claimed to have inherited the business from the original Alberti family, but Tommy knew the real story, that he'd run an unsuccessful excavation company that was bought out by Alberti, but retained partial ownership. Then he sued for full ownership once the third generation of Albertis decided not to continue the family business. Old man Alberti was so furious, he counter-sued. It backfired badly, and Adam Morgan now sat at the head of a successful excavation, construction, surveying, and paving company that traded in more construction jobs and building permits than Morgan traded in golf outings and martinis. Tommy had never met the snake, but his general manager, Bill Wyatt, was a pretty forthright guy. He couldn't imagine working for someone like Morgan, a self-important phony who always wore khakis, even to job sites.

As long as Morgan stayed on the golf course, the work would get done in a reasonable time.

But Morgan liked his surprise inspections, and would find ways to pad costs on the site, often by taking his workers out for long lunches (business expense) and charging for better materials while using cheaper. He was exactly the kind of contractor Tommy hated for giving contractors a bad name.

Tommy had a coin flip chance that he'd escape Morgan's attention. If he did, Bill would make sure he came in on time and budget. If not, well, that's what the extra 20% was for.

He stared at the number on his phone for a full minute before he finally dialed.

The pause between rings was an eternity. The click that signified an answer made him flinch.

"Alberti and Sons, Bill Wyatt speaking," came the reply. Tommy let out a breath of relief. The hard part was over.

"Bill, hey, it's Tommy."

"Walker! Sure plays a mean pinball! Hey, how are you?"

"Good, Bill. Good. I need an oil tank installed on my new property. Is this a good time?"

He could hear Bill smiling on the other side. "You mean, is the Captain out to sea? Florida far enough away for you?"

Tommy grinned, "Thank God. I've got the particulars worked out, how soon can we get the land surveyed and the ball rolling?"

"Well shit, Tommy, for you? Hmmmm..." he paused for a moment, the sound of flapping calendar pages audible on the line. "I might be able to get a team out in a couple of weeks. The bitch of it is gonna be that the Captain is due back in port by then. You know what he's like."

Tommy rolled his eyes. There was more paper flapping on the line.

"Oh, hey, wait... I think I can get things started next week. When was that damned cancellation? Shit... Ah! Looks like I got a window here... Yeah, how's Wednesday next week?"

"Done!" Tommy said, "I'll get the info to you so you can pass it along to your people."

"You need septic, too?"

Tommy's relief evaporated. He hadn't considered that part yet. That would be a totally other contracting job. "... Shit."

"That's the idea. Hey, don't worry, Kid. I still owe you for that Morrone gig. I'll see if perhaps our computer billing has a bug in it, get you a discount."

"Thank you, Bill."

"Send everything to my email. I've got your back. You still working for that greasy weasel?"

"Different greasy weasel. Aliman Bros."

"Ah, they're not so bad. Well, if you're ever looking for work, I could use good people. If you can put up with the Captain."

"I'll think about it, Bill. Good to know I've got options."

"I've seen your work. You're a good kid. Email the specs and I'll look them over this weekend and get back to you."

Tommy agreed. Oddly, this was the lift in his spirits he needed. This was progress. This was what he had planned for.

A week later, there were two huge pits in the yard.

Roots and stones were ground beneath the might of hydraulic-powered steel. Huge bucketfuls of earth came spilling out from each pass as the backhoe tore up virgin dirt. Tommy didn't know how rocky the yard was, but the various jagged stones and huge boulders kept rising from beneath. The chug of the engines filled the air, and at one point, the workers had to use a length of chain to secure a particularly huge chunk of composite granite to the backhoe so it could be exhumed.

Tommy watched all this from the camper. The new septic system sat on a massive flatbed truck in his yard, and the future oil tank sat on another. Some old dead roots came up with the crumbling dirt, and Tommy began to wonder if he'd have to even out the yard afterward, or if they would smooth everything over. He guessed it depended on when the boss came back to town.

And then there were the boulders to consider, what would he do with those? The huge stones were a mix of unrelated old rock, dropped onto the land long ago by receding glacial ice. Now he had to do something with them or else have huge rocks dotting his picturesque home. Would bill haul them away? What would that cost?

But that wasn't the thought that kept Tommy rooted to his spot. It was the terror of uncovering yet more horrible secrets from this apparently cursed place. Tommy didn't believe in actual curses, but he sure did know the problems associated with finding another corpse. Even if it was properly buried in a coffin, if the headstones were moved, but the bodies left behind like in that haunted house movie, then his property was going to be rife with problems. None of the machines needed to go deep enough into the thicket to reach that old graveyard, but if there were bones in the cellar, who's to say there wouldn't be some other burial around here?

What could he do, but sit and wait?

Every time the dirt tumbled from the ground into the huge dump truck, Tommy waited for a skeleton to come tumbling out, or some disjointed piece of rib cage, maybe a broken femur. It felt like years went by, though the excavation took only the single day.

The crew left the tanks to be installed tomorrow, and Tommy stared into the gaping holes with a mix of sickening dread and grateful release.

Mac had stayed inside all day, afraid of the big machines and their grinding, scraping squeals as they scratched stone and strained against rock. He was a whimpering mess at the end. Tommy comforted him with belly rubs and beef jerky, but both residents felt a cold terror at the prospect of the diggers return.

No bodies surfaced, but the deeper they dug, the darker the dirt became. That night, Tommy dreamed they dug down and pulled up massive loads of black dirt, dripping with blood, and pale crawling things emerging, tumbling, screeching and hungry. Each time he drifted into sleep, he'd find himself back in the same nightmare. The pale grub-like things oozing from the blood dirt would crawl towards him on tiny thorny legs and cry out with hunger. He'd awaken, shudder and kick at phantoms, before realizing he was in his own bed, safe from any crawling fears.

The silent dark was a comfort, but not nearly as much a comfort as the rifle kept by his bed.

Despite the nightmares, Tommy's morning runs went on. He chose a different path through the dense woods to avoid the insect swarms, especially after the vivid dreams. On this new trail, he could see the roofs of homes perhaps a mile or more away through the breaks in the trees: his nearest neighbors. One great big structure across the lake seemed to be some kind of apartment complex, or maybe condos. He wondered if those were one of the ones he passed as he snaked along the back roads to get into town. He also wondered if it might not be more financially sound to just sell the land he had to the guy who put up those condos. There was space enough here, and then, while it wouldn't be retirement money, at least he'd pick up a small profit and be free of this mess. He pondered this while his feet ran off calories on the leaf-littered dirt trail.

The deeper into the woods he ran, the more he would find evidence of trespass by some of those distant neighbors. To the furthest North, there was a circle of stones providing a makeshift fire pit, scorched black and surrounded by crushed cans of cheap beer and shattered glass of the same. A rotted couch, car seat, old deck chairs and more were scattered lazily around the central pit. Cigarette butts were stamped flat and half smashed into the ground, and a huge tarp flapped gently in the slow breeze, suspended above the couch. It looked like the kind of hideout frequented by teenagers looking to avoid parental authority and personal responsibility. He wasn't entirely sure if this was his land, but if it was, this garbage would need to go. He paused a little in his run to look it over. The plastic, aluminum and glass seemed invasive to him, like a weed. He didn't have a problem with teenagers having fun, but he didn't want anyone doing dumb things on his property. He'd be liable for anyone getting hurt. He didn't think the insurance he had for the construction would cover dumb teenagers, but he'd rather not take the chance. He decided to come back later and start hauling this stuff away. Whether it was his property or not, he couldn't abide this much of a mess. With his decision made, he ran onward.

The insect swarms had been less and less as the hot, dry weather drove them towards more boggy areas around the pond. He rarely even sensed the buzzing of a mosquito as his feet kicked up dust around him. He'd be messy, but this was much preferable to the miniscule air force that had assaulted him before. And he was intentionally staying far away from that hidden graveyard. The Worthington's could rest in peace, for he would not be treading on their burial ground. Not intentionally, anyway. He considered himself a rational man, and as such, it seemed a rational precaution to avoid spooky things in order to prevent further spooky things. Maybe it was only superstition, and maybe superstition was irrational, but erring on the side of caution, at this point, was very reasonable to him.

He was still lost in this train of thought when Mac shot off ahead of him, which wasn't unusual, as he often ran after small prey, or what he perceived to be small prey. Instead, Tommy heard him bark and saw his dark form vanish into the thicket. Seconds later, a sharp, high cry of shock went out, and Tommy could dimly see some day-glo orange through the sticks.

He soon caught up with Mac, who had adopted an excited, playful stance, with his tail up and wagging furiously. His prey, much to Tommy's surprise, was a five-foot-six, fit, coffee-skinned slim woman who seemed to be pulling earbuds out of her ears to look down at Mac, at first frightened, but then calming as she saw his playful demeanor. Mac barked once, then bounded in a circle and started sniffing the ground as he approached her.

Tommy took a moment to catch his breath before approaching. "Sorry," he said, "I'm sorry if he frightened you."

She smiled at him, a slightly guarded smile, which he caught and understood. That was a smile that said she was friendly, but not too friendly. He was panting, short of breath, and had just burst through the thicket, after all. If someone looking like he did had just appeared out of the woods, he'd be a little on guard, too. He held up his hand while he caught his breath, keeping his distance.

She was gorgeous. Slim, but with great curves, and the spandex running shorts only drove that point home. Her hair was dark, tied up in a ponytail, and though she was sweaty and a little grimy from a run in the woods, her sharp nose and dark eyes had a naturally sultry look to them. Tommy had trouble catching his breath. There were day-glo orange highlights along the sides of her running shorts, and her sleeves. That was smart, as the locals might be drunk and hunting in these woods. He probably should have been wearing an orange vest himself.

Mac rolled over onto the ground, and she carefully knelt down to rub his belly.

"Awwwww, look at you," she said sweetly, "So cute. What's your name, big guy?"

Tommy sat down on a rock and wiped sweat from his eyes.

"He's Mac," Tommy said, "I'm Tommy."

"Tatiana," she said, an accent slipping slightly into her speech, "I'm surprised to run into anyone way out here. Do you live at Bramblewood?"

She seemed to be a little more at ease, so Tommy remained sitting, and was grateful for the moment of rest. Meanwhile, Mac rolled back to his feet and started slobbering doggy kisses all over her. She laughed and tried to appease the dog without getting too slobbered upon.

"No, I just bought the property to the south," Tommy said, "Flipping it."

"Oh yeah? So that's what you do?"

Tommy shrugged. "Kind of a long story, but it's gonna pay for my retirement. In the meantime, I nail boards together for union pay. How about you?"

She waved a dismissive hand, "Call center. I get yelled at for a living."

Tommy nodded. "I take it Bramblewood is, what, an apartment complex?"

She shrugged. "Condos."

Tommy rolled his eyes. She caught it and gave him a look. "What?"

"Nothing," he said, "Condos are not my thing."

Mac took the sudden silence to pad off, sniffing the phantom trail of some unknown animal.

"Well, it was nice meeting you," she said, and turned.

Tommy stood up. "Wait... I'm sorry, I just..."

She turned back to him, apparently allowing him a moment to redeem himself.

"That was rude," he said, "I'm sorry. Can I-?"

"Make it up to me over dinner?" She said, cutting him off. It seemed more of a practiced, or perhaps, often heard and unwelcome comment.

Tommy wasn't prepared for such a direct swerve into the topic. "I suppose you get that a lot."

"Yeah," she said, "That's why I jog alone where nobody is around."

"I'm sorry," he said, "Would it be okay if I pulled my foot out of my mouth now and slunk away?"

She laughed at that and seemed to regard him a little differently. "I'll tell you what, Tommy. I'll let you start over."

Tommy smiled and nodded with humility. "I apologize if this comes off really forward, but I really enjoyed meeting you, Tatiana, and would like to get to know you better."

She considered him for a moment. "Not bad," she said, "You're pretty direct, aren't you?"

"I don't do pick up lines," Tommy said, "Even if I did know any good ones, I would be terrible at them."

She smiled and clicked her tongue. "Well, I can tell you from experience, there aren't really any good ones. I get them a lot."

"I get that," Tommy said, "And I wouldn't waste your time with anything insincere."

Her smile broadened. "Huh. What do you know. There is a good one."

They laughed together, and it felt genuine.

Tommy walked home with her number in his head and a tentative plan to meet and talk. He felt better than he had in weeks, and the eerie atmosphere of the house evaporated in the vibrant summer sun.

Through several texts, they arranged to meet at a little cafe that sat on the side of the highway halfway to civilization. He'd seen it before, but never given it a second thought. Now he gave it a lot of thought.

Chapter Eight

A wonderfully appetizing smell filled her nostrils and went right to her belly. It gurgled with fury, and pulled her from the black oblivion. There was a smoky edge to it that warmed her inside. Stinging light came to her brain through reluctant eyes.

Above her, the rough-hewn timber and straw-padded edges spoke of a world very different from the comfort of her own home. Her first thought was that God had purified her at last, and brought her to this cozy heaven in HIS house, where Jesus promised a room would be waiting. But the face that greeted her as she stirred was not the almighty. God was not black.

But the face was soft, and kind, with pure eyes and a voice as smooth and comforting as silk. The smile was round and cherubic, like her mother's had been in the years before the agony.

She could barely understand the words, but she was hushed back to sleep, an order she obeyed without thought.

In the bleeding dark, she drifted. Her body was caressed by the gentle cold of something distant and alien. It spoke to her in words she could not understand, and yet they were as clear and true as the word of God. Was this god? Was this truly god?

No... This was bigger than God. It did not lie like God. This vacuum of blackness told her wicked truths of the dark. She realized she had met this cold black love before, in that cellar, waiting for a breath of light. It sat with her, held her in her tears like a lover, and now, only now that she was skirting the edge of death, could she really hear its voice. It spoke naked truth, and that God was false. No heaven waited for the righteous, no hell for sinners, all was blackness and oblivion, but for the few who could hear the music of the voice in shadows. It sang to her while she drifted, and all that she knew was washed away. The lies in her head shattered, and for the first time, she felt free. Her essence danced to the music of black spheres in a starless void, bereft of the false promise of light.

Her second waking was less peaceful than the first, and between a booming voice of protest and a sharp feminine reply, she realized that she came to awareness mid-argument.

"The master gonna kill you dead," said the booming voice, "Shit, he almost kill his own baby girl. What do you think he's gonna do to us?"

"I don't care, I see a dying person, I help. He gonna kill me for that, I'll die a righteous death."

Her eyes focused on the figures. At first, the world was a blur of dim light and dry wooden beams, but now she could see them, the man tall and broad, the woman half his height, but looked stout enough to easily stand up to him. She recognized them, of course. The bigger man was one of the groundskeepers, and the woman was their cook, Martha.

She remembered other things now as well. She remembered the lashings, the punishment, and the banishment. She remembered she had the honor of being named after the Virgin Mother, and how she had sullied that name with her dirty blood.

She remembered firelight and darkness, fear, and waking to rats going to take nibbles from her cold toes. Here, she was warm, safe, and the pain from her wounds seemed to be gone. She remembered the voice in emptiness and its siren song. She remembered to vital dance, and it brought a spark of glee to her chest.

"Why..." she rasped out, and the pair seemed stunned that she was awake. But her question wasn't directed at them.

Martha came over to her and put a hand on her forehead.

"Fever's still going," she said, "You're gonna be okay, though."

Mary wanted to tell her that it was a lie, but that would come in time. She was safe now, and the oblivion would wait for her to heal before the work could begin. These two would be the first of her instruments, as they had already been instruments of the dark beyond. They preserved her body, now she would reward them, and then turn her eyes to the cold stars for guidance on taking back what was stolen by her ignorant father. But this was not vengeance, no that was what God and his disciples did... This would be balance. This would be order and truth. Her father believed that if you spare the rod, you spoil the child. But she could see now, the rod came no matter what. And it would now come for him.

• • • •

By the time Tommy rolled up in the truck, freshly showered from a day of nailing up drywall, and hunger was creeping through his stomach, battling his excitement. Tommy hadn't done much dating in the last few years, having spent far too much time and energy on work. But then, he hadn't done much dating in general. Deep in his soul, there was a flickering flame of fear from long, cold, lonely nights. A man could go insane living alone all the time.

Relationships were never his forte. Tommy was always afraid to get close to people, in case they discovered that he was a terrible person. He battled with that. He knew he wasn't as bad as his father, or his mother, but when the cold loneliness or the bitter anger welled up, he was capable of being very cruel. When he felt someone was playing games, he would lash out. In younger days, if he'd just been kicked out of one school or another for his outbursts, to the delight and revulsion of Margie, he would wind up alone and cold. She would push him, intentionally, until he couldn't take it, and then play the victim. Over and over, shoving him deeper into a self-imposed isolation of the soul.

He was assigned a social worker at one point, and she didn't believe him about how Margot would twist his world around on him. It was a decade before he heard the term gaslighting, but that's what it was. And for years he thought he really was an awful, bad seed. And yet, now, he knew better. But the bitterness and old mental habits remained. The queasy grumbling deep in his gut refused to quiet.

His fear almost caused him to back out entirely, but his father's words found their way into his head, telling him to accept, to be happy, to *live*. He forced himself past those long-held fears.

The small gingerbread-house establishment looked as if someone had nailed two big gambrel-roofed sheds together. The place could almost have been a hot dog stand, it was so cramped, but the tables were laid out well and it seemed to somehow be more spacious inside than it appeared from the outside. The smell of coffee and cinnamon greeted him, and his stomach demanded attention. He awkwardly ordered a coffee and their last stale muffin. He took several small bites, then slid it to the side. It was a lot of sugar, and he just needed to fill the hole so he could concentrate on his social anxiety instead. He'd be distracted enough just trying not to say something dumb, like he usually did. The many times he fumbled his words to judgmental women bubbled in his head, and the subsequent rejections threatened to send him to a nasty emotional place.

She looked amazing, even in drab business clothes, as she walked through the door. She exuded both confidence and feminine beauty. She walked in like she owned the place, and she seemed almost like a perfect snapshot of a professional in her natural environment. He inhaled sharply and caught a hint of perfume under the cinnamon atmosphere. Over a steaming cup of coffee the same color of her flawless skin, she leaned forward, an eyebrow slightly arched as she asked a simple question.

"So how is Mac?"

Tommy smiled and told her that he'd left the pup with a full dish and his favorite chew toy.

"He's a strange breed, isn't he?"

"Part husky, that much I'm sure of, but the rest..." Tommy shrugged.

"Did you adopt him from a shelter?"

Tommy smirked and shook his head. He liked telling this story. He took in a breath full of the lively aromas.

"A few years ago, I was out in a storm. It was bad, and my truck was hydroplaning all over the place. I pulled into a MacDonald's to take a breath, get some bad food, wait out the storm. Well, I'm walking out of the place, and I hear this growling noise. I turn and there's a little black puppy with a half of a McNugget, and there's a raccoon trying to fight him for it. Well, I chased off the raccoon, and almost the puppy, too. He hopped away into the dark where I couldn't see him. But I knew he hadn't gone far, I could hear him whimpering. So I coaxed him out, wrapped the wet little guy up, and bought him a Big Mac. He ate all of it, even the lettuce. He's been my little pal ever since."

"So the name comes from..."

"Yup," said Tommy with a grin, "I tried to see if he was someone's pet, but no chip and no one in the area seemed to know anything about it. The guys at the restaurant said he was a frequent dumpster diver, but no one had been able to grab him yet. So... There it is. The vet thinks he might be part wild dog, but they don't do ancestry tests for dogs. He's a good pup, though. Well behaved and just true blue."

"That's amazing. He's a lucky pup."

Tatiana smiled a wonderful, warm smile, and Tommy lost all interest in his beverage, or what he was saying. His fear melted under the gaze of her approval.

"So I've been doing all the talking," Tommy said, suddenly feeling very warm.

"Oh! Yeah, okay... So I'm a supervisor at a call center. They just made us start coming back into the office, which is stupid. And my team are good people, but burn out super quick because the job sucks. And management has no clue. They think changing how we phrase questions is gonna make things better. Like, listen, nobody is gonna think they got what they wanted if you verbally trick them, you know? That's some desperate Sales Department bullshit. Ugh, listen to me, I don't wanna talk about my job. Sorry."

"It's okay, my boss still thinks one guy can do the job of five if he yells loud enough."

She laughed, and Tommy found himself adoring the sound.

" Exactly. So yeah, let's see... I'm kinda boring, you know. My parents are immigrants, I'm second-generation. I, uh... was in a long relationship recently that I've slammed the door on real hard."

"Oh," said Tommy.

"Is that bad?"

"No no, just... I'm sorry it went bad."

She shrugged. "It happens. Most guys are jerks. You're not a jerk, right? Because you don't seem like one, but they never do at first."

"I try not to be. And would it help if I said I own a mansion?"

She laughed and gave him a hard look.

Bullshit," she said.

"No, really. I mean, it's a run-down old husk and I have to spend the next few years working on it to make it shine."

That genuine smile came through again. "I like men with long-term investments."

It was decided by looks, by furtive glances, by the way the corner of her mouth upturned and she slowly slid her legs apart. Tommy would barely remember the way to the Bramblewood complex later, but following her little silver Prius became his all-consuming thought. The conversation had taken more twists and turns than the country road, but the faux-pas and worries seemed to melt away the more they talked. They weren't teenagers looking for love, they were lonely adults, looking for companionship.

He'd never remember the building number, or the apartment number, just the way her lips felt against his, and the slow tease of her thigh against him. They barely made it to the bedroom, and it was there that Tommy felt his first twinge of doubt. He hadn't been with a girl since prom night, and that had been less than stellar. But she guided the way, brought him over to the bed and guided his lips down her perfect tummy to the little cave of her navel, and lower still to the sweet, salty treasure. He tried not to be clumsy, and her little moans and gasps were wonderfully encouraging. Eventually, she pulled his head up, guided his still-sticky lips to hers for a deep kiss.

She pulled him into her greedily, and they locked in a mutually shocked gasp.

The following hour was intense. Tommy either had better stamina than he thought, or she definitely knew what she was doing, and they teetered on the edge together for a brief eternity. When she came, her fingers raked across his back, and the sudden sharp pain pulled him back from the brink just a little, but soon she was riding a second, then a third wave and Tommy finally crashed along with her.

It was still light out as they parted, and Tommy felt a distinct and pleasant soreness in his muscle. Tatiana curled up around him, gripping him and letting out happy little noises and shudders as she came down.

No one spoke.

Amber stripes of light hovered above them from the setting sun drifting through her blinds.

Neither one of them was entirely sure what to say. Conversation seemed trite, so they both kept their mouths shut and just enjoyed the sweaty and smooth skin of the other. Tommy watched dust dance in the light. He enjoyed feeling her nuzzle against him. The affection was real. Even if they were only doing this because they were both lonely, and even if they never saw each other again, the sweaty dark was their private, temporary Eden.

Their peace shattered when a piercing and grating chirp invaded the dark, before it turned into a rattling noise. Tatiana let out a curse in Spanish and rolled over to grab her phone as it danced along the bedside table. She looked at the screen for a moment, then sat bolt upright with a sharp gasp.

"*Shit!*" She dropped the phone back onto the nightstand and leapt out of bed, still glistening in the dim light. Tommy was going to ask what was wrong, but his words fell away, drowned out by the banging noise on the door.

"I'm so sorry," she said, her explanations bouncing between English words that Tommy could follow and Spanish ones that he couldn't.

"Whoah, wait, slow down," he said, pulling his boxers on.

"God, I'm sorry. Just... Aw, *madre de dios,* that *estupido*... What's the word... Fuck! My... not *esposo*. Ugh, shit, the word..."

"Oh shit," said Tommy, then his mind decoded the Spanish word from his dribblings of remaining high school knowledge. "Wait... Your husband?"

"No, it's... It's complicated, but just get dressed fast."

Another series of knocks sounded on the door. She was already wriggled into some skinny jeans, which Tommy tried not to get too excited watching, and she had a loose sweatshirt on a second later, no bra. Tommy himself was pulling on his clothes, and wasn't sure if he was going to be pulling on boots or not for a quick escape, or possibly an ass kicking. He wasn't a meek or weak man, but he also wasn't going to straight up start a fistfight with some stranger if he could avoid it.

The pounding broke his thoughts again, and Tatiana seemed to strain, holding back another string of Spanish profanity. She took a second to take a deep breath, then beckoned for Tommy to follow.

Once out in the living room, Tatiana gestured for Tommy to take a seat. She quickly checked herself in a nearby mirror, running her hands through her hair to straighten the mess it had become in the tussle. Then she spun, grabbing the door handle. She took a deep breath before throwing the door open wide.

"*MOMMMMMYYYYY!!!!!*"

The child's cry was enthusiastic, and the little pigtailed figure barreled into Tatiana with glee. She caught the girl and hugged her tight. Tommy could see the facial resemblance, the vivid dark eyes, but a different smile than her mother's.

"Oh, my baby girl!!! How was your week with daddy?"

At this, the smile seemed to slip away from the girl's face.

"Daddy said I have to give you something..." she slid a little purple backpack off her back with a cartoon character on it that Tommy did not recognize, and pulled out a little piece of paper from a side pocket. Tatiana took it and unfolded it. Tommy could tell from across the room it was an invoice of some kind. He looked down at the girl, who seemed to finally notice him, and stepped closer to her mother.

"*Tacaño...*" She stopped herself and looked back at Tommy, then to the girl. She bit her lip for a moment before speaking. "Maya, this is Tommy. It's okay, say hello."

Tommy affected a smile and waved. Maya seemed a little too shy to return the greeting.

"Mommy, can I go play X-Box?" she asked.

Tatiana smiled at her daughter and nodded. "Go ahead, but not that shooting game!" The girl was already off and running for a corner bedroom that Tommy hadn't noticed in their earlier haste.

"It gives Mommy a headache!" Tatiana called after the scrambling little feet. She took a few steps, then dropped down onto the couch beside Tommy, clutching the invoice in her hand. Tommy was able to glance over and see the words "*Science Day Camp*" at the top.

"I'm sorry," she said, folding the paper up and slipping it into her back pocket. "My ex-husband likes to test the boundaries of our separation agreement whenever he can. He was supposed to drop her off tomorrow morning. And now he's not even watching her, he's dropping her off at this day camp and sticking me with the bill."

"I'm sorry," Tommy offered, and she smiled a little at that.

"It's not your fault," she said.

There was a silent question between them, and it seemed like Tatiana was terrified to ask it. Tommy wasn't sure what it was, but he'd seen it before somewhere, and it made him both sympathetic and afraid. It dawned on him slowly, and tore at old wounds when it did. He answered her question by putting his arms around her and pulling her close. She met his eyes. At first there was confusion, then something like disbelief, but then a sorrowful welling of tears as she buried her head in his shoulder and hid her tears from the world.

He just held her. His eyes wandered to the room in the corner, where he knew, a young girl was trying very hard not to wonder if this stranger in the room was her new daddy, if he would be a good daddy, like the kind on tv, or if he would be like the one she'd been stuck with. She'd be trying hard not to wonder if it was her fault. And she'd be ashamed, for reasons she couldn't understand. She'd sit in her dark place, and wish and wonder, afraid. She'd be mad her mother for not having a father, and scared that she might wind up the same way.

Tommy had been that child. And he would not be surprised if the girl had watched her Mommy have some wine and cry and get mad at something random because the real thing she was mad at wasn't here.

"I'll stay if you want me to," he said.

A single sob burst against him, and Tatiana's arms hugged him more tightly. She seemed to shake her head a little, then pulled back slowly.

Her tears were wiped away so fast one might never know they were there.

"No, it's... It's *my* problem," she said.

"Really, I can-"

"*No,*" she said, placing a gentle hand on his chest, "It's sweet of you, and I thank you. I need to talk to Maya and... And explain. It's hard for her as it is."

Tommy nodded. "I get it."

There was a small silence, and Tatiana studied his face. She seemed to make up her mind about something, then. Some small change in her face, maybe a shifting of lips, or a twitch in her cheek. He wasn't sure. But he was sure he'd seen a decision somewhere in her eyes.

She slowly pulled away, and stood before him, looking down on him like she was the adult, a grown woman, trying to bring her authority together through a heavy heart.

"Listen, Tommy... I really like you. And tonight was... Well, amazing! I want to see you again, things are just so crazy right now."

"It's okay," he said, "Take your time, and... Well, let me know if I can help."

She seemed on the verge of tears again, but with a deep breath, a mask of calm came over her and she nodded, giving him a resolute smile. And then she put her arms around him and he felt wetness dampen his shoulder. He couldn't help losing some tears of his own. He looked again towards that corner bedroom. He felt certain there were little eyes watching through the crack.

His mind conjured a parade of angry, drunk, tattooed and violent men who would put out cigarettes on his arm, or slap him for being too noisy when he was that child, peering through the door. He still had the scars. He took that pain and channeled it into the hug. He didn't want to let go. He wasn't one of those men, and he never would be. He would never hurt a child the way he'd been hurt.

And she was not the drunk looking for her quickest fix. She was not the shattered soul who had no business raising a kid. This was different. Broken, true... but not the same. He knew what it was to live in a life of broken glass, always afraid of getting cut on the shards, always walking on tiptoes so no one ever had to clean it up.

He kept making himself believe it wasn't the same. His head knew it wasn't the same. His heart was terrified that it would be the same.

He could still smell Tatiana's sweat on him as he drove home, and frustratingly tried to navigate the bare roads around the massive pond. The sun was just below the horizon now, and though Tommy had been lost in the dark in these woods before, he'd never have recognized the handful of landmarks that brought him back to the manor if not for the receding orange sun. He didn't want to leave, but he couldn't stay. Maybe it was just hard to focus through the roiling pain in his gut. His entire life, feelings like this kept him held back. And a year ago, he'd have shoved them away in a vault in his soul rather than face them. But that was what his father did. He needed a better way. It was almost an inner terror, as if he were so close to being exposed somehow that he needed to cover up, armor that spot against the world.

• • • •

It was still early, and the sky was only barely dark, when his phone rattled on the dash. He waited until he let Mac out for a bathroom break before he answered it. It was a text from Tatiana. It simply said "Thank you," surrounded by little hearts. He smiled, waited for Mac to do his business, then called the pup inside. He slept in the bare bedroom again that night, but for the first time in a long time, he slept deeply, and with peaceful dreams.

Chapter Nine

Harvest time was always an interesting time for the little village. That's how Mary came to think of it. Though the housing was crude, they were slaves after all, they had a community all their own, and they had great celebrations when times were good. Some spoke in that beautiful tongue from their native land, and she found there was an agreeable harmony in it. It sounded like magic, like the magic her god in the dark was teaching her each night in her dreams.

Mary had been hiding out with them for a few weeks now, slowly regaining her strength. At night, her dreams brought her to the void where the secrets of God were exposed as lies, and by morning she would scribble all she had learned in her diary. She'd had one of the young boys steal it from the house, his little ebony face grinning ear to ear with glee at being asked to break such a strict rule. These people had a certain innocence about them. Perhaps it was the innocence of ignorance, as they were the children of the displaced. What she had learned of their homeland from the remaining elders, it was a hot land, alternately very wet or very dry, a harsh place, but they spoke of it wistfully and with an English peppered by strange sounds. Still, she had learned much from them, and saw where they had many qualities to love.

Mary had begun teaching the slaves as well, how to read, write, math, science, and the secrets of the spheres that she thought they could understand. When her monthly blood came again, she was not ashamed, but recognized it as a sign of something new. The old God's hatred had been washed away that cold rainy night, and now what remained was stronger. Her God did not hate. It could not hate. The concept was beyond it, or perhaps, it was beyond the concept. Hate was a human failing.

Mary would never shy away from the darkness, because she had seen everything it had in store. The darkness sheltered her from cruelty, protected her from hatred. The darkness was warmth when all else was cold and dying.

The younger boys and girls eagerly ate up what she taught, and the pretty brown boys her own age were awakening feelings within her she once thought shameful. She would test them, touch their muscles and stroke their faces. She understood the growing hunger within her, but something was not right yet... No, not yet. Appealing though it was, and no longer burdened by the shame of sin, her body would become alight with electric excitement watching them dance in the firelight.

Now that the harvest was in full swing, and the heathens here were preparing their great celebration, she found a coincidence of ritual that she could use. She knew they did this every year, down in their little valley village, but in her previous life, she had never known just what a joyous and beautiful thing this celebration was. Her father tried to scare her into thinking there were all manner of terrible sins being committed, but as she lived among these people, she saw they were not sinners. No, quite the contrary, they were the most loving and giving people she had ever known. The old men and women were grandmothers and grandfathers she had never known she could even wish for, and the slew of new aunties and uncles showed her kindness and compassion that the Man of God would not even show his own flesh and blood.

But then... that's what it all came down to in the end... the blood.

Mary smirked and watched the beginning of the torch lighting. Sunset was approaching. Barrels of fermented cider were rolled out. Though these people were slaves, this one night of the year, they considered themselves free.

Mary would see that they were free. And she would make sure that the man who kept them in chains was, himself, bound and shut up in darkness forever.

They chanted in their broken language something soulful and joyous, and Mary soon joined in. This was her family now, the one she would kill to protect. It was nothing so paltry as a promise, for a promise could be broken. It was truth.

They welcomed her with calloused hands, gentle but strong. She joined a circle of chanting, and whispered her own little oath to the void. It would begin soon, the real harvest, and when she was finished, the bones of her father would be her throne in a new, endless night.

Little Peter was in his favorite hiding place in the cupboard when the men arrived. Father had been in a very strict mood since Mary was taken by God, so he and the other children were like to hide whenever they sensed his presence. It was only chance that he was here, making no sound, that he heard the heavy footsteps cross from the other side of the house.

"May I offer you gentlemen tea?" said father.

"No, thank you, Jedediah," said another man, a man with a deeper voice that Peter could feel through the wood of the cupboard.

"Well then, what can I do for the two of you?"

There was a small pause, and Peter could almost feel a rising heat.

"Well, my old friend," said another voice, this one a little softer, perhaps older, it seemed slightly raspy, but then cleared its throat, "We're concerned. You see, there have been some... unkind rumors about you and your missing daughter, Mary."

"Mary was taken by God," said Father, his tone somber, but somewhat proud.

"So you have said," rumbled the lower voice, "May we ask exactly, how?"

"Why, Magistrate, you doubt the almighty?" Father snapped.

"I doubt you," said the low voice.

A tense silence fell over the kitchen. Peter stopped breathing, afraid they might hear in this noiseless emptiness.

"What the Magistrate means, my good sir," said the raspy voice, "Is that we... Well, we wish to put the general town at rest concerning these, um... raptures, I suppose. First your wife, then your oldest daughter..."

"And possibly some of the foundlings," rumbled the low voice.

"Get out of my house!" Father said, his ire shaking the floor. "You, Marcus, are supposed to be a fellow man of God! You should be ashamed, questioning my faith! Both of you, out!"

No other word was exchanged. Footsteps left the kitchen, and Peter carefully slipped out of the cupboard. He wanted to get very far away, very fast, before his angry father caught him. He did not want to be raptured like Mary was.

But as he scurried out the kitchen door, into the back yard, one of the little black boys from the village was there. He smiled at Peter and waved. Peter backed away, but the boy ran up to him and pressed something into his hand. He winked at Peter, then turned and ran back down the hill towards the gazebo, and the stone steps down to the village. Peter looked down, and the tiny silver cross in his hand glinted in the sun. It had been Mary's.

That night, while Peter slept in his soft bed, cradling the little cross and praying for Mary's soul under his breath... She was listening.

She smiled and waited for him to sleep before she slid out of the darkness and took that breath.

• • • •

Doctor Curruthers did not enjoy this country. Back in England, people were proper, respectable, and so was the climate. But here, he had quickly discovered, the mere change in wind could turn a hot, sunny day to blistering wet cold, and nowhere else had he seen thunder and snow in the same storm. He had planned to return to

England before the frost hit this year, and whatever plagues God had planned for this land could be unleashed far away from him.

His bags bounced as the old buggy hit a rut, more common on these old excuses for roads than signage. But at last, they rolled to a stop.

He checked his many glass vials, then used a mirror to straighten himself. His mustache needed a quick touch of wax. He then gathered his belongings and waited for the coachman to open the door.

He was greeted by a well-dressed negro woman who gestured that he follow her to the house. The plantation's vast fields erupted with corn, pumpkins, and apple trees stretching away in all directions. Grape vines were latticed up along tall old fences.

But the house was what truly snared his attention. Dr. Curruthers looked up at the house, and felt as if the octagonal eye of the top spire was looking down at him. He did not believe in omens, he was a man of science, but it was unsettling, nonetheless.

The negro woman opened the door, and Curruthers stepped into an extremely beautiful painted room. Coals quietly sizzled in the fireplace, and there was not a speck of dust to be found.

The Negro woman excused herself and stepped away to go fetch her master. Curruthers took the time to look around the room. There were crosses everywhere, which he had expected, they told him Mr. Worthington was a very religious man, but he was not prepared for the portrait above the mantle. He had given it very little thought, since at first glance it was simply a crucifixion scene, but now that he looked at it, he could see the graphic detail.

It was nearly a study in crimson, the blood matting in the Savior's hair from the crown of thorns, the ghastly gore coming from the wounds of his hands and feet, and of course, the spear wound, which was lovingly painted with such dedication to detail that one could just see where the artist had hinted at the internal organs beneath the pierced flesh. The skin was emaciated, ribs poking through like the keys of a grim cathedral organ, and a pale, pallid gray. Beneath the dying savior, men and women prostrated themselves, each of them covered in the drippings of the savior's blood.

"Doctor Curruthers," said a raspy voice. The suddenness of it snapped the doctor from his gruesome reverie. Standing behind him was a tall man, his hair frizzled white, his skin old and dry, and he smiled with yellowed teeth.

"Mr. Worthington," said the doctor, regaining his composure. He stepped forward to take the man's hand. They shook hands like gentlemen, but Dr. Curruthers noted his thin, bony fingers were as cold as ice.

"Thank you for coming," said Worthington, "I would normally leave matters such as this up to the Lord, but I remember hearing of an illness like this before, and hoped you might be able to do something."

"Of course, I'll do my best," said Curruthers, "You said it's an illness? What sort?"

"I don't know the name," Worthington said, gesturing for the doctor to take a seat. Curruthers sank onto an old wooden chair. Worthington remained standing. "But my son, Peter, expels blood from his mouth in great fits of coughing, and he is feverish and weak."

Curruthers stood up. "My God! That sounds like consumption! This is no time for formalities, my good man, I must examine him immediately!"

The boy was dreadfully pale and weak. His lips were stained from the blood, and his fever was terrifyingly high. Dr. Curruthers listened to his lungs and subjected the boy to various pokes and prods, which he endured with no comment. His eyes seemed empty, vacant, as if he were not there at all.

Curruthers began to sweat. He could feel the watchful eye of Worthington on him as he worked. It was more than just disconcerting, something about the man was off-putting, casting a pall over the whole estate, like that tower with the eye.

"Well, Doctor?" he asked, as if he could sense Curruther's discomfort.
"It certainly looks like consumption. How long has he been like this?"
"Three days," said Worthington.
"My god! I only got your summons this morning! I'm so sorry..."
"Is there nothing to be done?"

Curruthers paused and considered, his finger idly running along the line of his jaw.
"It's difficult to say," he said, "I have some tonics that may be of use, but at this late stage... I'm afraid there's the very real chance the boy will not survive."
Worthington closed his eyes and put his hands together, dropping to his knees. He appeared to be praying.
Curruthers turned back to the boy, who seemed to suddenly be very alert, staring into the doctor's eyes. Curruther's mouth hung open, and something like a scream began to form in his throat. The boy was so close, the heat from his skin was blistering to Curruther's face.
"She comes at night," he said, his voice more raspy than that of his father, "And steals my breath."
Peter's eyes then glossed over, and he seemed to fall back onto the bed.
Dr. Curruthers looked back at the praying Mr. Worthington, then again to the boy, now inert, his eyes empty but staring at the distant wall. He'd never seen someone sick with consumption do

that. He swallowed hard, then began preparing a mixture of opium and alcohol to make sure the boy slept and that the germs in his throat were subdued.

. . . .

A summer storm in New England is a chaotic beast, delivering winds and rain that can chill to the bone, but cracks of hot white lightning, and then within minutes, the storm will recede, and the hot sun will burn away the wetness leaving the world in a mire of foggy heat, broiling the land in a choking cloud.

It was this heat Tommy woke to, and felt seeping into his big empty bedroom. Mac was curled up in a corner on the cooler hardwood floor. The poor pup was probably desperate to cool off under all that shaggy fur. Tommy rolled out of bed and got water for the beast, before getting ready for yet another day of work.

He and Tatiana had been texting, but she hadn't yet been able to arrange for any free time. Apparently her ex husband, or as she liked to call him, *El Mierdo*, had been using little Maya as a bargaining chip, or a pawn, depending on the circumstances. It boiled him to know that someone was willing to do something like that. Tommy may have some unkind feelings towards some ex girlfriends, but you don't make that the problem of a kid. A kid's only problem should be math tests and peer pressure, not a manipulative parent in a messy divorce. He'd endured that. He knew the wounds that could inflict. He had daydreams of holding the man with his arms behind his back while little Maya could punch him in the gut. That's what he would have wanted, all those years ago, scared, confused, desperate for a sliver of warmth.

But the rational part of his mind, the one that saw the fruitlessness of rage and violence, the one that knew how being pushed that far could be used against him, kept his temper in check. Though he still simmered beneath, and likely always would.

He also gathered that Tatiana was very lonely. It wasn't just that they'd wound up in bed so quickly, it was how she talked, and the little details he didn't notice until later. He remembered only much later the little red marks on her skin from shaving down below, and apparently in a hurry, as there were little nicks and scratches. Her little condo had been spotless, but for the single wine glass on the counter, and several bottles in a recycle bin.

And of course, there was *El Mierdo*. Tatiana said he would drop Maya off early, pick her up late, and sometimes Maya would be holding back tears. God only knew what he was telling her. He would flake on plans to take her, and then blame Tatiana for not reminding him. He knew that kind of behavior.

"Tommy, you didn't tell me you needed a ride today, so this is your fault."

He shook his head, trying not to let the cork on that particular bottle pop. Instead he went to the partially-functional bathroom and wet his face from the sink. His stubble was itchy, especially in this weather. A dollop of creamy shaving foam dispensed into his hand from the aerosol can, Tommy went to work covering the shadow. He took the dollar-store razor and began carefully running it along his rough skin.

"Well how was I supposed to know you had detention, you never told me."

A scraping noise, a rough cut, slight blood running into the whiteness. He rinsed off the little razor, then went back for another pass.

"It's not MY fault your drunk of a mother never showed you how to do this."

Another echoing voice in his mind from a distant past. More rough resistance on the razor, and more blood. He grunted and tossed the little plastic thing into a small trash can. He found the plastic bag full of more of the same, popped off the protective cover, and went back to work on his face.

Those words of Margot made him feel as if his stomach was filled with poison. Maybe it wouldn't work out with Tatiana, and in fact it probably wouldn't, just because of who Tommy was. Maybe he didn't consider himself caregiver material, but he sure knew when someone was doing a shit job of it. Nobody had this much trauma from being with a healthy person.

He looked at his half-foam covered face in the mirror.

Maybe this wasn't the face of father material, now or ever, but he wasn't going to stand by while someone even worse screwed up some innocent kid's childhood.

His internal trauma treated him to an imagining of Maya, locked in a bare room, no light, while sounds of moaning, then shouting, then angry violence filled the emptiness. His hands shook. He decided shaving was not a good idea right now.

He washed off and went to dress. He had some ductwork to put up. But with every nail shot into the woodwork, with every screw nailed in, the queasy poison in his gut simmered. He slipped and cut a finger on the sharp aluminum edge. The explosive curse that came out of his mouth surprised him, just as much as hurling the piece of duct into the corner where it smashed against a toolbox and scattered screws and nails all over the floor. This only enraged him further, but before he could engage in another violent outburst, he halted himself.

"You're as bad as your mother," said the voice in his head.

He stuck the bleeding part of his hand into his mouth. He sucked and spat to get as much crud out of the cut as possible. Then, still fuming, stomped up the stairs to go clean the cut.

Washing out the blood in the sink, thinking back to the shaving cuts, and the half stubble, he knew he was not in a good headspace. That outburst, and another one bubbling under the surface, shook him.

"I'm *not* like them," he said to his reflection.

And this was where the drink would have come in, once upon a time. Even now he wanted to drown this feeling in beer. Even now, all these years later, those old wounds had never closed. Bubbling up from deep within, his anxiety forced something to the surface.

. . . .

His last night at that house. His last night at a permanent home. Tommy had the lean muscle of youth, stood several inches taller than his father, and had skipped school every day for the last week. He had returned to that house only to keep up appearances, but he knew that eventually the letters or notes or phone calls would catch up.

He didn't care.

He only stayed there long enough to shower, change clothes, and then sneak out again. Margot would throw her passive-aggressive comments at him, and he would march past, ignoring every word. He learned long ago she could not be trusted.

His father would be where he always was, down in the basement, working on something or other. Likely he was just hiding out from his wife. The loud noise of sawing or grinding or some other machinery would make it impossible to hear her lies.

Back then, the stairs were new, not even stained, just raw wood already getting scuffed by the rushed running of children. As Margot shouted words after him, Tommy climbed those steps to the narrow hall that led to his little room.

His room had been an afterthought, like he himself had been. The old man had partitioned off some of Tim's room and given Tommy his own space. The younger boy, just growing into a disgruntled teenager, was listening to some terrible thrash metal. He didn't know where his sister was, but she was likely reading a book whilst hiding in her closet.

Suddenly, Tim's door opened, probably responding to the footsteps on the stairs. He looked at Tommy and made a disgusted face.

"You again," he said, in just the same way Margot would say it.

"Fuck off, twig," Tommy said, turning to go into his own room.

"I'll tell Mom you swore at me!"

"Yeah, that'll make her hate me," Tommy spat with syrup-thick sarcasm.

"You gonna sneak out again? I'll tell her that, too!"

"Twig, it doesn't make a goddamned difference. If I cured cancer, she'd still shit on me. Tattle all you want."

He turned the knob and went into his room. He locked the door behind him, fully expecting an enraged Tim to bang his fists against it, shouting. This time, he didn't. Tommy should have known then that there was something different.

He swapped out his threadbare Alice in Chains tee shirt for a plain black one in better condition, and started slathering on deodorant. A glance at his digital clock told him he was already going to be late to the party, but he was going to try to smell good. Tracy Demillo was going to be there, and Tommy had been inching closer to her socially for a while now. She was unpopular, like him, but whereas he was seen as the messed-up poor kid, she was the pretty goth girl with purple lipstick. He had dreams about those purple lips. Against all reason, they somehow both caught wind of a party tonight in the woods. It was the kind of surreptitious joy an adolescent could sneak out to where someone would likely have snuck beer, weed, and maybe more.

Tommy, himself, intended to contribute to the good times. Under his bed was a flathead screwdriver. He used that to pop up a loose floorboard and recover the small metal tin. It was covered in Christmas decorations, but inside was a small bag of green buds, rolling papers, and a lighter.

The smell immediately hit him, and it would likely be a damned sight better than whatever skunk weed his peers might bring. It hadn't been easy to get, but it made life in this shitty house bearable.

He opened his window. Down below was soft grass, and he had no problem making the jump as he had many times before.

On foot, the walk to the edge of the woods from the heart of suburbia was two miles. The sun was throwing orange light against black shadows when he reached the tunnel, a circular tube of brick beneath railroad tracks that led to a small park with a plastic playground and seldom-used basketball court. Beyond that, out of range of the awakening streetlights, stretched dark woods, growing darker by the minute.

The rumors were true, though, and before long Tommy heard the distant low-baseline thrum of something like Nirvana, or its many imitators. When the headlights appeared in the distance, he realized he was close. He followed that beacon of rebellion to a clearing where someone's shiny Jeep blasted out a Butthole Surfers song.

In his memory, the faces and names washed away. Maybe because he'd started drinking beer immediately, or maybe the weed, or shock, trauma, whatever. But what he remembered most was through the haze, he had looked up from talking to Tracy, or maybe more than talking, he remembered his lips were sticky, and standing there in the field was Jamie, his kid sister, looking lost, but also wandering with that wide-eyed curiosity that comes with youth.

Tommy broke away and stormed right up to her. This was no place for a 14 year old girl, but that wasn't his main reason. He knew what the Old Man or Margot would do to him if anything happened to her. And this was a field of horny, drunk, high teenage boys with dick brains. As it is, they were surrounded by couples in deep kisses, feeling up each others bodies.

"What the fuck are you doing here?!" Tommy demanded, seizing her by the arm. She gave a yelp, and he had probably hurt her.

"I... I..." she stammered. Immediately, Tommy felt stupid. She wanted to see what he was always up to. She was a younger sibling, after all. They did these things. And since she'd been the older sibling of the family for a while, she thought she was mature enough to see what was happening.

"Do you have any idea what Dad will do to me if he finds out you were here?! Goddamnit, Jamie, you're smarter than that. Come on, I'm taking you home."

"But... but wait," she said.

"No!" he snapped, "You don't want to do stuff like this! You're the smart one!"

Somehow, that seemed to deeply affect her. She started to tear up, but Tommy didn't have time to calm her down. If Tommy didn't come to dinner, that was normal. But if Jamie didn't show up, a search would begin.

"Look," he said, "Just... Go run home. Tell Dad you went to the library or something. He'll believe that. But DO NOT ever follow me again!"

"But-" she began.

"No! Wherever I'm going, you don't belong there. You're better. I'm not. Now go! Run!"

She didn't have the chance. A voice rang out through the woods, a figurative gunshot, one that shook him to his core. It wasn't just the voice he recognized, it was the tone. It was the tone he knew would bring pain. It would bring terror, and isolation, utter horror.

"*Boy*!" said his father. He was marching across the field. Not far away was that big white Chevy he drove. How he had found them would always remain a mystery to Tommy, but it mostly didn't matter.

He didn't get two words out of his mouth before that steel-hard fist connected with his jaw. Tommy went to the ground, his world rolling around him. He heard Jamie scream.

"No! Dad! It's not his fault!" She pled with him, but the old man just pushed her aside.

"She's fourteen, you sick little bastard! And your sister!"

Tommy looked up. People were watching, people in school, the people who already judged him every second of every day. *Like*

Margot did. They used any and every possible twist of words and meanings to torment him. These two awful worlds had never collided until today. There was no way to run from this now.

The fury took over. Tommy was on his feet, and hurled a punch of his own.

"I didn't *bring her!*" he screamed. His hand connected with the old man's nose, and Tommy felt a crunch. He caught sight of a red arc, and only a few seconds later, when the gravity of what he'd done brought him out of the rage, did he look down to see his father's blood on his hand.

He remembered thinking that god didn't bleed.

His father reached up to his nose, looked down at the blood running down out of both nostrils. His eyes lit with mad fire then.

Tommy saw that rage, and his own flared back. People were watching the fight now, some cheering Tommy on, others cheering against. They were nothing but distant voices as Tommy and his father hurled fists.

Eventually, people pulled them apart. Tommy would learn later that it was the police that had broken up the party. They hadn't even known about the fight until they chased away the crowd around it.

He remembered sitting in the back of a police car, handcuffed, bloodied, while looking out at his father, sitting in the back of an ambulance while an EMT set his nose, and put his arm in a sling.

Tommy was not afforded medical treatment until just before they threw him in lockup.

It was Tommy's first and only night in a jail cell. He'd heard stories about what happened to people in prison. But he never had the opportunity to find out. The next morning, he was released, unmolested.

But he was released to Margot.

She didn't say a word, and neither did he. He climbed into the back seat of the minivan, and stared out the window until the vehicle stopped in their driveway.

Once inside, Tommy went straight to his room, threw everything in his drawers into a backpack, and walked out the door again before Margot or anyone else could talk to him.

He knew what they were going to say. He'd heard it before. He hiked down to the bus stop, and took a bus up to Hartford, where he walked into the first law office he could find and asked what he needed to do to become emancipated.

He had two reasons for wanting this. The first, was that he knew he didn't deserve the hell that was waiting for him. He intended to leave that behind.

The second, was that the only person in that family who seemed to have the intelligence and the kindness to become better had just come within inches of losing her potential, because of *him*.

It was better for everyone if he just vanished. That's what he did. He didn't even pretend that he looked back. That house was not his home, and never really had been.

Reliving that memory, and the millions of memories that led him to that point in his life, left Tommy sitting in the middle of the trailer, needlessly tinkering with his collection of drill bits and checking to make sure they all fit well. It was idle, pointless, and required no concentration on his part. It almost felt like work. But eventually he realized he was accomplishing nothing. His gut continued to roil with his past mistakes for the rest of the day.

· · · ·

As evening set in, Tommy would find a novel of text messages, most likely sent over a few glasses of wine. But Tommy would read them, respond, give her a sounding board, while he made a quick cheap dinner and prepared for bed. This became their pattern for a few days. It helped him pull his focus from the depth of his own memories and concentrate on the here and now. This was borrowed pain, which he could handle.

And he lived for those texts, as it was the only time he was able to spend with her. Unlike her ex-husband, Tommy cared about whether his presence might be difficult for Maya. He didn't want to come for a visit while she was there, not if life was confusing enough. He was worried Tatiana would be disappointed by this, but she responded with a big heart emoticon.

A week seemed to pass like a grinding eternity, but finally, *El Mierdo* picked up Maya for the weekend, and Tommy made arrangements to meet with Tatiana for a morning run, and then maybe something more.

No, definitely something more. And not just the sex, though he very much wanted that, it wasn't all about him. Even if it was, seeing someone in this situation was making him relive a lot, and revisit nightmares he had thought long forgotten.

Before the broken home his father had chosen, Tommy had been beaten regularly by his natural mother, or someone she had brought home. He'd been scarred. He'd been yelled at for being too loud, or coming out of his room at the wrong time. His adult mind suspected his mother had been a prostitute, but as a child, all he knew was that she kept bringing men home, and none of them were happy to see him. The few that hung around longer than the others all made him feel like he was unwanted. That was probably how he first learned to love solitude.

Alone was safe.

When Tatiana confessed that she'd rather Maya's father be dead than be the sad human that he was, he was temporarily tempted to oblige her. With a few beers under his belt, he let slip that he owned a gun. She didn't respond for a long time, but then said no, because "we are better people than that."

No one had ever implied that he was a better person, and he needed to take that in, too. Sure, he knew he was trying not to be a bad person, but then, he kind of still was. Maybe not the 'beat your kids,' kind of bad person, but he honestly didn't know. Was he the kind of bad person that would punch out an old man? He certainly felt that way sometimes. Deep within he had a hungry fire for retribution against the people that hurt him, the people who sucked away his childhood and left him half a man.

By the weekend, he was so overwhelmed with emotion that he wasn't sure what was going to happen. In the span of seven days, his entire life had been turned around, its dirty secrets tumbled out into his mind, and concentrating at work was becoming a labor all of its own. He hadn't done a stitch of work on the house. Instead he checked his phone every spare minute, waiting for the next text. He drank up the beer he had, then forced himself not to buy any more. No, he knew what lay down that road.

Saturday morning, just after dawn, he was in his running clothes, heading to go meet her in the woods. He wasn't in the mood for a run. He was in the mood to vomit out his heart and hope she wasn't cruel enough to stomp on it.

Once again, her tight outfit was distracting as could be, and Tommy felt like a pudgy potato in his baggy tee shirt. They ran along the path in the woods where they first met. Thankfully, Tommy was not assaulted by any swarms of tiny flies, and Mac, of course, scrambled back and forth, marking trees and sniffing out potential prey.

The running helped. He couldn't explain why, but the rhythm of his feet on the ground, the beating of his heart, calmed the squirming anxiety deep within him. It did not depart, but it remained still.

They jogged on through the trees, and Tommy showed her the manor, his work in progress.

They came to a stop after breaking through the tree line, Tatiana leaning against a tree to take a long pull on her water bottle. Tommy did the same, but remained standing for lack of anything with sufficient support for him.

The property looked incredibly different now. Where once the manor had been a complete crumbling wreck, there were signs now that the exterior was at least partially built. Tyvek panels showed through where the construction was nearing completion, and the spire lost some of its ominous overtones with the cluster of tarp-covered lumber and tools resting below it.

"Wow," she said, "That's the house?"

"Yeah," said Tommy, "Got it for peanuts. Gonna turn it into a gold mine."

"It's huge! My god, I thought it was just a big, like... regular house. That's a fucking mansion."

Tommy shrugged. He was not motivated to contradict her being impressed. The thought of the body he'd found itched at the back of his head, but he dismissed it. There was no way he was mentioning that to her. Instead, he decided to highlight the good points.

"Twelve rooms," Tommy said, "Huge dining room, fireplaces everywhere."

"What's that over there?" She motioned across the field to where the top of the old Gazebo at the water could be seen.

"There's a pond down there," said Tommy.

"Wow," she said, "Can I see?"

Tommy hadn't been down there since the first walkthrough, but now as they stood beneath the pines and looked at the wide, still waters, she seemed thoroughly impressed.

"Do you ever go swimming?" she asked, quirking an eyebrow.

"No, I'm, uh... Not much of a swimmer," Tommy said, trying not to sound too embarrassed. She gave him a cheeky wink and stepped toward the edge of the water.

"It's a nice way to cool off," she said, in a tone that clearly meant to be enticing. She kicked her running shoes off and somehow slid out of her little socks at the same time. She stepped carefully into the water in bare feet while Tommy watched from where he was.

"It's perfect," she said, "*Vamanos.*"

Tommy stepped forward, trying not to be too hesitant. He really wasn't much of a swimmer, and it was something he tried very hard to hide. In fact, he couldn't remember a single time he'd gotten into the water and hadn't been utterly terrified.

His brain was echoing old memories of water seeping up his nose and down his throat, choking the air out of him as he sank. His old memories were full of the taste of soapy bathwater, and a hard hand pushing his small head down. *Wash that fucking hair or I will!*

He stopped at the edge of the water.

"I dunno," he said, "I mean, I haven't even had this pond tested for-"

She scooped a wave of water and sent it sailing at him. He betrayed himself and jumped back in fright. The look on his face must have given him away, as she came back up to him with a frown.

"Are you okay?"

Tommy didn't respond at first, but Tatiana put a gentle hand on his face and made him meet her eyes.

"Oh, I'm so sorry," she said, "You... Why don't we go look at the house, hm?"

Tommy wasn't sure how to react. He felt naked in front of her, and deeply ashamed. She took his hand and they climbed back up to the open field. Tommy soon recovered, but cast one final glance back at the pond. The dark waters seemed like a shallow grave.

They stopped at the camper so she could wipe off her feet and put her shoes back on, then Tommy showed her around the house. He talked about the work he was doing on it, and she seemed to comprehend none of it, but she sure had an eye for detail. She immediately noticed the fireplaces and the old stone work. She practically squealed at the size of the kitchen and the dining room.

"This is amazing, Tommy!" she said. He didn't understand her excitement, but she seemed absolutely fascinated, even by the absolutely gutted kitchen. The only thing Tommy had left intact were the brick fireplace ovens, but she ran her hands over them almost lovingly.

"It's like one of those old houses in those... what do you call them? Those old English dramas? Like Jane Austin or something."

The term didn't come to Tommy's mind, either. Tatiana turned to the brick ovens built into the wall and looked them over. He wasn't sure what she was looking for, but he sure did enjoy her bending over and looking. She peered inside, and for some reason, up the chimney, where a cool draft of air was sinking down from above.

"Hey," she said, "There's something in here."

"I'm not surprised," he said, "Usually squirrels or bats nest in old chimneys."

"No, no, it's... Hang on..."

She wriggled her body into the brick archway, and a moment later, emerged with something soot covered. It was an old glass bottle, stoppered with a cork, and apparently sealed with very old wax, wax that seemed to be flaking away from age. Whatever was inside was also black as soot, some sort of liquid onyx. As she shook it, something rattled inside, muffled by the liquefied contents.

Tommy had a deep frown on his face. "What the hell is that?"

"You think it's old wine?" she asked.

"I wouldn't drink it," he said. She handed the bottle to him, and he turned it over, holding it up to the light coming in through the window. The liquid did have a slight translucence to it, and as he looked, some of the rattling items settled where he could just make out some detail.

At first, he thought they were pieces of carved wood, but the ends were slightly bulged, as if they were tiny bones. He shook the bottle slightly, and as they moved, he could see more detail, and the bones of tiny human fingers danced in the morbid ink.

Tommy almost dropped the bottle, but managed to put it down on the still-standing bricks of the old oven. Tatiana frowned at him, as his face had lost color, and he seemed to be slightly shaking.

"What is it?" she asked. She picked up the bottle, and peered in herself. Tommy tried to make coherent words form, but nothing was coming out. It didn't matter. Tatiana saw for herself the tiny bones dancing in the black slickness.

"*Dios mio,*" she breathed.

She looked to Tommy, who was too horrified to say anything. He thought back to the body that he'd found, the strange old diary, and the stories of the crazy old man who'd owned this place in the distant past.

Chapter Ten

Peter had always enjoyed the little garden in the back where the grape vines grew. He used to eat them right off the vine and spit the seeds everywhere, hoping to grow more grapes. Ever since Mary had told him it was also Mother's favorite, when she had been alive and could stand in the radiant sun, nurturing the warm fruit on hot summer days. It seemed a fitting place to bury him.

The funeral was small, the family only, and of course, the foundlings. The consumption had taken Peter in the night, and now there were only two natural children, and eight of the foundlings.

Worthington delivered a eulogy, directly pulled from the psalms, and told the assembled children that Peter was now with the Lord, and having lived a righteous and clean life, was now in paradise where all the love of the Lord would comfort and protect him.

Four boys and six girls, dressed in rough black clothes, stood in the oddly hot morning sun while he prattled on. Doctor Curruthers lingered at the trees, feeling awkward. He had been amazed at the old man's vigor in preparing the body for burial. He seemed almost happy in work. The man clearly had either worked with or been an undertaker at some point.

During his stay here at the manor, he'd observed a lot about Mr. Worthington that concerned him. No more so than the boy's deterioration. Lucid and happy one evening, on death's door the next day that no amount of medicines or rest could restore. It was as if the life simply leaked out of the boy, draining away like the water on the other side of the Ardham Dam they were building up the road. That great ambitious wall of brick and rock was to open up land for farming, in the hopes it was as fertile and plentiful as Worthington's own green fields.

He snapped back to the moment, watching Worthington gesticulate wildly in the middle of some rant against blasphemy. The look in his eyes made the doctor's blood ice up even in the hot mid-day sun.

He'd checked the other children for any signs of consumption, or other ailments, and while mercifully there were none, there were other issues he had become concerned about.

There were scars on the backs of the girls, long scars, as if from a whipping. Curruthers had treated many former and current slaves, and knew those marks well. But to see them on children in this fashion... He understood the principle of 'spare the rod,' but this seemed excessive. Some of the wounds were old, and starting to fester. Had he not been there to treat them, the children might have come down with all manner of fevers and other maladies. Infected wounds often led to serious illness, especially out on these isolated farms where calling for a doctor was a long process. The fastest message and the fastest coach could not deliver assistance quickly enough once the fevers began.

But Peter, he had no scars. Indeed, if any child had been spared of the rod, it was he, which made his ailment all the more perplexing. He could be made to sleep by drugs, but his ailments were worse each day, until finally, one morning, he was simply gone. His small body cold, and his eyes locked open in a rictus of fright, as if some nightmare visited him in the early hours of the morning, before the moonlight dew had settled.

The foundlings, he discovered, slept in the barn, which had been converted into crude bunks for them. They were treated well, and Worthington would read to them every day from the Good Book, but when one of them would do or say something he didn't like, there was fire in his eyes, and the child would shrink back as if under the hot sun, often averting their eyes. The young boys had rough, calloused, hands with broken nails and many scabs and scars. The backs of their hands seemed to have lash marks, but not as severe as what he found on the backs of the young girls. The poor orphans would tell him their stories, and they seemed to all coincide.

Once every few months, Mr. Worthington would venture to some far-off place along the coast, collect a child with no living parents, and promise they would learn the value of good, honest Christian living. They would be given food and shelter until they were stronger than the sickly thin wretches they were begging or stealing on the street. Then Worthington would begin preaching, and forcing them to confess any sin they had committed. Then the lashings for each sin, or things Worthington considered sins, that were simple acts of the maturing human body. Boys were whipped for touching their own private parts, even to urinate, but the girls were practically brutalized if, or more likely when, their monthly blood came along.

And of course, the barn still had the stink of animals, and the children seemed to seldom have been bathed. He saw better care taken of the slaves, whose children seemed remarkably happy and healthy by comparison. One young girl had a bloated belly, and though she would not speak, one of the boys said Master Worthington had forbade her to eat until she had fasted herself clean.

Doctor Curruthers gave her some soft bread and told her to eat it slowly. It was appalling to think Worthington's dark-age treatment of these children was even possible, much less permissible. He intended to have some words with the town Magistrate when he returned. This could not continue.

The thought of confronting Worthington crossed his mind, but for a man of his advanced years, he had a terrifying energy. Watching the alacrity of his work when he preached and administered punishment made even a grown man like Curruthers reluctant. Even now, as he preached to the children, that mad fire glowed in his eyes. The children were visibly terrified, trembling, and holding perfectly still with their heads bowed lest a single movement or twitch of their face inspire additional fury.

Worthington finished his sermon, and dismissed the children back to their house, the foundlings to the barn. Dr. Curruthers approached, and tried to remember his manners. The old man still at least deserved a modicum of manners, if only for the Doctor's sake as a man of culture. And besides, the tempest of words from him during the sermon could have shaken stone itself.

"Doctor," said Worthington, "I thank you for your efforts. Peter was... my... my..."

"Naturally, Mr. Worthington," he said, eager to appease what would likely be a newly invigorated ranting. "I'm only sorry I couldn't do more. I do have a concern that I'd like to address with you, though."

"Yes, Doctor?"

Curruthers found his courage leaving him. But quickly he devised a way he could mask his intentions and learn more.

"The boy must have contracted the illness from somewhere. With your permission, I would like to examine your slaves as well."

Worthington visibly flinched. Sparks began anew in his eyes. "Why?"

"Well, consumption is not a disease that simply comes from nowhere. It requires contact, quite a lot of contact. And none of the other children have any symptoms. If there is a plague among the slaves, we don't want it spreading."

Worthington considered this, and looked the doctor up and down. The old man was wily, despite his devotion to doctrine, and seemed to detect that Curruthers was hiding some other intention. He did not divine what it might be, though, from the scrupulous examination of the man. They stayed locked in a silent battle of wits for several tenuous seconds.

"Very well," Worthington relented, "You may examine the slaves. Perhaps their savage ways brought this wrath upon me. If you can determine that, I will be very grateful indeed, and effect an immediate solution."

Curruthers hid his revulsion with a smile, and shook the old man's dry hand.

Descending the stone steps to the slave village was an interesting journey. Though it was only a handful of yards, it seemed worlds away from the cold and empty Worthington Estate. Here, crude shelters had been built around one or two solid wooden shacks. Some seemed to almost be made of a hodgepodge of bricks and sticks, the roofs built of mismatched wood.

He realized the first sound he heard was one he'd not heard since he arrived, and the startling realization tugged at his soul. He heard the sound of laughing children.

Little brown boys, shoeless and covered in dust, ran around the field of cleared trees, chasing each other and shouting in giddy glee. A pair of women were hanging up wash on a long line that stretched between trees and huts. Everyone was clothed, but most were barefoot, and their hands rough with hard work. Their eyes watched Dr. Curruthers approach, slightly wary.

He nodded to them. "Good Morning," he said.

They nodded back, with curt little nods of no actual welcoming gesture. "Good morning," said one, she seemed to be a little younger, but also more robust, likely a mother of several.

"My name is Doctor Curruthers," he said, "Master Worthington's son, Peter, has fallen victim to a terrible illness. I was hoping you would allow me to examine some of your people to ensure the disease has not taken hold here among you."

The two women exchanged a quick glance, then in unison turned to one of the nearby shacks, where a woman with pale skin and honey-colored hair emerged.

"No, Doctor," she said, "There is no disease here."

Curruthers jaw fell. The face before him was one he'd seen in the portraits, but even if he hadn't, the resemblance was impossible to deny. Mary stood before him, her hair wildly unkempt, and unlike the others here, her features were still soft, telling of youth untouched by the labor of these people. She walked on open ground with bare feet, her steps small and graceful. She approached the Doctor with a wide smile, and the beaming beautific eyes of a child.

"I'm Mary Worthington," she said, "And if you'll come with me, there is much we must discuss."

They sat in the small shack, the one where Mary first regained her senses, and where now Dr. Curruthers sat on the same bed and held a small tin cup of weak tea. Mary sat on a crude wooden stool and hooked her feet into the legs.

"Miss Worthington, forgive me," said Curruthers, "I was under the impression you had..."

"Died?" she said bluntly. She shook her head. "My father is a fiend, Dr. Curruthers. It was only a matter of time before his madness really did take a life." Here, she looked at the floor, and a small shudder escaped, as did a glistening tear that fell to the floor. "Poor Peter."

"I've seen the wounds on the children," said Dr. Curruthers.

"I know," said Mary, her voice almost a whisper. "I've been watching. Hiding. My father thinks I'm dead, and that's the only way I'm safe. Please, you must go back to Ingham, tell people the evil that my father is doing! Peter's death will only be the beginning."

Curruthers nodded. "I had intended to already," he said, "To be quite frank, Miss Worthington, I am concerned that the source of the illness is not these people. While one cannot always tell the source of such maladies, I do believe the consumption that took your brother may have something to do with your father. Sadly, I have no proof of this, nor of any other sources of the malady. I'd hoped to find more answers if I could stay here and investigate."

Mary Worthington smiled and reached out to touch Dr. Curruther's arm.

"Thank you, Doctor," she said, "You are so kind. But you must understand, it *is* my father that is the source of malady. He must be stopped before any of my other siblings die. And if you stay here, he will also infect you."

"With the consumption?"

"With the madness," she said, her voice flat and low. Curruthers found his stomach no longer welcomed the tea he was sipping on. He placed the cup down beside him.

"Perhaps," he said, trying to make sense of the mismatched feelings in his belly, "What if you, yourself, could go to town? I'm sure your word, especially in light of the rumors about you, would be more than sufficient. Meanwhile, I could gather the necessary evidence to document and prove the cruelty."

Mary shook her head. "No, I couldn't. I've no decent clothes, and who would believe the word of a girl my age? No, doctor, it must be you. A respected man of knowledge, only you could persuade them to come and bring my father to justice for what he has done."

Curruthers frowned and realized the wisdom of this. Mary was quite a sharp girl for her age. She couldn't be much older than 12, and yet here she was, as bright as any grown woman. Curruthers nodded. He stood, straightening his jacket with conviction. He was not accustomed to these feelings of doubt. He was a man of medicine, and though medicine was as much an art as a science, there was a certainty in it that he held on to as his rock-solid foundation. For some reason, since he had arrived, that foundation had begin to crack.

"Very well," he said, "I will go inform the Magistrate. They already do have their suspicions. And it would be best if they were to hear the testimony of a doctor. I will go and beckon them to bring the law, Miss Worthington, I promise you that."

Curruthers almost stuck out his hand to shake hers, but frowned at the odd impulse. She was a child, and here he was thinking of her as a full equal. Bright, surely, but a mere girl. Clever, of course, but he was a doctor. He shook these queer notions from his head and gave her a steady nod.

"Thank you," she said, rising and embracing him tightly. He blushed a little, and muttered a farewell as he slipped out of the shack. He couldn't stop his skin from crawling. It made no sense. Something about the girl was just... off. A little coldness of the touch, or maybe the way her eyes seemed to glisten a little too sharply, like her father's eyes.

Dr. Curruthers climbed back up the stone steps to the great wide field, and found Worthington standing there by the grave of his son. He turned to Dr. Curruthers with a strange look on his face.

"Did you find the plague?" he asked.

Curruthers shook his head. "No, Mr. Worthington. None of the slave children show any signs of the illness."

"I see," he said quietly. After a long moment, he approached the doctor. It was then Dr. Curruthers saw the pistol in his hand. "Then where did the illness come from?"

Dr. Curruthers froze at the sight of the iron barrel, and chose his words very carefully.

"I have not determined yet," he said, "Mr. Worthington, why are you armed?"

Worthington ignored his inquiry. Instead, the thin old man regarded the weapon with curiosity, as if he hadn't even been aware he was carrying it. "Answer this question, Dr. Curruthers," he said, "Do you believe in the Devil?"

Curruthers found the question far too relevant to Worthington's wild eyed look. He nodded slowly. "Yes, sir. I do."

"Then seek your answers there," said Worthington, lowering the pistol the barrel now aimed at the Earth itself as if in rebuke, "I only let a handful of the savages into my home to do work, and Peter was a devout, good boy. It can only be the work of devilry that took him from me."

It was only now that Curruthers noticed the despondent tears running down the old man's face. They'd been invisible before, the pistol and the mad eyes overshadowing them.

"Yes, yes he was, Mr. Worthington," said Curruthers, "It is a great tragedy."

Here, Worthington met the Doctor's eyes with that wild, mad rage again, the fiery coals of insanity burning behind the leaking orbs.

"No, sir," said Worthington, "It is not a tragedy. It is a challenge. And my faith shall overcome."

With that, Worthington turned back to the house and strode away, saying no more, the pistol still gripped in a firm, bony hand.

Curruthers swallowed hard. The old man was clearly mad, if he hadn't been before. The grief of losing his only son so soon after his oldest daughter must have sent him even deeper into the depths. Lord only knew what he was capable of, and seeing him march back to the house, pistol in hand, sent shivers of fright through him. The doctor followed at a good distance, determined to pack his things and leave for town at dawn.

The night was silent as a tomb, with nary an owl nor cricket to be heard. Only the soft, sighing wind, dancing invisibly beneath the cold crescent moon. Curruthers found sleep to be difficult, his dreams haunted by the discoveries he'd made since arriving. Something troubled him deeply about things here at the Worthington estate, something beyond the horrible treatment of the children. There were secrets here. There were deep, intentional secrets that Worthington would kill to preserve. He was sure of this.

The deep pain on Worthington's face, contrasted with Mary's calm, deceptively warm pleas, demure, mature... It could be madness, but there were two different flavors of fear at work on this land.

Mary pretending to be dead and hiding with the slaves, the consumption that came from nowhere, Worthington's lurking madness, the mysteries were too myriad and their connections fleeting without resorting to religious imagery or superstitious balderdash.

He rose at the chiming of midnight and wandered along the hallway. The doors to the children's rooms were all locked, which was odd in and of itself, but what truly perplexed him was the set of stairs leading up to a door. It seemed to be a recent construction, at least compared to the rest of the home. The stairs were a little more steep, and turned at an angle to rise up to a thin landing. He guessed this would be the spire atop the manor that gazed over the property. He stepped quietly, not wishing to rouse Worthington or his Old Testament wrath. He carefully shifted his weight, slowly, ensuring the creaks were gradual and quiet.

He reached the landing, and paused for a long, terrible silence after the wood beneath his slippered feet groaned terribly. His heart thumped in the silent gloom.

A terrible odor lingered here, one he had known before, from his younger days... from the war... His throat wanted to choke on that smell, but he held the hem of his dressing gown up over his face. Now he absolutely needed to see what was behind this door. He knew this stench, had smelled it in the fields of the dead.

Oddly, this door was not locked, and he gently pushed it open. Within was a pristine nursery, one not used for years judging by the layers of dust, but one that likely had seen the raising of at least one Worthington child. This room was different from the rest of the house. Wooden carvings of happy animals and smiling suns adorned the walls, painted in bright colors that were beginning to fade from time.

He was just about to leave when his eyes picked up the dark stains in the crib, not mere shadows as he'd thought, but actual black patches now clear in the moonlight. He approached, and saw the old sheets were crusted with something thick and black. The residue was well dried, but he knew what this was. He cringed. Had something happened to another child? Something in the light shifted, perhaps the moon coming from behind a cloud, because the light in that room changed imperceptibly, just enough for him to notice a darker shape in the corner.

The darkened mass was hunched over, and soon the shapes began to resolve themselves to his eyes as they readjusted. There was a face in that darkness, an old, dry, rotten one emaciated and gray. Curruthers stepped back, and saw the dark stains all over the floor now, previously hidden by the gloom. The spots that could only be sloppy drips. The shape in the corner laid back in the chair, some sort of old blanket had been lain over it, or perhaps a shroud, but now it was moth-eaten, threadbare, more of a dark veil on a dead bride. The doctor stepped back out, no longer concerned about the noise, shutting the door behind him and moving quickly to get out of that ghastly air. He nearly fell, but caught himself by the bottom steps where he vomited on the wooden floor.

He wished, in that moment, he was not a doctor. The knowledge of what he saw, from a medical perspective, painted a macabre picture of what happened. There had been a birth, and something had gone wrong, terribly wrong. The mother clearly did not survive. For whatever insane reason, the mother had not been buried, and perhaps this was where Worthington's madness had begun. The corpse in that room, left to rot, to cook in the sun, to dry out and shed dust and spawn maggots, to gaze forever with liquefied, dead eye sockets into silver moonlight, alone.

Dr. Curruthers rose from the floor, desperate to hide the evidence of his bile, but in the darkness he would find no rags. He stepped down the hall, now dizzy from the expulsion. His progress halted at the sight of dim light up the hall, and the man illuminated by the lantern, old man Worthington. In his bony hand, once again, rested the pistol. He was not dressed in evening wear, but his normal clothes, as if he never went to bed or even attempted it.

"You had no business in there!" he hissed.

Curruthers was unable to think of a reply. Thunder rushed up the hallway, tearing into him. Curruthers fell backwards into the puddle of his own sick, a pain he knew from his war years throbbing through his chest.

He knew the bullet had torn through his dressing gown, broken a rib, and possibly lodged into his lung. His medical mind knew that his chances for survival dropped every second he couldn't take action. He knew that there was no way he could treat a wound like that here. No, this would take the work of another doctor, and there would be none within reach. His clinical mind clashed with his panic, his desire to live, but he knew his fate was sealed before he hit the floor. Worthington approached, and in his other hand was a woodcutter's axe. The blade gleamed in the orange lantern glow, but the shaft was obsidian black as the night sky.

Odd as it was, the doctor's thoughts were of the dead woman, how she must have suffered, and how Worthington was completely ill equipped. Perhaps he was too ashamed of his own ignorance, perhaps he was just as mad then as he was now.

Worthington stood over Curruthers. He tossed the pistol aside, and hefted the axe.

"Please..." said Curruthers, "Please, no. It wasn't your fault. You weren't a doctor. You couldn't save them."

"I saved the child," said Worthington, "And we just buried him."

Curruthers saw the axe rise above him.

Events blurred together in his panic-fogged mind as Curruthers made his weak, staggering escape. He remembered hitting the first door he came across, and tripping into brisk night air. He didn't remember how he got past the old man, or down the stairs. By starlight, he could see the old rutted road, and the only possible escape he had. He was bleeding, from multiple wounds, and only his sheer panic and ability to outpace a man of Worthington's years had gotten him this far.

He heard shouting, but the words were lost in the endless echo of trees and distance. He fumbled, sometimes in complete pitch, but his feet always landed on hard packed earth, and when they didn't, he corrected, and wandered back across the cold dusty ground.

Great clouds had rolled in to smother the moon and stars sometime since he'd left the Worthington house. He could only hope to find another house where he could hide and perhaps get some help. The fact that he was still moving meant the bullet probably hadn't gone all the way through to his lung, likely thanks to the antiquated pistol and dumb luck. Maybe there wasn't enough powder, Worthington didn't seem to be well versed in firearms.

Curruthers did know bullet wounds, though, and even if he had been lucky, he was already feeling weak from losing blood. He could scarcely tell which direction he was walking half the time. He was grateful Worthington didn't have a passion for hunting, or else there might be dogs after him, too.

A distant rumble made him jump with fear, but it was only thunder from a gathering storm. He looked back and saw no muzzle flashes in the pitch. But when the sky crackled with incandescence, he could see he was not far up the road, and through the trees, that ominous eye of the manor still watched his retreat.

The cold rain that began to splatter against him was another shock that brought him fully to his senses. He tried to push forward, away from that hulking cyclops and out towards the main road, where he was fairly certain there were other farm houses, someplace where he could get some help. If he didn't find something, or someone soon, he wasn't sure he could survive the length of the storm, much less the night itself.

An animal howled, reminding him of the hot blood leaking from his chest, and that if he did not move quickly, he would be prey.

· · · ·

· · · ·

It was almost an alien world as Tommy pulled up to the big stone gates of the university. It was purely for show, there was no actual barrier, but there was a small squat security building there, unmanned and apparently regarded as formality. It was of little surprise, this time of year, a big university campus would be nearly deserted. It would be a few weeks yet before the students arrived in droves, but Tatiana said the professor would be here already, getting things prepared.

He passed a strange conglomeration of mixed-generation architecture, one moment a gleaming modern building of marble and glass, the next an old ivy-covered brick and wooden shingle affair that reminded him of colonial homes. Eventually he came to the building she described, a big, oddly circular neo-modern structure of metal and glass like a space ship had landed in an old colonial town. He pulled up on the curb and hopped out. He carefully picked up the bundle of rags in the seat beside him and started for the door.

It was warm, even for August, and he could feel the sweat starting to leak out. The wind from his ride had kept him moderately comfortable, but now he was starting to feel the hot air begin to cook him inside his clothes.

He pulled the glass door open, and once inside was met with dry, more temperate air, but it was a far cry from comfortable. The air conditioners seemed to just remove the humidity, not actually lower the temperature. He wondered if they'd only just turned it on an hour ago, or maybe all that glass just turned this beautiful lobby into an accidental greenhouse.

No one was at the big reception desk, so Tommy went through the only open door, a metal frame and glass pane bearing golden letters "History, Social Sciences."

There were only a few people there, either inside small offices and talking loudly on the phones, or bustling from cubicle desk to printer and back. They seemed stressed and busy. Tommy didn't see the need to bother them, and no one even seemed to notice he was there.

He found the offices with the numbers on them and with only one or two wrong turns, he located the right one down a hallway lined with cubicles.

The door was open, and inside an older man in a tee shirt and jeans was rummaging around on a shelf for some elusive object. Tommy gently knocked on the door frame. The older man turned, his eyes icy blue, but sharp and very aware.

"Hello!" he said, extending a hand, "You must be Mr. Walker."

"Doctor Reid," said Tommy, shaking the offered hand, "Hi. Um, thanks for taking the time-"

"Oh, it's no trouble. How is Tatiana?"

"Oh, she's good."

"Great. I'm glad. Bright girl, dreadfully unfortunate she had to drop out. Still, I'm glad she thinks well of me. Not all my students do."

Tommy shrugged. "Only person she seems to not like is her ex husband."

"Well, as an ex husband myself, we can be bastards," said Reid, smiling. "So let's have a look." He gestured to the bundle of rags. Tommy put it down gently on the professor's cluttered desk and unwrapped it from its oily prison. Dusty green glass peeked out from within.

Reid whistled, impressed. He picked up the bottle and turned it over in his hand.

"Wow," he said, "Looks like they used an old rum bottle."

He held it up to the light and turned it over and over.

"Looks like... nails, bones... Well, Mr. Walker, what you have here is what's known as a Witch Bottle."

Tommy let the phrase run through his head in silence for a moment.

"A what?"

"It was kind of a fad for a while in superstitious circles. If you thought you were being plagued by a witch or an evil spirit, you'd make one of these and put them in chimneys or crawl spaces, anywhere you might think an evil spirit could get in. It was supposed to ward them off. They were usually homemade, but a handful of hucksters would sell them to scared and ignorant people."

"Jesus," Tommy said. He started to feel that sinking feeling again that this project was more trouble than it was worth.

"Oh, I wouldn't worry," said Reid, "The worst thing about these old things is if you break 'em."

"Why's that?" Tommy asked, suddenly worried.

"Because they're full of pee."

He couldn't help it. Tommy laughed out loud, his relief escaping. "Pee?! Why? What?"

"Lots of reasons, but I think the main one is that if you used blood, the person would probably bleed half to death filling it, and god knows the infection. The bones are a little worrying, though. Part of me wants to crack it open and run some tests."

"Feel free," said Tommy, "I don't want the thing."

"Ah, but it's an artifact," he said, "You always have to be careful with artifacts. Sometimes in the pursuit of the secrets within, you can destroy the knowledge you're looking for. I'd be very interested to know the specific story around this, though."

"Oh, I bet," Tommy thought, but what he said was "Came from a property that I guess used to belong to an old guy named Worthington."

Dr. Reid carefully put the witch bottle down on his desk. His demeanor changed. He looked at Tommy with a cold, suspicious stare.

"Jedediah Worthington? Of Ingham?"

Tommy nodded slowly. He was startled by the professor's sudden change in demeanor.

"Oh, my boy... You've got quite a local legend on your hands." A smile grew on his face that had no business being that bright and cheerful.

Dr. Reid made a beeline for a shelf across the room. From it, he produced a thin binder full of photocopies of old newspaper clippings and pages from library books. He opened it, and flipped plastic-coated page after page as he looked for something. Finally, he tapped the page he was looking at.

"Right here... Jedediah Worthington and Mary Worthington. Really a fascinating piece of local history. It's a big hit around here on Halloween. See, Jedediah was a minister once, but he had some fairly medieval ideas on religion. That house you've taken on was once a plantation growing all manner of crops. But old Jedediah, see... I guess today the best way to describe him was as an aspiring cult leader. He essentially bought a bunch of orphans that he supposedly intended to convert and raise to be his disciples, but things went very very bad. After his oldest daughter died, his children began to die off one at a time. They would say they saw Mary at the foot of their beds at night, stealing their breath. Of course, Jedediah went even more over the edge than he was already, thinking Mary had become some kind of vampire. So, he did the only rational thing... He dug Mary up, cut out her heart, burned it, and fed the ashes to his children with holy water and gruel."

"That's rational?" Tommy balked.

"Hey, when you believe in vampires, witches, evil spirits, and resurrecting jews, you can believe anything. Besides, that's just the myth and rumor. Truth is probably more that he was an ignorant man in the 1800's with the medical knowledge of a slug. But where the story really gets crazy is the fire."

"The fire that burned down the barn?"

"Exactly," said Dr. Reid, happy that Tommy had a little knowledge of the story. "See... lots of theories have come about as to what happened. Some people say that night there was a slave revolt, others say the orphans all ran away in the middle of the night and Jedediah set the fire himself out of insanity. Some say it was an accident, but my favorite theory is the conspiracy. Apparently Worthington's lunacy reached the ears of the town Magistrate, and they raided the place, taking the orphans away, killing old Jedediah, and burning down that barn because what was inside was 'too horrible to be seen.' No one knows if that last one is true, but there's a journal fragment from the Magistrate, man named... God, what was it? Baker, I think? Some general name like Smith or Carpenter, something relating to a trade. Anyway, it mentioned taking testimony from a Dr. Curruthers on his deathbed about Jedediah, and being shocked at what he heard. But it's the only piece of paper we have, AND it's burned at the edges. Whatever happened, there's three big mysteries around that house. The first is that no one ever found Mary's body. The second, is that no one ever found Jedediah's body. The third is that no one ever found the slaves!"

He closed the binder for dramatic effect, his Cheshire Cat grin stretching his face.

Tommy listened to the story quietly, his skin growing cold. He chewed his lip and looked back up to Dr. Reid, his eyes full of guilt.

"I... Um... I did find Mary."

Tommy told him of the body in the crawlspace, how the police reacted when he called it in, and the grisly experience of collecting and re-burying the bones. Dr. Reid watched with deeply keen interest, his ears drinking in every word, his posture more and more tense as Tommy spoke. He was not just interested, he was enthralled.

Tommy finished his summary with how he had cemented the rock back into place in the empty alcove.

"Damn!" Dr. Reid said suddenly, slapping his hand on the desk. "I'd have liked to examine that. And the bones themselves, of course. Pity you buried everything. Damn! To finally solve the mystery of the Worthington Manor..."

Tommy almost didn't mention it. A certain part of him fought the urge to do so, but he blurted it out anyway.

"I do have her diary."

Dr. Reid's face went white with shock. He spluttered for a moment.

"Her diary?! My god man, why didn't you say so?! May I see it?"

Tommy was taken aback by the man's passion. Apparently local history, to him, was what working with one's hands was to Tommy. It was strange to see him get so excited over an old book. But that fervor, bordering on madness, maybe that was the same kind of gleam that was in his own eye just a few months ago.

"Yeah, I mean... It's back at the house. I could go get it and bring it back."

"Yes!" said Dr. Reid, but then his face slowly fell. "No... Damn, I've got a department meeting for the upcoming year in an hour, and those administrators love the sound of their own voices." Tommy bit back a comment.

"Listen, why don't you and Tatiana come over to my place this weekend? Bring the diary, we'll delve into the mystery a little over dinner," said Reid.

Tommy was uncertain, but he seemed a harmless enough old man. And though his eyes had a fiery passion in them for his work, they were soft, kind eyes, grandfatherly eyes. Tommy had only met his Dad's father once, and far from a kindly old man, he was just an older, more bitter version of his own father. No, this man had an authenticity to him, like he didn't have the presence of mind to be deceitful if he wanted to be. This was an oddly comforting notion to Tommy.

"Sure, Doc," said Tommy, "I'll go run it by Tatiana."

"Wonderful! Wonderful, I can't wait. Oh, and tell Tatiana I said hello, will you?"

Tommy nodded, and looked back at the witch bottle.

"And what about that thing?"

"Oh, right! Well, I can run some tests on it if you like. See what it actually has in it. My bet is urine and chicken bones, a few needles, things like that. But I'll let you know if I find anything unusual."

Tommy smiled at that. He'd been terrified there'd been tiny human bones, he didn't even think they might be animal bones. Finding the body had really turned his paranoia up, and only now confronted with the light of day and knowledge did he realize how ridiculous he'd been. He chuckled and shook Dr. Reid's hand. His panic hit the brick wall of reason, and fell apart.

"Sounds great, Doc," he said, "Can you email me your address?"

His drive back was completely unconscious as he swirled the thoughts around in his head. He expected a creepy vibe from an old decrepit manor, but this was a lot more than he bargained for. Still, it made him feel a little more at ease, finding actual explanations for some of the crazy things he'd found so far. Besides the body, the diary, that crazy witch bottle thing, but all of it was solid, real, and bringing it to an actual expert massaged away the eerie feeling that had been creeping in since he'd first laid eyes on that bony hand in the foundation.

Not only was it all explained, it was explained perfectly. He was creeped out by the house because something bad *did* happen there. But more importantly, it was over two centuries ago and he had no reason to worry now.

The fact that the home was a piece of obscure local legend might even increase its appeal to the right buyer down the line.

He also thought about what Tatiana would say about the dinner invite. He was sure she'd come along. It would be extremely awkward for him to be visiting some professor he'd never heard of before all by himself, but he was prepared to do so, especially if it could give him more peace of mind or helpful info for resale value.

He felt like he was on solid foundation once again, with a strong grip on what was, and wasn't real. Nightmares? Just him getting spooked. The injuries to his back? A frantic, scared puppy in a new place. And the real, tangible creepy items were not his problem, nor really an obstacle in his way. He could handle this. And he'd make some giddy professor's day, maybe get a little cash for the diary, and get another glimpse into Tatiana's life.

He didn't even know she'd been to college, but apparently she'd gone through to her sophomore year before *el Mierdo* convinced her to get married and start having kids. She'd wanted to wait until she graduated, but the man was utterly without patience or sympathy.

Tommy couldn't help but wonder if that was the kind of man he'd almost become. He didn't care for that idea. But it was certainly the kind of man he could have been. He felt like all the right ingredients were there. Abused kids grew up and abused unto others, wasn't that how it worked?

He'd heard something like that somewhere. And when he was angry, he felt like it took all of his strength to hold back. What would he do if he couldn't hold back? That anger always simmered beneath the surface. But maybe with some people, they liked their anger.

Maybe they confused it with strength, and just needed an excuse to let it out.

That Saturday night, Tatiana took forever to get ready. Tommy sat in awkward silence on her couch while beyond the door to her bedroom, the rustling of clothes, and the mini jet-engine noise of a hair dryer would intermittently fire off for a brief flight.

The bilingual curses and occasional English ones also concerned him. Tommy had girlfriends before who would have their beautification rituals, but most of the time, his waiting involved getting grilled mercilessly by a protective father, or an overly curious mother, and more disturbing combinations of parental scrutiny as well. Sometimes even a sibling with decidedly hostile intent would show up, and Tommy would stutter over his words, or try to pull himself up to meet the challenge. He was never good at it, but then, awkward angry teenage boys rarely made a good impression. Especially when, at the time, he rarely had a good intention. There was never a polite way to say 'I'm using your daughter for a little temporary pleasure because my life sucks and I need to escape.'

But this silence and emptiness as he sat with nothing but his phone and the ticking of the clock to keep him company, he was starting to miss the awkward interaction. At least it would make the time go by. Terror-filled, anxiety-ridden, at least it wasn't boring, and it didn't leave Tommy alone with the worst company of all, his own thoughts.

Tatiana finally emerged from the bedroom after a long silence. She said nothing, and it took him a moment to realize the noise had fallen away. He turned and nearly jumped to his feet at the sight. She'd done her hair in loose curls that fell around her face like a glamor model. The dress she wore was modest, but it complimented every single thing about her, from her figure, to her dark eyes, to her self-satisfied little smirk. The latter was what really made Tommy's jaw drop. Her confidence alone made the outfit work, the rest was just icing. Those lips had a seductive curl that made him lose breath.

"You ready to go?" she said.

"Oh, oh, yes. Absolutely. Ladies first," he said, gesturing to the door.

On the drive, Tommy filled her in on the details he'd learned from the professor. Sitting on the dashboard was the infamous diary. Tatiana smirked and picked it up, looking over the old crumbly leather binding.

"This is amazing," she said, "Can I?"

"Sure," Tommy said, shrugging.

She opened to a random page, and her eyes scanned the paper. Tommy peered over briefly, but stopped himself and looked back to the road.

"Well, what does it say?" he asked.

She laughed and gave him a look. "You've had this book all this time and you've never read it?"

Tommy shrugged. "I've been busy."

"Uh huh," she said, her eyes and tone teasing. She looked back to the book, and proceeded to read.

"The slaves have shown me the barn where Father keeps the foundlings. We were never allowed to go there before, and now I know why. Father keeps the poor children chained to their beds by their ankles and a short length of chain. Their only respite is his daily sermons, where he allows them food and trips to the outhouse. He treats them worse than the slaves he keeps. But now that I have seen what he has done, I am certain he must be stopped. The night is coming quickly, and these foundlings shall have their part to play in his downfall. Very soon, I shall..."

Tatiana slowed her words, and looked up at Tommy. He glanced back over to her and met her eyes briefly.

"... Take the blood from his body, and make fertile the land with his corpse."

Tommy chewed his lip for a moment.

"Wow," he said.

"I think I'm done reading," she said, closing the book and putting it back on the dashboard. They endured the rest of the ride, and its tense silence.

The professor's home was on the coast on the Southern edge of Norwich, on a large plot of land beyond a curvy state route filled with beach traffic. Off to one side of the yard was a large pond, where someone had made a diminutive stone garden on an island, and a storybook little wooden bridge over the water. The house itself had a dark wooden exterior, like a modest country home. but after ringing the bell and peering through the window, Tommy could see the interior was a stark contrast. Some of the scenery and decor had him reconsidering some of his plans. The professor had some very nice features to his property. Apparently college degrees did pay well if you never left college.

Dr. Reid opened the door, an older woman by his side, presumably his wife. She had a face full of laugh lines around cherubic cheeks and hair just tinted with silver through fox-like red.

"Tatiana!" said Dr. Reid, "and Tommy, please, come in. This is my wife, Anna."

They stepped inside, and Anna gently shook their hands.

"It's so nice when Daniel brings students home," said Anna, "I'm delighted to meet you both. Please, come in, sit down."

The stone facade was made of actual stone, polished just enough to maintain the appearance of natural rough edges, but glossy and smooth. Varnish-drenched wood formed the contours and edges. Huge wooden shelves full of books adorned the walls where there wasn't some piece of framed artwork under the glow of installed lighting specifically designed to highlight it from within the frame.

It took Tommy a moment to realize there was no television, only a gas fireplace with a mantle covered with pictures. Many saw Dr. Reid standing next to or embracing a younger man and woman that shared a number of his facial features. Then there were pictures of him with little bundles that had newborn faces sticking out, which seemed to almost have more of his facial features. Apparently that nose didn't just run in the family, it sprinted through each generation. Matching photos of Anna with similar-aged younger people, though no pictures of babies. She wasn't a grandmother yet, although maybe she got to rent his grandchildren on alternating weekends.

He marveled at the happy smiles in the little pictures. They seemed unreal, like those pictures that come with the frames in the dollar store, and he half-expected to see a young child in a yellow coat, in the rain, holding a duckling with a wide grin that showed only two front teeth.

They sat down on the plush couch, while Dr. Reid took a seat in an easy chair. Anna sat in an equally comfortable-looking chair beside him. Tommy briefly thought of a king and queen ruling over their court. Somewhere he could hear the sizzling of something in an oven, and his nose told him it was going to taste like rosemary and salt.

Tatiana put a hand on his shoulder, sensing he wasn't quite at ease. This was true. While he very much wanted the house he was working on to reflect this level of expense and luxury, seeing it here in the flesh, so to speak, was unnerving. He knew how much these materials cost. He could almost tally up the bill in his head, labor included. It was more than a little intimidating.

"Your home is beautiful," said Tatiana. Tommy shot her a look, not sure whether to be insulted that she somehow read what he was thinking, or impressed for taking the pressure off of breaking the ice.

"I can't take the credit," said Dr. Reid, "I'm the moocher. Anna here makes the big bucks with that big brain."

"Men, always obsessed with body parts," she said with a smirk. "I write code for Apple."

"So I can bring you my phone next time it goes weird?" asked Tatiana.

"Chances are, I'm already working on what the problem is and it'll be in the next update."

"Slick," Tommy said, despite himself. He was impressed, and perhaps a little intimidated, but something about her demeanor put him at ease. He wasn't used to seeing two people, married, and actually happy to see each other. They lived in a nice home, they had a happy family, each. Is this the kind of house rich kids got to grow up in? When their families broke, did they just get bigger? It didn't seem fair to him.

"So... Can I see it?" asked Anna, breaking his train of thought, which Tommy was actually grateful for.

"Anna," Chided Dr. Reid.

"Oh, come on now, I haven't seen you so excited since Rome. Come on, let's see this diary, then. He looks calm, but his eyes are about to explode."

Tommy had the book between his sweaty palms. He handed it over to Dr. Reid. Reid took it with a small smile, and flipped it open to the first page. He ran his hand along the edge of the paper, then the interior of the spine, as if looking for something. Finally, he started scanning the writing itself.

"The book's age, the pen strokes, binding... This all looks genuine."

"God, I hope so," said Tommy, "I can't imagine why someone would go to these lengths to prank me."

"Oh, of course," said Dr. Reid, "Sorry, it's nothing personal. We always have to check for authenticity. You could hand me the ark of the covenant and I'd have to check for signs of welding."

"Well, Daniel, what does it say?" Anna asked, trying to peer ever closer. He took a moment to sneak a kiss on her cheek before looking back down.

Dr. Reid went back to the first page. He skimmed it quickly.

"Normal daily chores and routine," he said.

"Skip ahead a little," Tommy said. Tatiana pursed her lips, a worried look crossing her face.

Dr. Reid flipped forward in the book, settled on a page seemingly at random, and peered closely, beginning to read.

"The night is nearly upon us now. The sickness has taken my siblings, freed them from my father's wrath, as the dark ones said. Now, with the slaves as my followers, and the foundlings hungry for freedom, the time to strike is nigh. I have..." Dr. Reid frowned and peered more closely, "I have sealed my covenant. My soul burns. But this fire is a balm. I will burn, but I will burn as bright as the morning star. The ritual begins at dusk tonight, and I have prepared all. My father's madness comes to an end before dawn tomorrow. And then we will vanish, into the night. The townspeople will arrive to find nothing but the dead, and missing. I will lead my people into the world, and set it ablaze."

No one spoke as he finished reading. He flipped backwards in the book, and his eyes went wide.

"My God... there's a whole ritual in here..."

Another heavy silence fell over them. Only the distant popping and sizzling of cooking meat broke the quiet. Everyone nearly jumped when a loud buzzing sounded from the kitchen. Anna was the only one to get to her feet.

"That will be the rolls," she said, "That means dinner is ready."

They were grateful for the change in tone, but Reid kept the book beside him at the table while he ate, flipping backwards and forwards, mesmerized by it.

"Daniel," urged Anna. He looked to her. There was a stern look on her face. He went slightly red, and put the book aside on a credenza. He turned to the others and muttered a sheepish apology.

"It's all right," said Tatiana, "So what was all that about rituals and dark ones? It sounds like devil worship."

Reid nodded, cautiously. "Not... Not exactly the devil, but definitely occult. I never would have imagined the mystery had this kind of side to it. I mean, to some people of the time, if you got a hang nail, it was the devil's work, but this... This is incredible. It's almost like Mary Worthingon invented a whole new mythology. These rituals are like nothing I've ever seen before. And she doesn't even seem to have a name for these higher powers, it's all vague euphemisms. I don't think I'm exaggerating when I say this is going to be the talk of the Academic circuit for the next few years."

"Oh good," said Anna dryly, "More cocktail parties and fundraisers."

"Yeah, uh, no offense Dr. Reid," said Tommy, "But, um... I'm trying to flip that property. And having it as a well known haunted house might have an appeal, but devil worship and ritual sacrifices... That tends to put buyers off. I don't suppose you could, uh... *Not* show that thing around right now?"

Dr. Reid's lips tightened and he stared into the distance for a moment.

"Mr. Walker," he said carefully, " I can appreciate your situation. But you must understand, this diary is going to completely change the profile of your little town. There's no way around that. Frankly, based on everything you've told me, I don't think it's even possible for the Worthington Manor to be any less famous than, say, Salem Massachusetts."

Tommy seemed to visibly deflate. Tatiana sensed this, and patted his shoulder, but he didn't stay deflated long. He stood, and took the diary from where Dr. Reid had left it.

"Okay," said Tommy, thinking out loud, "Okay, look... You gotta let me finish this house and sell it. I mean, you just have to. I sank every penny I had into this, and even some I didn't have. Please, I'm begging you, keep a lid on this for a while. Otherwise, I have to take this back and... I dunno... burn it."

Reid's face inflamed with horror, his eyes nearly bulging out to the lenses on his glasses. "No! No, you can't!"

"Daniel," said Anna, "Boys, please..."

"Dr. Reid," said Tatiana, "Won't it take time to authenticate the book anyway?"

Reid's expression settled, and he tilted his head at her.

"Authenticate... Well, yes, of course, but..."

"How long?" she asked.

Reid sighed and folded his fingers together, thinking.

"I suppose... depending on the equipment we'll have access to... A few months."

"All right," said Tatiana, "And Tommy, how long will it take you to finish that house?"

"God," he said, "My plan was five years, doing it mostly myself. But maybe if I really hustle, hire a few guys... like... eight months, a little over a year. But then I have to sell it, too. Hell, it could take up to two years, and that's really polishing the silver lining."

Dr. Reid drummed his fingers on the table for a moment, his eyes drifting back to the book in Tommy's hands.

"That's a lot to ask, time-wise," said Dr. Reid.

"Nothing worth doing is ever easy or quick," said Tommy.

Reid smiled at that and nodded. He took a deep breath. "No, no, I suppose you're right. I'm sorry, I guess I just got carried away."

"Men," said Anna, looking to Tatiana with a smile "What would they do without us?"

Tatiana laughed, but Tommy winced a little, his pride having taken a blow. He put the book back on the credenza and drifted back to his seat.

"But here's the question," said Dr. Reid, "Can I at least read through it? Take some notes? If only for my own curiosity's sake. I swear, I won't divulge anything beyond these four walls. I'm just going to take notes, start some research, see what corroborating sources I can find. Who knows, it may yet be a fake invented by a very clever scammer."

Tommy considered this idea for a moment. "There were a lot of prior owners before me. Maybe one of them was really creative." He thought back to the stories, people stumbling around basements, the bees nest, knocking noises. Tommy could see it now, and it could be true. If the house was too expensive to flip, he sells it, but first he hears about this local legend, doctors up some creepy stuff, invents some stories, lets it go on the market for a while. Eventually someone gullible like Tommy buys it, invests a lot in flipping it, but then the house's reputation catches up. Tommy becomes desperate to sell. Here he comes in, buys it for well under value, then has a big laugh as he sells it for an inflated price after Tommy put in all the work. It wouldn't have been the craziest scheme Tommy had ever heard of. The housing market had been insane for decades. There were reality shows about house flippers, for god's sake, to say nothing of the way every other telephone pole had a flyer for people looking to buy junk houses. Those were pretty much all scams, to a one.

Tommy nodded. "Okay," he said. Reid picked the book up with trembling hands. He almost looked giddy.

"Not a word," said Tommy, jabbing a finger at Dr. Reid.

"Cross my heart," he said, but his eyes never left his prize.

"Good," said Anna, "See, you two can play nice. Now who wants some sponge cake?"

To his credit, Dr. Reid put the book down and left it alone for the rest of the dinner. Tommy was grateful. Instead, they talked about Tatiana's time at the University, a topic of some mild embarrassment based on the little blushes and slight squirming in her seat.

"Do you regret it?" asked Dr. Reid.

Tatiana shrugged. "Sometimes," she confessed, "But I have an amazing daughter I wouldn't trade for the world. She's so wonderful. Smart, and such a kind heart."

Dr. Reid nodded. "Sometimes the path to happiness is a strange, winding one."

"I hear that," said Tommy, chuckling, and thinking of his last interaction with his father. Suddenly a lot of the photos seemed to make a lot more sense. Reid didn't seem like the kind of guy who left his family in the dust, or who would slap his kids around for being disobedient. And yet there he was, divorced from the mother of his children, but still close to them.

He idly wondered why they didn't have families like this on TV? Every time two people on TV are divorced, they hate each other. There's no smiles, just occasional sexual tension and the threat of reconciliation until the main character learns some lesson and the episode ends on a joke.

Here was a man who had "left his family," but had never left. From the pictures, he was there at birthdays, graduations, and right after actual births. This was an alien idea to Tommy. Maybe because he always wished his father would divorce Margot. He would pray for it, back when he used to believe in things like God.

"And what about you, Tommy? Where did you go to school?" asked Dr. Reid.

"I didn't. I finished high school, just went right to work. Could never afford college."

"More's the pity," said Dr. Reid, "Everyone should get an academic education. It's a tragedy that it's out of reach for so many."

"There's the internet," said Tommy with a shrug.

Dr. Reid chuckled and waved a dismissive hand.

"Internet is information, not knowledge. Not wisdom. Half my students give me internet sources and I spend half my night marking their papers down for them. Most of them are bunk. New age hippy psuedo-science or politically-charged nonsense. It can't compare to the actual learning process, to the very art of learning something new. You can read what the War of 1812 was, but it doesn't give you the slightest idea of the millions of details around it. You're a carpenter, right? The knowledge and experience you have gained, is that something you can get reading articles on a blog?"

Tommy chuckled, nodding his head. "Okay, no, you got a point."

"There's always something lost in translation," said Dr. Reid.

"Sometimes literally," said Tatiana, bursting into laughter a moment later. "Oh, my English was so bad back then."

"Oh, I remember," said Dr. Reid, also having a little chuckle. "Still, you didn't let that slow you down. You worked twice as hard as any other student. I was tempted to give you a full A just for the work."

"I could have used it. I was failing math."

They shared another laugh. Tommy watched Dr. Reid again, and that smile, that look in his eyes, it was something he had seen on TV, and occasionally in real life with other families. This man thought of Tatiana as another daughter.

The idea made him feel nervous, but he couldn't put a finger on exactly why.

It was late into the evening when they finally said their goodbyes. Tommy helped Tatiana climb into the truck, then happily slid in beside her. He hadn't had a relaxing evening in a long time, not like that anyway. Tommy usually felt extremely awkward in social situations, but this flowed very smoothly for him, and without a drop of alcohol. Tatiana, though, had enjoyed a few glasses, and looked very satisfied. She was still giggling about some parting joke, something that flew over Tommy's head, and was probably referencing something from those college classes.

"This was a lot of fun," she said.

"Yeah, it was," he said. They shared a look, a silent agreement that very soon, the clothes would be shed, the inhibitions abandoned. Tommy started the truck.

The ride back felt like an eternity.

Hours later, they sat in the warm dark of Tatiana's bedroom, naked and glistening while soft light played over the room from outside the window. Tatiana sat up, smiling down at him, and even in the dark, he could see her playful eyes.

"You still awake?" she asked.

"For the moment," he said, enjoying her shapely silhouette in the gloom, "Don't tell me you're ready for more. I can't even feel my legs."

She laughed and cuddled up to him. "Oh, no, very happy right now. Happier than I have been in a while. I'm just curious about you."

"How so?"

"Well it seems like all you do is work. Work at your job, work on that house. I know it's important to you, but what else do you do?"

He bristled a little at the question. "What do you mean?"

"Well, what do you do for fun?"

"Well, I... I go running, or I read sometimes. Watch internet videos."

"What about your friends? Family? Any crazy characters I should worry about long-term?"

Tommy sucked in a breath and pulled away from her a little.

"No one I'm likely to go visit anytime soon," he said, his impatience coming through his voice. It was her turn to pull away, and she frowned at him in the gloom.

"Whoah, what's the matter?"

"Nothing," he said, "It's just... I just don't have anything like that in my life."

She cocked her head to the side for a moment, looking at him. It seemed to Tommy like she was trying to make up her mind about something.

"Can we just drop it?" he said before she could speak again.

Tatiana sighed and slid out of bed. She paced a little, her posture going rigid. Tommy felt a flicker of guilt, but it was a glimmer against his anger. He felt like she was pushing at him, and was mad that she wasn't getting anywhere. He folded his arms and stared off into the distance. He heard her make a sniffling noise. He didn't budge.

"I'm sorry I brought it up," she said, "You don't want to talk about it, I won't make you."

"I really don't," he said, and was surprised at the bitterness in his own voice. She looked to him, her expression changed. Where she had looked hurt and sad before, now she had a gleam in her eyes that, even in the dark, he recognized. His belly squirmed uncomfortably. He stood from the bed and started gathering his clothes.

"Tommy," she said. He didn't answer. "Tommy, wait..."

"I should go," he said.

"Hey, hey..." she said. She slid her arms around him, "I said I was sorry."

"I'm not looking for pity," he said.

Her eyes exploded with fire. She stepped back from him, and her voice took on a volume and power that shook Tommy to the core.

"Pity?! *Un momento, cabron!* I'm just trying to get to know you! What's wrong with you?"

"You *do* know me. This here, is me," he said, gesturing to himself.

She put her hands to her head, then raised them out as if pushing away some invisible force. She shook her head, then looked back to Tommy.

"Maybe I made a mistake," she said.

"Maybe I did, too," said Tommy. He pulled his pants on and walked for the door. He pulled his shirt on as he walked through the living room. He had the feeling that her eyes were on him the entire time. He left without making a further scene.

Tommy spent the next ten minutes sitting in his truck in the parking lot. His first impulse had been to speed away out of there and not come back, but when his fingers touched the ignition, he hesitated. Something just didn't feel right about this. He sat back and stared out at the diluted night sky for a long time. He couldn't go. He had to go, but he couldn't.

The part of him that was angry was quieting down now, and he started to feel more and more empty. Part of him kept saying that this is what women do, they get into your head, twist you around, play with your heart and then screw you over. They look for any way to get inside and pull your strings.

But when he thought that way about Tatiana, it felt hollow. The untruth of it rang louder than his rage.

He drummed his fingers on the dashboard, and thought of a dozen reasons to go back home. Mac would need to go out, he needed to get up early to start the next phase on the house, he would look like a creep just sitting here in the parking lot... They all felt forced, unreal.

He thought about going back up and apologizing, but would that make him weak? Would he just be giving in? Giving in to what?

He couldn't figure it out, but the more he tried to put it into words in his head, the more he felt a gnawing panic and claustrophobia. He pushed the door open to get some air. The cool night immediately stuck to his skin. It felt better, but he still couldn't move. He couldn't go home, he couldn't go back.

A part of him found brief, renewed anger at being put in this position, but it, too, was short lived. It sputtered and flickered out in a moment. When it was gone, he simply felt cold and alone.

He wondered if this was how his father had felt.

Tommy sighed, his head falling into his hands. The weight of all those years of loneliness crashed down on him all at once. The empty house on Christmas day, the half-assed tree decorated with scant ribbons while his mother watched A Christmas Carol and drank straight from the bottle. He remembered his brief time living with his father, where opening presents was such a strange affair, tightly organized, and his pleasure or displeasure with each item judged and used against him later by Margie. Or worse were the years where the presents were taken away because of some sleight, real or imagined.

The tears started to flow, and he realized this is what he didn't want to happen, especially not in front of the woman.

No, not *the woman*. That's what his Dad used to call Margie.

"I'm not him," he said. He looked down at his shaking hands. His chest itself was trembling, threatening sobs that wouldn't come. This hurt lived deep in his chest, and it seemed determined to remain where it was, comfortable and snug. He choked out an unintelligible swear word. He shut his eyes until they squeezed some moisture out. His father would have ridiculed him for crying.

He climbed out of the truck and looked back up at the building. She was in there now, angry, upset, and maybe too much so to talk to him. He could still just get in the truck and head home. He shut the truck door behind him.

"*I'm not him*," he said again. His hand lingered on the cool steel of the vehicle.

Tommy felt like he trudged through miles of thick muck, each step a test of strength as he went back into the building. Inside, he wanted to run. He wanted to start drinking the first drink he could find.

But he wasn't like *her* either.

He thought of all of those happy pictures, and how neither of his homes had those. That was a child's pain, one that still lived in his chest.

His feet moved. He forced them to. Each wooden step creaked, and he was sure she could hear, and maybe would open the door just long enough to hurl something at him like a half-full bottle.

She's not like her, either.

His stomach twisted like he'd eaten broken glass. Was that how he had just treated Tatiana? *Like that woman.*

He swallowed hard. He knew the answer. He just didn't want to admit it. He didn't even know he would react like that. But now every step felt like trudging through three feet of snow made of his own personal burning shame.

He felt an inch tall as he knocked on the door. He almost hoped she wouldn't answer, and he could slink away again with only his shame as company. He could live with his shame, he had before. It was always there, and if she wasn't there for him in the dark, the shame would be. It would hold him and tell him to sink and drink and forget the pain because it hurt too much.

He thought he heard movement from the other side, but the door remained closed. He leaned against it.

"Tatiana," he said, his voice cracking like it hadn't in ten years. "Can you hear me?"

No sound came forth. He wondered if maybe she had just rolled over, gone to sleep, and forgotten him already. She could have any man in the world, she deserved better than the broken pile of human that he was.

He winced at that thought. That wasn't him, that was the shame, the grief, the fear. It made him angry. His stomach twisted into another knot.

"Listen, I, uh... " He stumbled a little, and choked back a sob that lurked in his chest and threatened to break free. "I'm sorry."

The door swung open suddenly, and that fiery fury was back in her eyes. She wore only a long sweatshirt and her tousled hair was a mess. She jabbed a finger at him, her words flowing fast, striking him in rapid-fire.

"You're *damned* right you are! How dare you treat me like that! Who do you think you are?! No, who do you think *I* am that you can push me away like that? I'm not allowed to get to know the man I'm fucking?!"

She continued on, and he let her, not interrupting once, despite some words and phrases triggering that familiar ire within him. He held his tongue, and waited, her words cutting him to pieces while he did. He felt like a small child being scolded, which normally would bubble up a vindictive fury within him. He could almost see himself letting the anger get through, argue with her on every point, riposte each remark with a put-down of his own.

But he bit his tongue. He held it back and let it slip away. She was angry, and had every right to be. He endured the storm of her fury, which included some words in Spanish he did not know, but could guess by context.

Eventually, she ran out of steam, and tears began to slip from the corners of her eyes. He waited precisely five heartbeats before he responded to her rant.

"You're right," Tommy said softly.

"What?!" she demanded, she sounded almost insulted.

"You're right. I was an asshole."

She stopped, her finger still pointed at him. She stared in disbelief.

"That's... No, what are you doing?! I'm mad, and I want to keep being mad at you! I really, really like you and you don't get to be a jerk and then just go back to... to... Augh!" She threw her hands up in the air. "Fuck you!"

"Yeah, I, uh... Look, it's... "

"If you're going to apologize again, I'm going to punch you. I've been sucking down wine and getting all good and mad since you left and I want to punch someone! Yell at me so I can punch you!"

Tommy bit his tongue again. He tried to put into words what it was he was grappling with, but it felt like trying to catch a trout with his hands.

"Look, I'm, uh... I'm really bad at, uh... feelings. Can I come in and, uh... try to explain?"

She let out a vicious-sounding curse in Spanish, but sighed and gestured for Tommy to follow her inside. He followed behind by several steps. She had an open bottle of wine on the table and a very full glass. She sat down on the couch and took a big sip while Tommy shuffled uncomfortably and took a seat as well.

"So, uh... It's kinda a long story," he said.

"Well, I'm wide awake at midnight, so hit me," she said.

Tommy heaved a sigh and tried to think of how to begin.

"Well," he said, "I, uh... Christ. I felt like you were trying to kinda... get something out of me. And, uh... Well, I... I mean you touched a nerve. It's the kinda shit my Mom and Stepmom would do. But... Thing is, I know you're not like that. It's just... Back there, I guess it was like a... flashback kind of thing."

"Oh shit," she said, "Don't tell me you've got these issues. I went through the 'dating men with issues,' and the last one knocked me up and treated me like shit for years."

"Well, that's what I'm trying to say. I... I don't wanna be like that. My Dad's like that. That's why I came back. Tatiana, I really don't want to be that kind of a guy. I know what that kind of guy does to women, and especially to... to kids."

Tatiana's eyes flickered over to a picture on the wall of her daughter, much younger, with missing front teeth and a big cheesy smile. She looked back to Tommy again, and set her wine glass down. She clasped her hands together and rested them on her knees.

"Okay," she said, "Well, I guess I am getting what I asked for. Keep going. Tell me. I want to know what I'm getting into."

Tommy gritted his teeth. "I was afraid you'd say something like that."

"Oh, no backing out now. You keep talking. You fucking piece of shit, making me care about you and then all this. Out, all of it. And no lies, or I will break your head open with this Merlot bottle."

Tommy squirmed. He didn't know how to tell her everything, or even how to begin. He was quiet for a long moment, trying to put his words together. She seemed to be impatient. He muttered some false starts, not wanting to sound cheesy or overdramatic, and he realized as he started to put the words together, he'd been afraid to even think them for a very long time.

He started with his father, how he and his mother were never married. What he had gleaned later, but no one really said, was that they'd dated for some time, but broken up shortly after he was conceived. His mother never said anything, not for years. How his father went on to marry Margot, leaving him with his biological mother. His earliest memory was having a lit cigarette flicked at him. He couldn't have been more than 3.

He told her his vague memories of being seven years old. He remembered his mother dressing him up nice to go meet his "Daddy," and how she spent the entire time telling him that he needed to pay child support.

He remembered sitting in a big, boring, cold room while his mom yelled at a man in a black robe who sat behind a big important-looking desk. He didn't understand it then, but she had taken him to court for child support payments. The judge took one look at her, and the obvious track lines, her senseless babbling, and then at Tommy, sitting there, scared and sad, caught up in something completely beyond his comprehension. The judge awarded his father full custody on the spot. His mother screamed and tried to throw a chair at the judge. She was taken away by police. He didn't see her again for years.

Suddenly he had a little sister and a baby brother in a house with a new family, and a mother he hadn't even met. How Margot absolutely hated him. She seemed to go out of her way to make him feel unwelcome. He learned that for his eighth birthday party, she put together a cake, decorations, and wrapped presents, but didn't send out any invitations, and told him nobody showed up because he was "a bad kid."

Tatiana's face fell. Her eyes darted again to the picture on the wall, it's gap-toothed innocent grin, before turning back to Tommy.

He talked about how his sister Jamie, had always been kind to him, and he to her. But he'd been downright evil to his little half-brother Tim, and even in the re-telling, he realized how much he had stressed half-brother versus sister. He admitted to some of the things he'd done, wiping tears from his eyes. He visited upon Tim what had been done to him, because that's what you did when little boys cried too loud, or broke something playing, or didn't go to bed when you ordered them to. But he didn't realize what he was doing until months later, sitting in some office with brown carpet, and a woman in a pantsuit who said she was a doctor for his head tried to make him understand what he'd done was wrong.

He didn't accept it at first. This was just the way things were, wasn't it? He hadn't had a concept of cruelty before that doctor showed him what it was. It changed everything in his world, but not in time to handle what Margot was doing to him.

The clock on the wall ticked away slowly.

Starting around his tenth birthday, his father started to teach him tools, woodworking, carpentry, plumbing, and how to build things. He ate up every moment, absorbed it, dreamt about it, as this was the closest thing to affection the old army veteran offered him. He was eager to learn everything, and at thirteen, he was already building his own little clubhouse in the backyard. One that the Old Man knocked over with a John Deere earth mover tractor when he failed a Math test.

School was always rough. It seemed like every year the teachers treated him with some hidden disdain, and it took him a long time to realize Margot must have been filling their heads with ideas on parent/teacher conferences. And rumors began to spread about him, how he was unstable, dangerous, psychotic. People said he was on meds or worse, off of meds, and he never could make long-term friends when those rumors started circulating. He was the bad kid, and that was that. It was just decided by some merciless world. He got tired of trying to dispel it. Life was easier when he leaned into it. When he started sketching little knives and talking about firearms, people at least paid attention to him. Girls paid attention to him.

When he was fifteen, his mother returned. Said she'd cleaned up, wanted her son back. She had some slick lawyer who used the sympathy of the court to get custody. He painted a picture of a woman abused and left by her boyfriend, and forced to raise a child she wasn't ready for. He remembered being in court for one of those hearings, being questioned, and telling the judge in no uncertain terms what a pile of lies his mother was spewing. He told them she was abusive, cruel even, and how his earliest memories were of pain. It didn't help his credibility that he sat there with long hair, a black eye from a school fight a couple of days ago, and dressed in ratty jeans and a black tee shirt showing how much he was in to Megadeth at the time.

She burst into tears, and pleaded for the chance to make things right with her "baby." The judge ruled in her favor.

She was... different. She wasn't overtly cruel but had begun taking pages from Margot's book. Her neglect was emotional, her cruelty was subtle, and she would openly mock him for not having a real girlfriend, not having a car, having poor grades or no friends. Meanwhile, she would hide her alcohol and think he wasn't finding it. Think he wasn't marking the bottles and measuring how much she was drinking. She didn't even think he was using a polaroid to track it so the next time he sat in front of a judge, he'd have proof. He kept it a secret from her and her lawyer. But after only a few months, there they were, in front of a judge again, Tommy showing his evidence to her utter shock. The judge was furious at her deception.

He was back with his father's family again a week later. But even that was torturous. When he tried to talk about what he'd gone through, Margot kept a not-secret smirk. She was delighting in the cruelty he'd suffered, and probably taking notes for the future.

He spilled about the party where Jamie followed him, and how he spent his last year of high school living in a tiny one-room apartment and after finishing, unlike his classmates, he didn't go out and get drunk. He went out and got employed.

He hadn't seen his mother since. And when he told her about that Christmas, and the gift from his father, it was well past 2 in the morning. She drank every word, but the bottle of wine hadn't gone down, not since the part about his biological mother.

When he finished, he was quiet for a moment. She had a very real, very sober look on her face, as if he were a math problem instead of a person. It made him feel even smaller now that he'd opened up and dropped all of his past on the floor in front of her. He wasn't even sure what to do now. But the one thing he didn't see in her eyes, the thing he was terrified to see, was pity.

When she finally did speak, she said "So you aren't used to opening up, have real issues with trusting women, and a lot of guilt and obligation to your father."

Tommy blinked for a long moment. "What?"

She slid over to him and put a hand on his chest "It's not your fault, Tommy. You're a good person, especially with everything you've been through. I know guys, they had the best life, good parents, good schools, money, and they treat people like dirt. You don't do that."

"I sure used to."

"Stop it!" It was a command. "You were a kid, Tommy! Christ, I can't imagine growing up in that kind of house... those kinds of *houses*. What happened to you, and what you did because of it, was not your fault."

"No," he said, "But... it's still there. And it's like... Like factory settings. But I have to keep changing it because it keeps resetting if I'm not careful."

"Yes!" she said, and slapped him upside the head, "Because you know it's not who you wanna be! That means you know the difference between right and wrong you fucking tool."

He took the smack with a little irritation, but swallowed his feelings.

"Yeah, right there! You didn't smack me back. A lot of guys would. Do you not realize just how gentle you are?"

At that he wanted to argue, but some inner, wiser part of himself said not to.

Instead, he just stared at her until she spoke again.

"This is what I wanted, Tommy. To know you. And now that I do, I just want to hold you for the rest of the night and tell you it's okay. A bad person wouldn't rescue a puppy. A bad person wouldn't have come back after a fight. A bad person would have..."

"Just run away," he muttered. She must have heard, because she gripped him more tightly.

Tommy felt strange, but oddly soothed by the touch. He was almost embarrassed, lying there in the dark in the arms of a woman, letting his feelings out. He felt weak, and it sent shivers of revulsion through him. He hated himself for being in this place, being vulnerable and letting someone else comfort him. That's not how a man behaved. A man held it in, a man carried his burdens, a man comforted others, and didn't allow his feelings to overwhelm him.

He barely realized he was crying. His soul came out with heavy sobs. All she did was hold him and let him be. She didn't judge, didn't advise, didn't do anything, just held him.

And then it was over. The vomiting up of his shame left him feeling lighter, but oddly, less empty. She was still there when he was finished.

He thanked her, but it seemed like hollow words.

"Anyone who's been through what you have would be completely broken. You've kept it together this long. You're allowed to shed some tears."

He turned away, feeling small again. "It's not right,"

"Hey, my daughter's father would never have done this. He would have kept it all bottled up and taken it out on me. That's why I was so mad at first. I'm not going through *that* again. But this... This, I can do. You got some really bad stuff up here."

She kissed him on his forehead, and his shame evaporated.

"But you've got a lot of potential to grow. None of your parents ever had that."

Chapter Eleven

D r. Reid found that sleep completely eluded him. For the first hour or so after he and Anna went to bed, he tossed and turned, his mind endlessly spinning with the implications that the diary held. It took all of his willpower to remain in bed for as long as he had, determined to try to find rest.

Sleep never came for him, instead, he rose, donned his flannel robe, stepped into his slippers, and went down the soft stairs to his study. There, the book rested on his desk, where Anna made him leave it after their guests had left. She had kissed him, lured him up to bed, crawled under the covers with him, and run her hand over his chest until she fell asleep next to him.

He wanted to follow her into dreams, but his mind could not let go of the excitement of his prize.

He fetched a fresh notebook and a pen, then set about making himself a cup of chamomile tea. Anna always had some around, and on occasion, it did help him calm down and drift off to sleep. Though, the tea would have an uphill battle tonight.

Sufficiently comforted by a sip of the warm tea, he opened to the first page of the diary. The first dozen or so pages were fairly standard for a young woman of the time. Mary read books, played with her siblings, and of course, attended her father's sermons on Sunday, which were held in the parlor.

He read a page which described her fear and confusion at discovering blood coming from her bottom, but could find no wound. She was afraid, and tried to find answers in her books or from her siblings, but none came forth. Reluctantly, she decided to ask her father. That was the last normal entry. The next page was about her punishment, how her father had found a switch and lashed her for her sin, one that she didn't understand and couldn't stop. The entries were spaced farther out now, but upon the next month, the blood came again, and so did the pain. Two daily entries detailed the ache in her knees and the stinging pain in her back, and the horrible cold, dead feeling in her limbs after a night in the cellar.

Dr. Reid turned the page, and his eyes almost fell out of his head.

Here, there was more than mere words, but detailed and intricate sketches of strange sigils, monstrous figures, and most puzzling, a series of long numeric equations. He tried to follow them, but their logic eluded him. He did find the continuation of narration a few pages later, detailing her strange dreams and visions as she found herself close to death from her father's wrath.

Dr. Reid flipped back to the series of numbers. He opened his desk, pulling out a scientific calculator. The fact that Mary had such a strong understanding of mathematics was almost beyond belief given the time she lived in, but as he ran the numbers, the formula seemed to check out as far as he could tell. Though he had no idea what it was for, the numbers and their processes balanced. He went back to some of the sigils and tried to figure out their significance. They were odd, angular designs, almost like Nordic runes, but significantly more complex, and often arranged in circles and alongside diagrams of geometric configurations he couldn't even begin to guess at.

He turned the page, catching another snippet of actual diary entry. It seemed to be a recounting of one of her dreams, where she met some formless thing she called the Dream-Maker, and the various things it told her.

According to this Dream-Maker, there was no God, no Jesus, no savior or powerful being watching over her or her people. There was only the vast, empty void and the things that dwelled within. The Dream-Maker was one such thing, formed of thoughts and fancies of all living things, having no solid form of its own, it could only appear to her as a parody of her father, like a lifeless corpse with hollow eyes that spoke with his voice, but not his cruelty.

Mary wrote down everything she remembered from these dreams, and taught it to the slaves who had saved her and taken her in. Some were resistant to the lessons of the Dream-Maker, but the rest, young, restless, angry and abused, rallied around her as if she were their new personal savior. Those who resisted were shouted down, shamed, but not by Mary... instead, by their peers. Mary felt rather proud on this point, having been able to turn them against each other to ensure they would be dutiful followers.

The chamomile tea was cold now, but Dr. Reid kept on reading, captivated. Some of the inscriptions and sketches could almost form a pattern he could see. He started copying the sketches into his own notebook. He flipped back and forth, pulling pieces from different pages, like putting a puzzle together.

And they did fit into a pattern, one that seemed not unlike the particles in an atom. The strange runic inscriptions seemed to be a key of some kind describing each particle, and eventually he determined the respective protons, neutrons, and electrons, but it was incredibly complex. Once he finished piecing it together, it looked like a very complicated atomic structure. This made no sense to him. Even if Mary had a truly excellent education, there was no possible way she could have learned of atomic structures, much less one this complex.

Resting on one of his shelves, he knew, was an old chemistry textbook. He sought it out to check against this atom pattern.

He found the periodic table in the middle, easy to open as it was a frequent index point. He counted the electrons and protons, then moved his finger along. He had to re-check it several times, because it made no sense. It described a Cesium atom. Upon a more in-depth examination, it specifically described Cesium 137, which wouldn't even be discovered for at least a hundred years. And the mathematical formula, when looked at in this light, was some very detailed chemistry formula that he was not experienced enough to put together on his own. His specialty was history. And history said that this was completely impossible.

He sat back in astonishment. It wasn't possible. And yet, the inscriptions and diagrams conformed to it perfectly.

Frowning, he sat back. He couldn't believe it was real. But if it was a hoax, it was done by someone who knew chemistry very well. He did not expect many people with this level of knowledge to fake a diary just to sell an old ghost story.

He flipped several pages further along, and saw more diagrams of different atomic configurations. He worked feverishly to decode the next, able to move more quickly now that he had an idea what he was doing with the first atom as a blueprint, and decoded the next atom. It corresponded to Thorium, another impossibility. With growing curiosity and horror, he looked back to the mathematical formulas and realized what it was they truly entailed.

It wasn't possible. No child in the early 1800's could possibly have knowledge like this. It didn't exist. And it was no mere fluke or misinterpretation, the math backed up the scribbles, and with the elements involved here in the equations, it painted a hideous picture. This was the kind of deep chemical mathematics they did in classes on nuclear physics.

Dr. Reid looked down at one of the sketches of the Dream-Maker, and he had a sinking feeling the strange figure was watching him, a gleam in its void-black eyes depicted in old charcoal. It appeared as Mary's father, but elongated, bones protruding from skin.

"No," he said softly, as much to himself as to any sense of dread. "No, no, there's a... there's a logical... explanation. It's a fake. It has to be..."

He felt an eerie chill, as if the temperature had suddenly dropped around him. Even in his flannel robe, the chill cut right through to his marrow. He picked up his tea and shuffled back out of the office to go warm it up. He had to step away for a moment, yes that was it, just get some distance and perspective. As he passed the window in the kitchen, he caught a glimpse of something, of someone, standing on the other side of his reflection, a hideous rictus of a smile on its pale, wrinkled face. His pale, wrinkled face. Porcelain shattered. Cold liquid seeped into his slippers.

He turned around, expecting it to be some optical illusion or some other figment of his imagination, but instead he met that grinning face of yellowed, broken teeth and void-black eyes as it seized his mind. It pierced his soul. He opened his mouth to scream, and the blackness swallowed him.

When Anna woke from the screaming, she naturally feared the worst. Never one to be shy of protecting herself, she reached behind the bed for the aluminum baseball bat she kept there for just such an occasion. No prowler was going to hurt her husband and get away with it. She crept down the stairs with the weapon raised, and heard the strange whimpering cry coming from her kitchen. She stepped into the doorway, her feet crunching on the ceramic shards. There was no prowler there, just her husband, curled up in the corner, something like whimpering sobs coming from him.

"Oh God," she said, "What happened?!"

She ran over to her husband, but recoiled instantly as he turned to her.

His face was frozen into a painful grin, the skin around his lips cracked from the strain of the taught muscles, the tears leaking blood down his face. He tried to speak through the gritted teeth, but she couldn't understand his words at first.

They came in a strange garbled and strained mess, but she heard them, and began to sob along with him while he gibbered "*It's not real,*" over and over again with clenched teeth, and a hideous grin that cried blood.

"It's not real!" he seized her by the collar of her nightgown, then by her throat, smothering her scream and crushing her windpipe. Her silenced scream could be seen in her eyes until the light went out of them, and only Dr. Reid's twisted face remained.

He stood then, sobbing his life out through his stretched face. He looked to the darkened window at his reflection... The void-black eyes looked back at him. He tried to open his teeth, but they crashed shut with hot pain. He felt a chip break off of a tooth and land in the mess of teacup on the floor.

It left the corpse of Anna lying on the floor with terror in her dull eyes. Only the book was important. And it was still not in the right hands.

• • • •

The cool morning dew still coated the world when Tommy climbed his ladder up to the roof. He had stripped several shingles off just by walking on it, and the scraper removed the rest with very little effort. They slid down the slope like an avalanche with every pass. Piles of old, crumbled mess rained onto the tarp below. Stripping took less than two hours.

AC/DC provided the beat that he worked to. He didn't expect it to go so quickly, but it absolutely made his day. He was back down the ladder and hauling away the old shingles before Tatiana even woke up.

She emerged from the trailer in his tee shirt and with Mac at her heels. She watched him for a few minutes, then went back into the trailer. She emerged soon after with an exasperated look.

"You don't have anything to cook with!" she yelled to him across the yard.

Tommy frowned. "There's a frying pan," he said, "Somewhere."

She sighed and shook her head, heading back into the trailer, a number of Spanish mutterings following her. Mac yipped happily and bounded back and forth through the tall grass and bushes. Eventually, he smelled warm, buttery food.

He came down the ladder, washed his hands at her urging, then sat by the fire to eat her improvised omelet. Tommy usually just ate eggs, or cereal, but Tatiana pulled some of his cold cuts and put together a surprisingly tasty breakfast. Though she chided him for having no spices besides salt and pepper, and most of that was in tiny paper packets. Tommy smiled sheepishly.

"I'm not really a great cook," he said.

"Oh, so you can build a whole house but can't cook a meal?"

"That seemed a little unkind?"

"Sorry," she said, "I just mean, it seems so much more complicated to rebuild a whole damned house than to learn a few recipes. I mean, when you get right down to it, it's all just about putting in the effort, right?"

He paused mid-bite. He never really thought about it that way. But she was right. He had never seen himself as much of a chef if it couldn't be cooked over a fire, but she seemed to think he had the potential to do it. That made him smile.

"Has Dr. Reid called yet?" she asked over her own omelet.

Tommy shook his head. "I tried giving him a ring this morning, but nothing. His phone keeps going to voicemail."

She frowned and put her plate down. "He didn't answer my calls, either. That's not like him."

"Maybe he's busy. I know that I'm shit at answering my phone."

"I know," said Tatiana with a sidelong glance. Tommy blushed slightly.

"Thanks for breakfast," he said to change the subject.

"You need cookware. Even over a fire you need more than a frying pan," she said.

"Never needed it before," he said.

"Okay, I'll put it this way... If I'm going to spend the night here, *I* need more than a frying pan."

"Stick around long enough, there'll be a whole kitchen you can play with," he said.

"Is that a promise?" she asked with a smirk.

He laughed and picked up his hammer, tossing it once and catching it by the handle. "Try to stop me."

"I could, you know," she said, stretching and making a show of arching her back.

"Damn, woman," said Tommy, "Even after last night?"

She laughed. "No, not really... I think I'm actually a little sore. But very very satisfied. You can go work on your big empty house with your fancy tools. I'm going to shower and have a run."

He smirked at her. She was being playful. A few days ago, he might have been a little insulted at the words. But this was different. He went back up the ladder, and it wasn't until he was hammering in the first nail that he realized the word to fit what he was feeling: respect.

The idea felt good to him. She respected him, and he respected her in return. It wasn't transactional, and it wasn't dependent on anything, it was just there. Some Foo Fighter song came on the radio, and even though he despised the song, he really just felt like singing. He was off-key, and somewhere he was sure Mac was howling, but he felt no shame. He wondered why he ever did.

By the time the sun was highest in the sky, and Tommy's sweat was pouring into the woodwork, he elected to call it a day and climb back down the ladder. He rested in the shade of the trailer with a beer, and checked the weather with his phone. He had three days until rain, according to the most recent reports. He had a lot of work to do, and none of his buddies were available to help. He didn't want to ask Tatiana. Among other things, he felt like the house was his responsibility. Maybe that was his Dad talking, but he wasn't ready to push that boundary yet.

Still, he felt different. A lot of weight he'd carried for years had fallen off of him. He stood up straighter, walked with more confidence, and felt sure of himself for the first time in a long time. He didn't feel like he needed to watch out for the next thing that lurked in the shadows because right now, he felt invincible.

He decided to take a stroll beneath the trees to clear his head. He walked out to the old, run-down Gazebo by the water. He took a tentative step upon it. The wood felt soft, spongy, even in the dry heat. He stepped back and approached the edge of the water. The great big lake seemed darker than normal, despite reflecting the big bright sun, casting a shimmering reflection of the beautiful day. Two suns blazed at him.

The dark waters lazily rippled while Tommy stood there. The contrast of bright sun and dark water almost hurt his eyes to look at. He scraped the wet dirt with the heel of his boot at the edge of the water, finding black griminess beneath the top layer. He had the strangest sensation of poking into an eye when he did that. He shuddered it away, then looked back at the crumbling Gazebo. It would be easy to collapse it into the murk.

He almost went back to the house, but stopped.

For so long he had been afraid. Today, he didn't.

He didn't have the vocabulary to explain why, but he kicked off his shoes. He peeled off his sweaty socks and drenched tee shirt. He slid off the jeans and approached the water.

The first few steps squelched mud under his toes, and he almost turned back. But he pressed on. The next step brought the water higher, and the coolness was taking the edge off of the heat. His next step, he saw tiny fish flee his presence. The water was up to his knees, and he stepped on hard rocks that almost made him lose his balance. He swung his arms, and steadied himself.

Another step brought him to a sudden falloff, and he slid down a few inches before sinking into more mud. It was up to his thighs now. It was just beginning to dampen the edge of his underwear.

He was trembling now, but pressed on, and made himself take a leap of faith. He splashed into the dark, cool water and felt relief embrace him. The hot sun couldn't touch him. Down here, no one could touch him. The sound of the world above, the sizzling wildlife and birdcalls all fell away. There was just the sound of water in his ears.

It terrified him.

And he almost could imagine that there was a hand holding him down. His imagination could still remember someone with sour-whiskey breath telling him he needed to wash his hair *or else.*

But there was no hand. No voice. No breath drenched with spirits and tooth rot, cigarettes and bile. No one held him here. He did not feel cold ceramic beneath him. Nor was there hot pain waiting for him should he rise. He was safe. He was free. He had *chosen* to duck beneath the surface, and he could choose to rise.

He came back up and shook water from his head and ears. He put down his feet and discovered he could still stand. So he walked out further until the ground gave way and he was forced to swim to keep his head up. But instead, he reclined himself and floated on his back. The water in his ears dulled every sound but the beating of his heart, and he felt the sun high above him. He drifted for a time, floating freely in the waters, his face hurting from smiling more than he had in years. He floated like that for some time, he wasn't sure how long, but long enough that he could feel his chest hair drying in the sun.

He lost himself there until he heard Tatiana call his name. He pulled himself upright, but realized he couldn't touch bottom and started to panic. He scrambled clumsily for a little bit. He was further out than he realized, but a few panicked strokes brought him close enough to touch the mud with his toes and start his journey out. She was on the shore, watching him. She had her hands to her mouth.

"I... I thought you were afraid of the water," she said.

He nodded. "Yeah," he said, "I... I was." He just laughed. He felt heavier for the water dripping off him as he trudged up onto the shore. His feet stepped in deep mud, and he didn't care. Tatiana wordlessly scooped up his clothes. He struggled to keep his soaked boxers up. They wanted to follow gravity all the way down.

"Well, you'll need a towel. Or do you want to take another dip?" She cocked a hip and gave him a look. He felt oddly giddy. Maybe this was what it felt like to be happy? To drift away from the shore you know for a little while, confident that you can always come back?

In soaked underwear and a warm towel, he jabbered about taking the plunge, how good it felt. She listened with a strange smile on her face.

Coming up from the trees, he saw, in the distance, a car speeding along the road, leaving a visible dust trail in the hot summer air. He frowned. He didn't get a lot of traffic out here. Even the mail carrier didn't come by very much, despite Tommy making the official request to forward his mail.

The dust trail from the car was already faded, and there was no sign of visitation. Tommy thought it was a little early for the mail, but he didn't question it. He dressed, taking his time, enjoying the feeling of having let go for even just a little while. Tatiana teased him a little, with glances, touches. He'd never known a woman like her. She wasn't like the reserved, timid women he'd been conditioned to think of. She was utterly open, as she'd proven already, hiding nothing and making no pretense. Her honesty was blunt, sometimes brutal, but never intended to hurt. It shattered his preconceptions, and he realized that was the best thing that could have happened to him.

His head was filled with those thoughts as he crossed the field of dead grass to the mailbox, newly erected and guarded from teenagers by some cobbled up brickwork. He felt the shadow of the house fall over him from that single towering eye that loomed above all. It felt cold in that shadow, but his head was full of delight.

He would never forget this house, but he was happy to be turning it into a memory already. He could complete his task, and move on with his life. No, that wasn't accurate. He could *start* his life, and really *live* it from here on out.

Inside the hollow aluminum interior of the mailbox was a familiar, leather-bound journal. Tommy frowned and removed it. It felt cold in his hands.

He looked back up the road where the car had gone. It was well out of visual range now, but it had to have been Dr. Reid. Why would he just drop it off like this? Had he found something? Why didn't he call? Was there at least a note?

Lying on top of the diary was a small piece of paper that looked like it had been torn from a notebook, but hurriedly, crudely, as it was little more than an uneven scrap. Scrawled in strained, forceful letters was one word, "*Dream.*"

His blood went cold. He grabbed his phone to text Tatiana, but it was already buzzing. She'd sent him a text, with a link embedded. The headline read: "*Anna Reid, 57, found dead in home, husband missing.*" The preview picture had a snapshot of the house they'd just visited.

The cold in the shadow of that house seemed to close in on him.

He dropped the diary into the dirt, and the note went fluttering away on the breeze. It swirled upwards once, the word *"Dream"* mocking him, before floating off into the woods to be impaled against a small, broken stick on a pine tree. The sudden wind caused the pages to flutter and dance with the breeze. Tommy left the book on the ground and ran straight back towards the camper.

Mac was inside taking a nap, but as Tommy pulled the door shut behind him, the pup whined and started peering out the windows, his hackles raising. Tatiana came out of the bedroom section, sheer panic written on her face. Gone was the fun, flirtatious day. They both now saw the cloud hanging over them.

Tommy leaned against the counter. He ran the sink just enough to throw some water on his face and try to calm down.

He thought about reading the article, but he did not want to know any details. He knew it wouldn't help him feel any better. Still, his mind conjured up a shadowy foe that lurked outside, someone crafty, hiding, menacing in a way Tommy couldn't fathom. He badly wanted to fetch his rifle.

Another gust of wind blasted past the trailer, and he was sure he heard more than wind. Wind didn't have a rhythmic footfall on the dirt, but he was certain that's what he heard, soft crunching of dried grass just a few feet away, past the aluminum walls.

The more rational part of him said this wasn't real. Despite all the creepy craziness, this was real life, and there was nothing to be afraid of. He jumped at shadows, and he was meant to. Maybe the professor had returned the journal, and that speeding car was just some dumb teenager doing weird stuff to be weird. Maybe the article was a misunderstanding, or a terrible coincidence? Maybe what he was afraid of wasn't actually real, and he could just open the door and nothing would be there. He could laugh about being spooked by a rude mail delivery.

He reached for the door handle, and hesitated. Something deep and animal inside him found the thought of opening the door horrific.

Mac barked, then ducked his head and whimpered. He alternated between growls and whimpers. Tommy watched the beast. It turned soft eyes to him, as if pleading to make the bad thing go away.

If he couldn't trust his own senses, he could trust Mac's. The pup could hear the peeling open of a hot dog wrapper from a thousand yards.

Tommy sucked in a breath and made a decision. He always kept the weapon secure and hidden. That's what responsible people with guns did. The drunken warnings of coyotes from a few weeks back floated up into his mind again. It was probably coyotes. But if someone or something was out there looking for trouble, he would be happy to give it to them.

He opened a compartment in the bedroom, and from the back of the closeted insert, he removed long black steel. Tatiana didn't see until he brought it out to the kitchen area. He slipped the ammo in, locked it, and braced himself.

Tatiana crossed herself and flattened against the wall.

He held the rifle steady, and quietly went through his safety steps. Load the round into the chamber, check magazine, safety off. Precise, rehearsed, as he'd done it before. He had only fired the rifle out on the range, or on unsuccessful hunting trips, but now he pointed that powerful barrel at the aluminum door. Nothing happened for thirty agonizing seconds.

Tommy lowered the barrel. His trembling hand reached out, turned the knob, and gave it a shove. With the same motion, he pulled back and hefted the rifle up again to about chest-height for anyone on the other side. He vaguely remembered his father talking about learning to shoot in the army, about aiming for the center of mass.

A part of him worried he was about to shoot a lost mailman, but as his sun-touched vision cleared, no one stood there.

The only thing in front of him was the leather-bound journal, resting in the dying grass and trampled dirt. He almost fired anyway, but removed his finger from the trigger. This was a prank. He was certain of it now. Then he considered that the prankster might still be around.

He cautiously stepped outside, head swiveling back and forth to scan the horizon with his rifle at the ready. He wasn't going to actually shoot whoever this was, but he was going to scare the bejeesus out of them.

He carefully ran his eyes over all of his property, from the distant glimmers of light on the lake to the crumbling cycloptic spire on the main house. He found nothing but wind-swept branches and the occasional dust devil spinning happily in the summer haze. He stepped towards the book. A breeze caught the cover and flipped it open, flapping pages until it landed on a sketch of a hideous, old, grinning face with black eyes. Tommy pulled the gun back into a firing position. Then he lowered it, feeling incredibly stupid.

He turned his eyes back around to the trees, looking even up in the branches.

He paced around the trailer, checking for footprints, or animal tracks, any sign of disturbance. He checked the tires, the wheels, the roof, and beneath. All he found was silence, and an ominous chill come through the shifting wind.

He could hear Mac whining inside, but once he finished his circuit, the pup was peering hesitantly out the door. Tatiana was behind him, and her lip trembled.

Tommy kept turning his head, whipping this way and that, trying to see if he could catch someone hiding. Nothing and no one appeared. He took a long look at the house, at that damned eye hovering above him and looking down.

"All right," he said out loud, "Joke's over. Get off of my property before we have a hunting accident!"

Silence answered him. Wind swept past his face. The trees swayed and somewhere far away, a hawk cried. Tommy slowly lowered his rifle. He looked back to the book sitting in front of his trailer. He picked it up, shutting it and tossing it carelessly into the trailer. It landed on the floor. Tatiana and Mac scrambled back out of the way to make room for it, like it was some dead, or worse, some live animal.

He closed the door behind him, then began disassembling the rifle for safe storage. He didn't begin to relax, though, even with the chamber clear and the safety on.

"Tat?" he said.

"Yeah?" She was close to crying, he could hear it in her voice. Tommy looked back at the book as it sat inert just inside the trailer. Mac sniffed it, then backed away with a frightened yip.

"Tat, is, uh... Is the Doctor the practical joke type?"

She was silent a moment. "What kind of question is that?!"

"Tat, the book's here," he said, "Someone just stuffed it in my mailbox and drove off. I left it in the road, and now here it is again."

She looked down at it. Then their eyes met. Hers were already glistening from the held tears, and now had taken on the sheen of fear.

He looked down at the book again, the way the old leather flaked off on his hands. The dust coated his fingers already. He felt like something was crawling over his skin. He wiped his hand on his jeans.

"We should leave, right now," she said.

Tommy thought that was a very good idea. "And we're bringing Mac."

Tatiana left first. She was already running late anyway, and expected that Maya would probably already be dropped off early with nary a text to be found. Tommy had never seen a hybrid accelerate like that, and he wondered if his assumptions on those vehicles was also wrong, or if Tatiana was just that scared.

He collected Mac and a few changes of clothes. Nothing crazy, just for a few nights. He packed up the rifle, and put it in the big toolbox in his truck. While he had the gun rack, he preferred not to advertise the expensive weapon to the world. Really, the rack was more of a statement, one that served as a better security system than a car alarm. No one cares if an alarm goes off, but if they think the driver is packing, most car thieves will select an easier target.

This wasn't the kind of state where cops ignored weapons that could down bears just being bandied about freely. But if ever he felt the need to be armed, it was now.

And, leaving nothing to chance, he packed up his more dangerous tools and locked the toolboxes.

The ride felt hectic, even though he literally could not speed on these roads. He couldn't fathom how Tatiana's little, low-to-the-ground car could stand these roads without blowing out the shocks or bottoming out. If they needed to flee, they were taking his truck. He'd rather have the four wheel drive. One bad rock could total that little car.

All through his drive, he paid close attention to any other cars, to any roads he hadn't noticed before, anything that looked strange or different. Clearly someone was out there. He could write off the spooky shadows and weird fears, and all the other distractions. But this was tangible, physical, real. Someone was messing with him. He suspected Samson. That's where most of this spooky stuff was coming from. His stories were the unnerving ones. Everything else was hearsay, legend, weird rumors and gossip. But Samson had owned the house. Samson had put on an Oscar worthy performance in that Diner. How far was he willing to push this con?

What was it? There was a name for it, wasn't there? This con? He'd heard it in a movie once. The fiddle game? Something about making a piece of garbage seem really valuable and then get the rube to buy it for a ridiculous price thinking they can turn around and sell it to a more interested buyer.

But that didn't work if Samson already said he wanted nothing to do with it. And wasn't he retired anyway?

In the end, it didn't matter. He was getting away from that house and that damned book.

Mac was oddly quiet in the passenger seat. He reached out to stroke the pup as much to reassure him, as to be reassured.

Tommy entered Tatiana's apartment with Mac at his heels. Tatiana threw her arms around him. She'd been crying. She let a couple of sobs into his shoulder. He just held her, then looked to see little Maya sitting on the couch with her phone.

"Mommy's sad because her friend died," said Maya, who hadn't looked up yet. But Mac was panting and suddenly she perked up, looking at him.

"Oh my god, a puppy!" she said, jumping to her feet, "Can... Can I pet him?"

"Go ahead," said Tommy, "He's friendly."

Mac stepped over to Maya and received a prompt head-scritching right behind the hears. His tongue lolled out, and he started licking at her other hand. She giggled happily. Mac went to lick her face and she fell instantly in love.

Tatiana gave Tommy a look, and wordlessly signaled her distress with wide, wet eyes and a quivering lip. Tommy nodded towards the kitchen.

"Maya, you and Mac play out here, okay? Mommy and her friend need to talk."

"You mean boyfriend, Mom," said Maya, "C'mon, I'm six."

Tommy couldn't help but smile. Tatiana seemed to bite back a reply, then just nodded. They stepped into the kitchen, where Tatiana stepped out of view of Maya and slumped down against the counter.

"That kid is very sharp," said Tommy.

"Tommy, what's happening?"

"I... I don't know," he said, "But I brought the book."

Tatiana stood straight up. He handed the book to her, and she acted like he was holding out a venomous snake. She recoiled.

"I don't want that *thing!* Get rid of it, Tommy!"

"I tried," he said. He dropped the book on the table, "I don't even know why it's so goddamned important."

"Well someone sure does, and they killed Anna, maybe Daniel," she said, "And if they were at your house, I just... I'm just *scared*, Tommy."

He nodded. "Well don't worry," he said, "I have a rifle."

"Good," she said, "But still, I don't want you to go back to that house until... Until Daniel's found. It's just too much, Tommy."

A weak, almost whiny digital tone rang out. Tatiana nearly jumped out of her skin, despite the pleasant, cheerful tone of the doorbell. Tommy tensed. He'd left the rifle in the truck, but now wished that he hadn't.

"Who's that?" Tommy asked.

Tatiana put a hand over her chest and took a breath. "It should be Miguel. I asked him to take her for a few more days. Whatever's gonna happen, I want her safe while it happens."

Tommy winced a little, but understood her reasoning. He didn't like the idea of dumping the kid off. Again, he'd been through that. But Tatiana wasn't doing it so she could go do drugs and drink herself stupid. She was legitimately scared for her daughter's safety. So was he. Still, the memories of being dumped off on random people bubbled up in his mind, bringing a familiar shudder of old pain. He pushed it to the back of his mind. He couldn't feel that right now. Not right now. He had a lot of other fear to work through without hauling more along for the ride.

Tatiana strode across the room, putting on a neutral mask. She opened the door. Standing there was a man with skin the color of varnished wood, flashing a wide smile that looked similarly polished both in shine and practiced, fake-friendliness. He tapped at his phone, only half paying attention, like she wasn't worthy of him even looking up.

"Hi Tatiana," he said.

"Hello," she said, "Thank you for doing this."

"No problem," he said, but his eyes were grinning as he slowly looked up from the screen. Tommy had seen that look before, too. The man caught Tommy's gaze and his grin faltered. "Who's your friend?"

"Boyfriend," Maya chimed in, and crossed the room. "Hi, Dad."

The man gave Tommy a look, one with a grin or a scowl, depending on how much you read into it.

"Hello," he said, holding out his hand, "Miguel."

"Tommy," He took the man's hand, and felt him tighten the handshake. He was muscular beneath the suit, he probably went to the gym regularly. His slicked-back hair and crisp businesswear spoke of someone who didn't work hard for a living, and here he was trying to intimidate Tommy with a handshake. Tommy tried not to grin. He squeezed back, pressing his hard callouses from day labor into the soft skin. Miguel flinched. Tommy kept his eyes locked for just a second longer than necessary. Miguel broke eye contact first, and the petty battle ended. Tommy was tempted to gloat, but that was what his father would do. As much as he wanted to drive home the defeat, this was still Maya's father, and he wasn't going to dress him down in front of his kid... for her sake.

"Good to meet you," said Miguel to cover his defeat, "Always nice to meet another of Tatiana's boyfriends. Ready to go, Maya?"

"Sure am," she said. She picked up her backpack and stepped through the threshold. Miguel cast a glance back at Tatiana. Tommy knew that look, too. Migul wanted to escalate. He was *that* kind of guy?

As Tatiana closed the door, Tommy turned to her, and spoke just loud enough for Miguel to catch what he said.

"So like I said, my rifle's in the truck if you're concerned."

Tatiana shot a horrified look at him, but then realized why he said it. Tommy glanced back at Miguel who had swiveled a wide-eyed stare back at them. The color had drained from his face. That was the last they saw as the door shut.

He could see the whiteness of her smile through the cascade of hair around her head.

"*Estupido,*" she said, but she laughed.

"Guys like that need a little jolt now and then," he said, "Prick tried to do that 'squeeze your hand' thing."

"Sounds like him,"

"I bet he's got cuts on his palms now," said Tommy, running a thumb over the rough skin.

Tatiana laughed. "He's such a girl. Uses lotion on his hands every day."

"On his *hands?*" he chuckled.

They shared a good long laugh at Miguel's expense, eventually sliding down and sitting with their backs to the door. It was wild, free, silly laughter that Tommy hadn't felt since he was very young. It was freeing, and slightly guilty, and full of glee.

Once the laughter wore off, Tommy bit his lip and tried to think of the best way to bring up his next thought.

"Go get the gun," she said before he could say anything. He smiled. They both stood up from the floor. Tommy turned the knob just as a knock sounded, a hard, rapid knock that reverberated through the walls. Tommy let go of the knob.

"Jesus," he spat. Tatiana seemed to be holding her breath. Tommy opened the door, too terrified and angry to care anymore. He was ready to choke whoever or whatever was on the other side. The afternoon light filtered down over a man in a police uniform. He frowned and peered at Tommy before taking off his sunglasses.

"You again," said Corporal Miles.

Tatiana sputtered. "Who... Who is, I mean you. Who are you?" asked Tatiana.

"Corporal Miles, Ingham Sheriff's office," he said, looking at Tatiana. "Are you Miss Herrera?"

"Yes..."

"I was wondering if you could answer some questions for me. We understand that you visited Dr. Reid on Saturday?"

"Oh my God, yes, have you found him? Is he all right?!"

Miles seemed guarded. His professional look was up. This was not the look of the man that helped Tommy bury a body, this was the look of the officer unsure what he was in for.

"I'm afraid I'm not at liberty..." he began.

"It's okay," Tommy said, "Why don't you come in? We'll tell you everything we can."

Soon, Miles was sitting at the table with a notepad out, and Tatiana poured some coffee for him. Tommy sat across from him, trying to remain at ease.

"So what can you tell me about that night?"

"Not much," said Tommy, "But, uh... Well, remember the last time we met?"

Miles simply nodded in silence.

"Well," Tommy continued, "Along with... what we found, there was this diary. Tatiana used to be one of the Doc's students, so she suggested I show it to him after we found a few other weird things at the house. Said he might know what they were."

"And what were they?"

"Well, there was a bottle of old urine," said Tommy.

"*Jesu Cristi,*" said Tatiana. "Witch bottle, it's a thing people used to do."

"Yeah," said Tommy, "Well, we went over to see him for dinner so he and Tat could catch up a little, and he could look at this diary."

Tommy had made a hand gesture, and when his palm touched the table again, the diary was underneath it. Everyone looked down at the book. Tommy slowly removed his hand, a slight tremor to his fingertips. It hadn't been there a moment ago, he was sure of it. There it was, flaked leather again lingering on his fingertips.

Miles picked it up. He looked it over.

"And what did he think of it?" Miles flipped open the cover.

"He seemed to think it was amazing. He asked to keep it for a few days. So... I let him."

Miles frowned and looked back to Tommy. "Then when did he return it?"

"I found it in my mailbox this afternoon," Tommy said, "Just about the same time Tatiana sent me a text about what happened."

Miles put the book down and looked at both of them.

"So you two were the last ones to see Anna Reid or her husband alive," he said, "And it was about this book here, which mysteriously got returned to you?"

"I guess that sounds bad when you say it like that."

"Hard to imagine it sounding good when there's a murder involved. But you're lucky at least that I'm pretty sure neither of you were involved."

"Oh... oh good... Um, why?" asked Tommy.

"You're an idiot," said Miles, "If you did do it, then you just handed me the kind of story that would get you locked up."

"Excuse me?"

"You're the last ones to see Anna alive. You have a piece of potentially important evidence. You claim it was returned to you but can't offer any details. You didn't contact us with any information when you heard about what happened, and I know you've got one body buried on that property already Mr. Walker."

"Okay, yeah..." said Tommy.

"Plus, I saw you almost lose your lunch over those bones, so-"

"Okay, wait, no... bones?! A body?" Tatiana demanded.

Tommy winced. "Yeah, I, uh... Well, when I checked the foundation there was this little, uh... hole... And inside was-"

"*Oh my God,*" she said, her voice cracking with fury and terror.

"Yeah, you don't strike me as a criminal mastermind," said Miles, sipping his coffee. He seemed to leaf through the journal for a moment, then shut it and put it down. "I'll be taking this book in as evidence, though."

"Knock yourself out," said Tommy, "Never wanted the damned thing in the first place. I just didn't want my investment to become some 'real crime' landmark. Kind of hard to move a property with a lot of bodies under it."

"Sure," he said, shaking his head, "Now, if you don't mind, I'd like to get to some details of the evening. What time did you arrive at the Reid's home?"

The interview seemed to go on for hours, but then for Tommy, every second was a minute eternity. He kept expecting the cop to suddenly rise and slap cuffs on him. He felt like he really had done something wrong, and a part of him was actually a little angry about being treated like a criminal. On some level, he knew Miles was just doing what all cops did, but from what Tommy had seen lately, cops had a nasty habit of getting rough with people. He glanced at Tatiana now and then, and she also seemed to be fidgeting, or working very hard to keep a placid face. It was the same one she had put on to confront Miguel. The eternal seconds ticked by. Corporal Miles eventually seemed satisfied and closed his notebook.

"Well, thank you for the coffee," he said to Tatiana, "There may be more questions in the near future, so neither of you go too far. And, uh, Tommy?"

"Yeah?"

"Good luck, man." he nodded at Tatiana and went towards the door. Tatiana opened it for him, her demeanor oozing a terrified politeness.

Once the Corporal was gone, Tommy and Tatiana sat on the couch for a moment and each tried to think of something to say.

The silence dragged on, with Tommy bouncing his knee nervously and Tatiana fidgeting.

Eventually, she slid up to him and rested against his shoulder.

"Please tell me it's going to be all right," she pleaded.

"It's going to be all right," he lied.

Then she smacked his face. It stung, and her nails left faint surface scratches.

"And tell me about this body you found, you *ass!*"

Sitting in the cruiser, Miles called in a basic report, then started the car. The journal was in the seat next to him, its flaking leather cover casting aged particles all over the seat. He felt an odd curiosity and decided to flip through it again, curious what might be so exciting about it. After all, he'd buried its owner, he might as well learn a little bit about it. Maybe it would even give a clue to where the professor had gone. He reached for the aged thing, his fingers dislodging more flakes as he lifted it up. He opened it to the first few pages. At first it seemed like the diary of a teenage girl in the early 1800's, with very ornate penmanship, probably well schooled either by a tutor or one of those old one-room schoolhouse classrooms. There were occasionally little sketches of flowers, or animals she'd seen around the house. He rolled his eyes. The book was probably worth money, but not necessarily a priceless item. Academics like Daniel Reid would probably go nuts over it, but not a blue collar guy flipping a house and single mother who was a college dropout. He was never more certain that Tommy Walker was innocent. While he didn't think the man was really stupid, literally handing clues over to the police of your own crime would be bad-cop-show stupid. Besides, Walker was just so brazenly honest. He just didn't see it. They had the means, motive, and opportunity, and a crucial piece of evidence. But fitting those pieces into place made the whole picture look askew. It was like trying to imagine Mr. Rogers and Glinda the Good Witch chopping up bodies. It just didn't fit. He couldn't speak to their virtuousness, but he could definitely see scared, and disorganized people who were afraid of what was happening.

You could tell the people who were afraid because they were about to get caught versus the people who were just scared because they didn't understand what was happening. Miles knew the difference. Most of his colleagues didn't, or didn't care, but he did. He had a kid, and there were different kinds of guilty nervous.

Tommy had the guilty nervous of someone who doesn't want more trouble. He's scared of something he doesn't understand. That's not the same as being scared of getting caught. People who are scared of getting caught tell much more creative, and reasonable-sounding lies.

He leafed through to some heavier pages where the sketches changed dramatically from local wildlife to circles of people in open fields, and incomprehensible strings of symbols and math intertwined. Maybe that was the part that was valuable, but if so, then how? Other sketches showed some dark figures around similar circles and symbols. Now it looked more like something out of one of those horror movies where you couldn't read it out loud without causing demons to appear or something. A few more pages in, there were silhouettes of people, and floating above them were these detailed drawings of black masses, many of them exuding tendrils and black vapors down on the human shades.

Now he could see how something so gruesome could be tied up in a murder, but besides there being a dark, creepy angle, he didn't know how it fit. He began to wonder if maybe someone else, maybe someone in academic circles who was less concerned with the legality of murder and theft, might be involved.

Their current suspect was Dr. Reid himself, as it was his fingerprints on Anna's throat, though how he put such force on her throat with his bare hands was absolutely baffling. They found tons of arthritis medication with his name on it. Unless he had some other interesting drugs, he wouldn't have that kind of hand strength.

A page turned over and Miles almost dropped the book. There was a face sketched there, an old, wrinkled face with empty black eyes. He shuddered and shut the book. There was nothing helpful about that, just some nightmare fuel from a long-dead girl. He normally came home complaining about the drunks he had to drop off at home, which could include the chief, or the teenagers he had to chase away from people's property, sometimes the occasional domestic dispute. Right about then, he'd have been glad to get one of those calls.

Miles sighed, and put the cruiser in gear. The engine roared, then settled. He slowly made his way out of the parking lot. He'd check back in at the station, turn in the evidence and his notes to the lead investigator. Maybe they'd even call in the Feds. A murder hadn't happened in Ingham since, what, the seventies?

Miles pulled out onto the long, dusty road that ran around the edge of the complex and back to the main strip. The sun was lowering in the sky, and it glared through his back window, blinding him for a moment. He flipped the mirror and slipped on his sunglasses. In the intervening time while he was distracted, he caught sight of someone in the road. He slammed on the brakes, the car skidding on the dust and almost fishtailing. As the spots cleared from his vision, he recognized Dr. Reid himself, standing there in the road... But he did not look well.

In his torn robe and pajamas, mud and muck up to his knees, and his face twisted into a painful-looking skull-grin, Dr. Reid looked both in distress, and darkly menacing. He also seemed hunched for some reason, his arms dangling at his sides. Miles unbuttoned his holster. He was not one to lose his cool, but something in that face... That was either insanity or seizure, but he didn't want to take the chance. The interesting drug theory gained a lot of ground in his mind.

He pushed the door open and stood up, keeping the door between himself and Reid.

"Dr. Daniel Reid?"

He didn't respond. He stood there, just breathing. Miles rested his hand on the butt of his gun.

"Dr. Reid, can you hear me? I need you to come with me. We'll get you to a hospital."

Reid didn't even seem to be looking at him. His eyes seemed glassed over, empty, almost like he was dead.

"Dr. Reid?"

No response. Miles drew his weapon, but kept it pointed at the ground.

"Dr. Reid, if you can understand me, please place your hands on your head."

Still no response. Miles clicked his handset radio.

"Dispatch, this is Miles. I have Dr. Daniel Reid here. He shows signs of physical distress and is unresponsive. Requesting an ambulance and backup at-"

Dr. Reid waved his arm, and the radio fizzled static, then emitted blue smoke and the scent of ozone. Miles looked back to him. Dr. Reid seemed to be closer, though he couldn't have moved, Miles would have seen him. He aimed his weapon at Reid.

"You stay right there!" he shouted, "Do not move!"

Suddenly, Reid was in front of him, Miles's hand screamed in pain, and the gun was gone. He staggered back, instinctively cradling his broken fingers. Dr. Reid had the gun, and was examining it as if it were some alien object to him. Miles tried to get into the car to use the car's radio, but Reid kicked the door shut with speed and force that dented the side. Reid struck Miles in the chest hard, and so fast the Corporal didn't have time to even register the movement. Miles felt the harsh crack of his armor, and felt heat sear through his chest. He'd felt the pain of a gunshot through his armor before, and this was twice as bad. Miles stumbled back. He reached for his taser and managed to fire it into Reid's chest. Reid did not slow down. He reached forward and grabbed Miles by the throat. Miles felt the electricity surge into him, sending his mind into white hot pain.

The next thing he realized, he was on the ground again, cold seeping into his limbs. Dr. Reid stood nearby, at the cruiser, removing the book from the cruiser. He turned his rictus of a smile to Miles, who lived just long enough to watch one of his eyes fall out of his skull and land in the dust. Behind the eye was blackness, and before Miles' vision blacked out, he heard Reid utter one word through his gritted teeth.

"*Dream*," he said.

Corporal Miles fell into darkness, surrounded by nightmares.

Chapter Twelve

D usk creeped over the world, receding its low amber light and
allowing the shadows to grow. Tommy and Tatiana sat in her
living room, the rifle sat on her coffee table, and Tommy, against
years of his safety habits, had it loaded, with a round chambered. The
safety was on still, but he could flip that quickly if something
happened. Now they sat, watching the sunset, sharing confusion and
loss.

Sometimes Tatiana would start up a round of questions that
Tommy couldn't answer, but all conversational roads would lead
back to silence and dreadful anticipation. The stars were peeking out
above the Eastern treeline when Tatiana stood, shaking her arms in
frustration.

"I can't do this! I can't just sit here and wait for something to
happen!"

"Well better this than getting killed in our sleep or something,"
said Tommy.

"And for a stupid book we don't even have anymore!"

Tommy just shrugged. Tatiana seemed to only get more
aggravated.

"What if we hook up that trailer of yours, drive a hundred miles
away somewhere? Somewhere nobody would think to look for us."

"Welllll..." Tommy said, drawing out the word as he considered
the idea, "Miles told us not to leave town, but it would be hard to
follow us along all those back roads without being seen. We could
probably drive out to the highway and buzz down to this truck stop
I know. It's not a hundred miles away, but it's away and safe."

"A truck stop?" She sounded venemously skeptical.

"We could hide among the semi's there. It'd be a LOT harder
for someone to follow us, and even harder still to start any trouble

without a lot of surly and probably armed truck drivers within shouting distance. Hell, it's safer than a police station."

"Truck... drivers... That's your plan?"

"A bunch of armed, bored, overblown tough guys who are sleep deprived and eager to prove how tough they are," Tommy said, "Trust me, nobody wants to invite the wrath of bored, armed white rednecks."

"That's... Yeah, that could work. Are you sure no one would follow us?"

"They'd need a 4x4 to take the back roads around the house at the speeds I drive at, and even if they did follow us, we'd see them coming a mile away down the highway. Late at night, in this town, the roads are gonna be empty."

She nodded. "Yeah, yeah, okay. That's not a bad plan."

"It's your plan," he said, "I just filled in the blanks."

She thought about it for a second. "I'm going to get some things."

She stepped into the bedroom. Tommy picked up the rifle and was about to take the round out of the chamber, but thought it might be better to wait until they were safely in the truck to stow the weapon.

Tatiana came out a few moments later with a small gym bag. She was now in her running shorts and sneakers, and he realized it was because she expected to need to run away very fast in the near future. He did not like this thought, but he couldn't help sharing that concern.

With an abundance of caution, he opened the front door, peering around the edges and trying not to look terrified. They descended to the street, trying to look as calm as possible carrying a long rifle and duffel bags. They passed under the dull glow of tungsten lights, approaching the truck. Tommy opened the door, then peered around inside just to be safe, while Tatiana held back

Mac. Once he was certain of the emptiness of the truck, Tommy took out the ammunition and the round in the chamber. He then stowed the weapon behind the seat of the truck.

The engine sounded like it roared when he started it, but it was just nerves. He wished they could be utterly soundless in their escape. Tatiana also seemed to jump when he turned the ignition.

He pulled out of the parking lot, heading back towards the house. Mac panted and rested his head on Tatiana's lap. She petted him for comfort, while Tommy drove. He took a long, winding, circuitous path. At no point did he see another vehicle in his rearview, but he intended to be completely certain no one was following him. Ahead of him, the halogens showed everything, nothing could escape their glare.

Behind him, no headlights ever appeared, just the receding dark trees and road.

It was deep starlit night by the time Tommy pulled into the driveway at Worthington Manner. It took a little time to hook the trailer up to the truck, but not as long as if he was being genuinely careful. He didn't bother trying to stow everything inside properly. He could clean up dropped knicknacks. He made sure nothing important or valuable would get knocked around, that was all. The whole time, his eyes were watching all around them. He was grateful for the full, open clearing here. Even with the wild grass, it would be tricky to sneak up on them. He briefly wondered if they might be a little paranoid, but Tommy reasoned that an ounce of paranoia was worth a pound of staying alive.

Soon the trailer was hooked in. Tommy pulled out onto the backroads, and felt the lurching of the extra weight as he drove. The ruts bounced them around violently. He slowed a little, hoping to avoid any strut-breaking road hazards.

In time, the rough dirt gave way to cracked pavement. No vehicles seemed to appear behind them as they passed the oases of light from the odd street lamp here and there. Tommy avoided going through town altogether, and wound up on the highway, driving South as hard as he dared push the engine. The trailer added a lot of mass, and once it was up to speed, it would take a lot of braking power to come to a stop if he had to come up short. But the road was vacant. Occasionally a meager SUV, or tractor trailer would appear over the rise, and Tommy would pass it with single-minded determination.

Between the rhythmic flare of the street lights, and the gentle sound of the tires on pavement, Tatiana seemed to lean her head against the window and drift off. Tommy was slightly jealous. All the worry and fear had them very worked up. Now it was time for the crash. He could feel it coming, that slowing down of thoughts. His eyes were drooping a bit. He shook his head to get the blood flowing again. He wasn't about to let that weakness bring him down.

At 85 miles per hour, it felt like the truck was crawling along. The old hand-painted road sign said that the "Kickin' Asphalt" Diner and truck stop was off the next exit. He glanced in the mirror and saw nothing but empty highway behind him. He dared to take his foot off the accelerator, letting the momentum run down a little before he started to carefully brake. He moved off the exit at a careful speed. The gray road curved and came to an awkward four-way intersection. To his right was a long median with the entrance to a massive empty lot. Several long metallic shapes gleamed under weak fluorescent lamps. He pulled in, and slid the camper between a pair of big rigs with full trailers behind them. There would be just enough room for them to get out and climb into the camper. They'd be nestled between big, packed trucks hidden among a nest of shipping containers on wheels. They would not be easy to find here.

Ahead of them, bathed in neon and fluorescent splendor was a diner done in a style of 1950's decor. Tommy's stomach rumbled. He jostled Tatiana to wake her.

"Hey," he said, "Hey, we're here."

She lifted her head, blinking at the lights of the diner. A group of late-night bikers were just now walking out, sharing guffaws and childish sneers with some chubby men wearing red hats. She wrinkled her nose.

"Really? We're safe here?"

"No one knows we're here. I know these types of people. I'm a carpenter, a laborer, you know, one of them. I'm-"

"White," she said, her voice tinged with bitterness "And a guy."

He closed his mouth, not able to think of anything to say that wasn't going to be stupid or insensitive.

She gave a grunt of frustration. "It's... It's fine. I'll stay in the trailer. But we're closing the curtains, and *you* keep that rifle nearby! I don't need to have some fat idiot try to 'deport me,' thank you."

Tommy nodded. She let out a curse in Spanish, then pushed the door open. Mac slipped out after her. He seemed tempted by the new smells and sounds, but Tommy let out a decided *stay*.

He stepped out on the driver's side, and walked around the truck to where the pup was looking at people walking with big greasy-looking sandwiches. He took Mac by the collar, gently tugging. Mac followed obediently, but reluctantly, his tail dipping down a little. Once inside the trailer, Tommy saw it was a mess. He didn't particularly care, but Tatiana was already pushing piles out of the way to clear a walking path.

"Think it's safe for me to go grab a burger to go? Bring it back here?" Tommy asked.

Tatiana thought for a moment. At first he thought she'd be mad, but she seemed to nod.

"And one for me," she said, "And any beer or whatever. If they have vodka, I'll take a lot of that. Like, a liter of that. With a side of more."

Tommy nodded. Before he went, he placed the rifle inside the trailer. She had the locks, the rifle, and Mac to protect her. Tommy strode towards the neon and smells of food. But still, he worried.

The little diner was surprisingly clean. Apparently they'd fixed it up a little since his last visit. The lights were brighter, the booths were clean and re-covered with new padding, fresh paint on the walls, and the smell of cooking meat instead of old cigarettes.

He stepped up to the long counter. It seemed like the bikers had been the largest rush of customers, as the place was a lot quieter now. The clock on the wall said it was nearing 11pm. Outside, multiple loud engines revved and choked, spewing heat as the bikes and their riders sped off into the night, sounding like a parade of rampaging dragons.

Tommy turned back from the window to find a woman about his age, a little rounder in the middle than he was, greeting him with a warm smile.

"Hi, what can I get for ya?"

"A couple of burgers to go?" asked Tommy. "Oh, and is it possible to buy some beers? I know it's late and all..."

"You'd have to drink 'em in here. Liquor laws."

"Damn," said Tommy. She raised an eyebrow at him. "I'm not getting on the road," he said, understanding her look, "My girlfriend and I are looking to crash in our camper in the lot here for the night. It's late, we've had a long drive, you know how it is. Safer to pull off and get some shuteye. Nothing else is open."

She nodded and smiled. "Oh, I get you. Well, as long as you stay put and don't make trouble, I guess I could let you take a couple bottles out of here. But behave." She pointed an accusing finger.

"Great, thanks," said Tommy, "Then that, please. Thanks."

She put in his order, and bustled back across the counter to pour coffee for an older man working on a pastrami sandwich. His skin was leathery and stained yellow at the fingers and mouth. He wore thick glasses that obscured his eyes, scratched and of questionable usage. He was the only other customer in the diner.

A few other waitresses were cleaning up tables. A TV was on in the corner turned to some talking head on a news show ranting about something Tommy didn't care about. He started to feel anxious, and kept stealing glances back at the parked truck and trailer to make sure everything was all right.

Outside, all seemed quiet. Inside, the wait for his burgers felt like he spent a decade of his life trapped beneath neon and the smell of charred beef.

Finally, his order was delivered in a big paper bag that had some fresh grease stains beginning to form on the side. He dropped an extra ten on the bill for the generosity of the beers, and headed back to the trailer.

Tatiana was asleep in the bed with Mac curled up at her feet. She snored in the dim light, blissfully unaware of his return. Tommy smiled, and put her burger in the fridge, despite the fact that it had no power at the moment. He sat down at the table in the kitchen area and ate, savoring the greasy cheap meat in all its caloric glory. Mac stirred tempted by the greasy delight he could clearly smell even in his doggy dreams.

He looked out the window at the reassuring steel between them and detection. The corrugated metal had some block lettering on the side that was too dark to read even if he cared what it said.

Outside, he could hear the occasional breath of a vehicle on the highway. Otherwise, all was quiet. Mac uncurled from the bed, roused from sleep by the smell of food. He stretched, and ambled over for some scraps. He sat down in front of Tommy and put a single black paw on Tommy's leg. Tommy smiled and tore off some beef patty for him, and let him steal a few french fries.

But mindful of doggy nutrition, he opened a cupboard and fished out a tin of regular dog food. The poor pup, he realized in their haste and panic they hadn't just forgotten to feed themselves. He was very glad little Maya was away and safe. Even if her father was a bastard, he wouldn't really hurt her, not like she might be hurt here. He almost wished he could have sent Mac, too, but the pup probably wouldn't go. This jet-black furball was loyal to a fault. Tommy gave him some reassuring pets, looking out the window again, hoping that if he couldn't see out, it meant that no one else could see in.

He stayed up for a while, gripping his rifle and waiting, sipping on his beer occasionally, but halfheartedly. It didn't taste very good, and did little to calm his nerves. He wondered what was even the point of the alcohol at a time like this. It didn't make him calm, it just made him less able to feel and respond. That wasn't what he needed now. Maybe it took the edge off the panic, but it then replaced it with a greater panic that his response time was off, and if something happened, he'd be less able to do something. It was only one beer, and a light one by the taste, but seeing it next to the deadly weapon in his hands, he decided he wasn't going to finish it. What he would do, is try to get some rest. Running along the same logic, a wired and tired man with a rifle was not a good idea.

He triple-checked his rifle's safety, then set it down beside the bed within reach. He left the beer bottle, half-finished, on the table. Then he crawled into the bed beside Tatiana. He put his arms around her, and she wriggled closer into his embrace. He was glad she was resting. He wasn't sure he would sleep. But the gentle sound of tires on pavement soothed him to much-needed slumber.

Tommy dreamed of fire.

A burning barn sent plumes of greasy black smoke into the sky, while figures danced in wild orgiastic glee around the inferno, nothing more than silhouettes. Tommy looked back towards the house, where a woman... no, younger, maybe a teenage girl, stained in blood from her mouth down her front, laughed with wild, mad eyes. She raised a long, curved blade, covered in crimson. She traced a circle over her head, and flung droplets of glossy black ichor on the grass.

Her mad grin was framed by long tears that streaked down from the corners of her eyes, and her cackle rent the starlit sky.

Tommy looked back, and could see now, in the flames, a man-like figure stumbling through the fire. Blackened, almost ash, a skeletal thing stepped from the fire, walking across the cooler ground, a single hand reaching out towards the cackling woman. It stumbled, then fell, landing with a sound like dry kindling landing on stone.

The dancing figures suddenly stopped. Murmurs and mutterings drifted among the crowd. They seemed to be looking across the field towards the road. Tommy looked as well, where the distant burning light of many torches marked the night. Men were coming, men from the village. They carried pistols and rifles, or in some cases, scythes and swords. The rifles had bayonets.

The cackling girl stopped. She looked at the approaching crowd. With a feline hiss, she threw out a hand, as if hurling something in their direction from her chest. The barn collapsed, and a wave of flames seared horizontally across the field. The fire seemed to glide like a great bird of prey. Tommy tried to turn from the fire, but was only carried with it. It came at the assembled men, catching some on fire, scorching others through and through, before fading away and leaving ashes and agony in their wake. Bodies smoldered in the moonlight.

Several pistols fired. Tommy tried to run for the house, his house, the Worthington house. He recognized that front porch, though it was neat, straight, all pieces at strong right angles and a roof that was solid and unmolested by the ravages of time. He only barely made it a few steps before that crazed girl was before him. She grinned with bloodstained teeth.

Several bursts of blood erupted from her as gunfire reached her, but still she walked with demented eyes. She gestured at one man, who let out a strangled scream as his throat seemed to crush from within.

She waved a hand at another, and his skin split at his hands, peeling away like fruit, curling back on itself and causing him to emit a shrill, agonizing cry. Tommy had once watched a man accidentally put a nail in his thigh with a nail gun. This scream was far worse, a cry of such pain that the man who made it was dead the instant it started, and the rest was just the pain and air escaping his lungs.

Everywhere the girl set her eyes, horror and death fell upon the poor man that dared get near. Nearly a dozen men had to have fallen to all manner of gruesome deaths. One man came within five feet, but she took some sort of slender, long pin from her hair and jammed it into his outstretched hand. He cried out, and fell backwards. His hand began to swell, but more than that, the skin split, and the thin spike that had been jammed in seemed to be growing into his body, swelling tissue and displacing it, causing muscle and bone to rupture out. His scream raised in pitch, his whole body swelling as if from some horrible allergic reaction. Then his skin finally tore open, and the horrible black, chitinous thing that had grown into him dropped to the ground. He was still screaming as this insect-like thing began to eat him.

The girl laughed with a hateful, spiteful laugh. She raised her hands to inflict a new horror on another poor man who had approached. But someone seized her from behind, taking one of her hands, and holding it behind her. She flailed, but he grabbed her by the throat. Tommy couldn't see the face in the chaotic dark, but soon he was joined by others, who bound the woman with rope and stuffed her mouth full of some kind of cotton or wool.

The silhouettes who had been dancing around the fire were now beginning to descend on the men, but the gunfire kept them at bay. They soon fled from the bullets, across the field, towards where Tommy knew the lake was.

From around the house came a man, older, with white hair and a priestly collar, holding a bible and a large wooden cross. He looked at Mary. She glared back with hatred. The old man opened his book, and recited some Latin over the girl, who snarled like an animal even through the gag. She tried to spit out or chew away the wool, but only succeeded in nearly choking. When he finished reading, he made a throwing gesture with his hand, and splashed wetness across her face. This seemed to further enrage her. He seemed concerned that she still fought back, and for a moment his look of resolve faltered.

"What do we do with her?!" demanded one of the men holding her.

The priest thought for a moment. "Bury her," he said, "Within the foundation. Let this home bind her dark spirit forever. May the Lord dispose of this witch, and seal her away!"

"And what of the slaves?" asked another.

A man stepped forward, Tommy recognized him somehow, and he wore clothes of greater quality than the others. He looked more like some kind of Victorian judge, but he held a pistol in one hand, and a sword in the other. The sword was darkened with blood.

"Take the black powder and destroy the dam. It will flood that plain. Let them drown, for their part in this devilry. Let this land be forgotten, the earth salted so nothing else evil may grow!"

Tommy took a step back, and only now did someone seem to notice him. The madwoman looked at him, a grin touching the corners of her mouth. He could feel the words in his very soul as she spoke without uttering a sound.

"Free me, kindred soul,"

Her eyes remained locked on his. He couldn't move, could not flee, forced to stare into those mad eyes.

Everything tilted sideways, Tommy's feet flew from beneath him, and his head banged against the ground hard. Something toppled onto him, and for a horrific moment, he was certain he was being buried alive.

Colors and shapes blended and the long, low rush of the highway turned to a chaotic groan and thump as the trailer bounced and lurched on rough road. Tommy was tossed from the bed, his head swimming as he came back from dream to sickening reality. Mac was barking, and a heartbeat later, Tatiana was screaming. She braced herself against the corner of the bedroom, her eyes wide and shining with terror in the dark. Tommy tried to hold on to something as the trailer jolted back and forth. He stumbled, landing face-down on the floor. He lifted his head up, focusing on the darkened interior of his trailer. They had been hijacked while they slept, and whoever was taking them for a ride had pulled them off of the smooth highway and onto an extremely bumpy old back road, just like...

Tommy's heart sank. He rolled to the window to try to glance outside. Tearing down the curtain, he could only vaguely make out dim starlight hidden behind the tops of trees. They were somewhere deep in the woods, and Tommy had a horrible feeling he knew exactly where they were going.

While the trailer rocked along the rutted road, Tommy managed to crawl over to his bedside table and remove a small flashlight. It shone brighter than daylight in the choking darkness. The trailer had been a mess before, but now it was a disaster, with plastic cups and dishes rolling around beside paperbacks and knicknacks. Mac was still barking and Tatiana had stopped screaming, settling into a panicked hyperventilating. Tommy was a hair away from that himself, but he had a security blanket nearby. The dark metal of the barrel gleamed in his light. He crawled over to retrieve the rifle.

It felt cold in his grip, and his sweaty hands slid over the long barrel. Whoever had hijacked them was going to be in for a real surprise once Tommy could get sights on them. He crawled up to the front of the trailer and tried to look out the windows up on top. He could just make out the outline of a big truck. Tommy's blood went from cold to white-hot as he realized that it was his truck. Someone had stolen his truck and the camper! Someone had stolen his truck, and his camper, and him!

Just as he realized this, the truck took a sharp turn, lurching the Trailer, and causing Tommy to tumble to the side. He almost lost grip on the gun. He was on the floor now, near the door to the camper. The whole vehicle lunged once, then came to an abrupt stop. Tommy tried to get his arms and legs to make sense, spinning his arms around until he could use the butt of the gun as a support. Soon he was standing, the flashlight lost on the tumble, but its light casting enough dim illumination so that Tommy could see. He was in front of the door. He braced himself against the back wall, leveling the barrel of the gun at the door and waiting. Whoever it was, he wouldn't even let them turn the knob. As soon as he heard the weight hit the ground outside that door, or sensed any movement, he would put a bullet through the door and the thief.

Everything fell into a torturous silence. Tatiana seemed to be trying to crawl into a nonexistent corner in the bedroom. Mac was putting himself between her and the door, and seemed ready to lunge. He was letting out a low growl, and sniffing the air, looking for the threat.

Tommy remembered the first time he'd ever taken aim with a rifle, out hunting with his Dad, long ago, during one of the few moments they had to bond with Margie and the other kids absent. Tommy leveled the weapon, his finger beside the trigger, his breath even and measured despite the terror in his heart. He flipped the safety off. If he was patient, his prey would come into sight soon.

He'd brace for the kick, then gently pull. Darkness and dust stirred around him in aching silence. The flashlight flickered out. His eyes briefly went to Tatiana, whose face was a study in fear, framed by her sweaty locks before the darkness obscured her. He looked back to the door, though he could see nothing. It wouldn't matter. He didn't even need to hit them, just scare them badly enough to put *them* on the defensive, and take the opportunity to turn things around on them. He'd burst through the door a half a second after shooting, knock them down, then hold them at gunpoint while they bled, and demand answers. He could see it all in his mind, and all he had to do was wait. The moment would come. He was ready.

The thought crossed his mind that he'd never killed anyone before. And any shot with this rifle would most definitely kill someone, even if the aluminum door slowed the bullet down.

He was content to forego the questions, if a single shot could end this whole nightmare.

Tommy heard the shrieking of broken glass a heartbeat later and felt the horrible sense of twisting, his guts spinning and then finally a hard landing on the ground with sharp pain in his back. Tatiana screamed again, and Mac was barking and growling with a ferocity he expected from wild wolves. Tommy looked up to see a hunched figure in the starlight, with long, thin arms and legs, his head at a strange angle, as if regarding Tommy with a dog's curiosity. The door of the camper was on the ground, bent and twisted, little more than plastic and metal scrap. Tommy didn't know how he got outside, but he had trouble filling his lungs with air. Mac charged at the figure. It swept around with one of its long arms and smacked Mac away like he was swatting a fly. Mac fell away, rolling with a yelp.

Tommy was still trying to get up, but his body kept trying to vomit. He saw light appear, bright, powerful, shining on their lanky attacker. He saw Tatiana in that light, and while he couldn't see her features, he could see the long barrel in her hands. It was shaking a little, but then she straightened it, and aimed it at their attacker.

Tommy could see the face of the thing now. He recognized it. He'd sat at a dinner table with that face not too long ago. His body was completely out of proportion, arms and legs too long, face stretched to a jaw that couldn't be human, one eye bulging and bloodshot, the other... gone. He still wore shreds of mud-stained pajamas, but his head above the hairline was not covered in hair. Whatever it was, it moved against the air in wild, random direction like wiry worms.

Tatiana fired.

Tommy watched the exit wound splatter thick, dark blood out the other side, but Reid did not even react. Tommy started to get up, but before he could get to his feet, a boot landed on his shoulder, pushing him down, and forcing some glass shards deeper into his back. Tommy cried out in pain. He stretched himself around to look, seeing a man in a police uniform, but with his head dangling from his neck sideways as if broken so completely that only the skin and flesh held it vaguely aloft.

But in its hands was a gun, aimed at Tommy's head. He looked back to see Reid pull a screaming Tatiana from the trailer by her hair. Mac made another charge from the darkness.

"Mac, no!" Tommy cried.

Reid reached out and caught Mac, with a hand made of spider-leg fingers. Mac went spinning back into the camper. There was another yelp and a whimper. Tommy felt tears running from his eyes, reaching out with his hand, impotent. A handcuff was slapped over his wrist, and a second later, his hands were bound behind him. The dead cop pulled Tommy up in a fireman's hoist over his shoulder, and started hauling him away from the trailer. In the starlight, he could see that rising cyclopean spire, and he knew where he was. They'd brought him back to that cursed house. The dead thing that was Dr. Reid, and the dead thing that was Corporal Miles were not figments or nightmares or conjecture. They were not elaborate pranks by a greedy, cheapskate flipper. They were not imagination or urban legend. This was happening, and the blood dribbling down Tommy's face was real, warm, and *his*.

The lanky Dr. Reid followed along them both, carrying Tatiana in its arms, who screamed, bit, kicked, all to no avail as they were taken into Tommy's own house.

The floodlights Tommy had set up to do detailed work were all plugged in and set up in the middle of the large dining room. Dr. Reid tossed Tatiana down, and the cop threw Tommy down beside her. The Miles corpse took a few steps back, and Reid leaned in closer, the skin on his face stretched and splitting in several places, stains of blood running down from the cracks.

"*The... Bones...*" he said, his voice a grating rasp. The teeth never parted while he spoke.

Tommy didn't say anything, he could barely even look at the hideous peeled flesh of Reid's face, much less focus on his words. One of those stretched hands seized Tommy's throat and held him up. He gurgled and struggled to get any gasp of air.

"*The bones!*" demanded Reid.

Tommy remembered, suddenly, that day in the hot sun burying the bones of that poor girl. He tried to spit out a response, but the choking grip was too strong to let air flow. He could feel the tension in the very skin of his face. His head was about to pop like a gruesome balloon. The hand released, and Tommy fell to the floor. He wheezed for breath and fought against the specks of blackness trying to cloud his vision. Tatiana was weeping next to him, whimpering and sobbing.

Tommy spluttered out a few words for the thing. "The... the field," he said, then sucked in air in case it might be the last chance he had to fill his lungs.

The thing seized Tommy again, but this time by the shoulders, bringing him face to cracked face.

"*Show*," it said.

Tommy nodded, and the thing pushed him towards the door. He stumbled, bouncing off of the door frame, still dizzy and out of breath. He was very close to crumpling to the ground just from watching the room spin around him.

Reid turned to Miles and hissed some inhuman speech at him. Then Reid seized one of Tommy's own shovels, and followed Tommy out into the night. Tatiana was left inside, with the ghoulish thing holding a gun on her.

The night air was cooler, but only because of all the sweat coating Tommy's skin now, and the slight breeze bringing some relief to his burning wounds. The glass in his back stung like a dozen angry wasps. He looked around, trying to get his bearings. He'd used the treeline as his reference point last time. He squinted, trying to see in the darkness. Reid stood behind him, easily a head taller than Tommy was, grinning at the gloom. The man had been under six feet, and now he towered above Tommy. Bits of overgrown jagged bone stuck out from torn flesh. It moved like some lumbering ape, but faster and stronger. It had torn the door right off the camper, and yanked Tommy outside faster than Tommy could see it and pull the trigger. It was so fast, he only barely remembered details now, how the metal exploded inward, torn like paper, and that hand grabbed, pulling him, using his body to help tear the door itself away. Tommy faintly remembered hitting his head against the door... That would be where the blood was coming from.

Tommy thought he recognized an area of trees, and started towards it. He didn't know what else to do. His mind still spun from the visage of this monster Dr. Reid had become, that these dark events were real, and linked by tragedy and time. All he knew was that compliance kept him alive for now, beyond that he had no idea.

He watched Tatiana put a shot from a .22 into Dr. Reid, and all it seemed to do was stain his ragged clothing.

Now Tommy marched through a field, probably to his own death. Once at the tree line, the mound of dirt where the bones were buried was visible. Only small patches of ambitious grass and weeds had grown in the upheaved earth. Reid stepped past Tommy and looked at the mound of dirt. It tossed the shovel down in front of Tommy. It wanted him to dig. Tommy shuddered. He bent down to pick up the shovel, but with his hands bound, it would be difficult to dig. The thing didn't seem interested in his comfort. He plunged the blade into the dirt and pulled up fresh, dark earth, tossing it to the side. He repeated, wondering what would happen if he put the shovel into Reid's head. Would it even work? This thing had taken a .22 shot and not even known it happened. Its skin and flesh seemed to just be accessories hanging off the warped bones beneath. It wasn't human, and whatever monstrous force kept it animate would not likely be defeated by a shovel.

Tommy dug, beginning to sweat more in the nightly air, guided by dim star and moon glow. The thing didn't seem particularly interested in anything but Tommy's labor, giving him a reproachful sneer every time he slowed even a little. He knew the bones were not buried very deep, but it sure felt like he was pulling up massive amounts of dirt. Was this even the right place? He started to have his doubts. It was dark, and he'd taken a lot of bruising to just about his entire body, his head included. If it weren't for the familiar ache of hard work, he'd have believed he was dreaming. Finally, Tommy's shovel made a plastic wrinkling noise as it hit the dirt. The Reid-thing straightened up and seemed suddenly interested.

It pushed Tommy aside, and swept its great arm in a wide arc. The remaining loose dirt exploded upwards, falling back down around them in dry, mossy rain. Tommy shut his eyes and staggered several feet away, dropping the shovel in the dark. He looked back to see Reid reach into the hole, and remove the plastic trash back. It seemed to lovingly stroke it for a moment, then tear the bag open so all the bones came tumbling out to the ground, landing in a pile. Once the bag was limp, it tossed it into the air to be carried off by the breeze.

Without even turning its head, it reached over and grabbed Tommy's neck again, pulling him closer. It raked one of its sharp, bony fingers across Tommy's chest, drawing fresh blood. He winced and coughed out spittle with his yelp of pain. The thing looked at its blood-stained talon-like finger, then shoved Tommy back.

It bent down to collect the bones. Its hissing, spitting, grinding speech seemed to intensify and as its hands worked in hectic ambition, flinging droplets of Tommy's blood on the assembled remains. Tommy started to creep back into the treeline.

"Just survive," he thought, "Just survive."

He slowly crept backwards until he could put a large, sticky pine between himself and the thing that was Dr. Reid. He peered around the edge of the tree to see a fiery red glow, then a sphere of hellish firelight bloom outwards, lighting up the whole field like silent fireworks, and vanishing just as quickly. Standing there in the dirt was a naked woman, gray in the starlight, looking down at herself, then up to Dr. Reid.

"Oh, Dream Maker," she said softly, "Thank you, great one."

She fell to her knees, throwing her arms up in supplication. Tommy could see her face just a little, just enough to recognize her from his insane dream. Her words came back to him now, "*Freedom,*" which she now had. This was Mary Worthington, the witch of Worthington manor, the one that the witch bottle was supposed to keep away. Or maybe, keep contained.

The one who talked in great detail the vengeance she would enact on her abusive father. The one who took lashings in the dark and cold, who was left to die in freezing rain. She was the one who set fire to men with a flick of her wrist, and danced in blood beneath a cold waxing moon.

Tommy waited, watching as Reid motioned for her to rise, then follow. It didn't seem to notice he had snuck away, or maybe it didn't care since he wasn't a threat.

He couldn't be a threat. He was alone, unarmed, and his hands were still bound. The creature and the nude woman walked back towards the house. Tommy watched them go, both gray in the starlight.

He knew they were heading back to Tatiana. He knew they had some hideous idea in mind for her, and he didn't want to take the chance that they might succeed. Tommy crept up behind them slowly, finding the shovel where he'd dropped it. In his mind, he would run up behind the woman and slam the shovel into her head as hard as he could. In reality, his steps were sluggish, slow, and noisy. Reid turned to him, caught the shovel, and an unearthly glow pulsed from its void-black eyes. Another shriek split Tommy's ears, and he fell into a deep, terrible blackness that seemed to go on forever, one that burned his skin and mind.

Chapter Thirteen

Tommy landed hard, his already aching body suddenly crashed into soft Earth after a fall that felt beyond the scope of time itself. He had no specific memory, only the vague sense of freefall, a stomach-lurching turn in the air, and a gulf of empty black void beneath him.

His eyes opened on a gray, misty morning, where the sky held roiling clouds full of the promise of storms, but eerily still, holding back their fury. Tommy pushed himself up, terrified he had blacked out, that he was too late. His heart sank at the thought that they'd done something to Tatiana, and he'd been unconscious and helpless the whole night long.

But through his panic and jumbled senses, something seemed wrong. The air was too thick with mist and fog, the ground too soft, and the house in the distance was not the rotting goliath he knew so well. The spire that watched him with its single eye was painted white, and at the top, there was a large gleaming metal pole flying a red flag. This was not his house, it couldn't be his house. The wooden shingles were pristine, the paint relatively fresh, and all around it were bushes and hedges, trimmed to immaculate shapes. This was the dream house, the house as it had been in Mary's time. Tommy turned around, seeing wide fields of corn and maybe wheat or barley. Other plants he could not identify, but in those fields were human shapes, toiling away. Tommy almost retreated from them, but he could see that their dark skin was defined by the brown and tan cotton clothes they wore.

Looking again to the house, Tommy saw several children playing in the back. A young blonde girl was chasing an equally fair-haired boy around with a small length of rope. They screamed and giggled like children do, but the sound seemed almost muffled by the thick mists.

Tommy walked towards them, through a bank of fog, and arrived before them in only a few steps. The young boy spotted Tommy, and hid behind his sister. The girl smiled up at him, cradling the rope in her hands.

"Hello," she said, "Do you want to hold my snake?"

Tommy couldn't form a response, he had too many questions, too many confused jumbles of thought. Instead, he simply held out his hand. The rope lunged from the girl's hand, and Tommy jerked back just a hair out of range of the sudden flash of small fangs. She giggled, and put the rope down on the grass, gently. It slithered off towards the house, disappearing into a crack between stones.

Tommy watched it leave, but when he looked back to the children, they were gone.

He stood alone on the North side, beneath the watchful eye of that turret.

He went to the back door of the house, a sturdy and fresh oaken door, sitting ajar and letting the must flow inside. Tommy stepped up to it and gently pushed. It yielded some, the iron hinges squealing. Tommy stepped inside.

The kitchen was stone and brick, but beautifully done, the old wood work done with care, despite the plainness of the times. A large pot sat on a hook over a fire. A pair of black women worried over it, adding ingredients and occasionally speaking in hushed whispers that either became stifled giggles or knowing glances. Tommy walked past them, they stopped to look at him, and their faces fell, becoming masks of indifference. Tommy knew that kind of reaction, he'd had plenty of practice at it himself. Never show any emotion, it could be seen as a sign of weakness. Or worse, as some sly affront that would earn someone a smack across the face, or a night sleeping on the floor with only a ragged Elmo blanket to keep warm with. He turned away from them, stepping into the living room. Here, several cozy chairs sat around a fireplace, with a short couch and a roaring fire. A thick bible sat on a table, its leather cover gleaming and new, and with no discernible words, but its ornate inlaid cross of gold paint gave away its title.

This is where Tatiana would be if he were in his house, but this was all wrong. It was like he was back in the 1800's, but even that didn't seem right. The surreal haze and people out of time... He was dreaming. He came to understand this, even though it meant he couldn't do very much about it.

Tommy reached for the bible, but before his fingers could touch it, he heard a voice, one that reminded him of his own father whenever he was angry.

"What are you doing here?!"

Tommy straightened up immediately, turning to the source of the voice. It was an older man, his thin white hair falling around his head, but partially contained under a very old fashioned hat. It had that pilgrim design, complete with a buckle. He wore a dark suit, his hands gnarled like old tree branches, currently clenched into fists. His face was a road-map of wrinkles and scorn, but the worst were his eyes, alight with something like madness, a delighted fury, eager to take his wrath out upon someone.

Tommy again tried to conjure words from his mouth, but what came out were not his words.

"I'm sorry, Papa," said the voice of a young child. Tommy felt two feet tall all of a sudden, and the man seized Tommy by his ear, dragging him by the thin tethers of cartilage across the room.

"You will be, girl!" snapped the old man. Tommy saw the old man reach down and seize a small iron ring from the floor, pulling open some kind of trap door. Part of Tommy's mind connected this with the floor plan of his house, and he realized this trap door was just over the spot in the foundation where he'd found the girl's remains.

The old man pushed him down a set of old wooden stairs into the dark cellar, then slammed the trap door after him. Tommy felt childlike sobs coming on, and the intense weight of loneliness closing in.

He wanted to stand, to force his weight against that trap door, but finding the will to even try to move felt exhausting.

When had this trap door been put in? Or more importantly, removed?

The rationality felt link an anchor. It didn't matter what the answer was, it was here now. He pushed himself up to his feet. He tried to press against it, but there was no give.

"It's no good," said a child's voice. Tommy turned, and in the scant light from the gaps in the floor above, he could see the face of a young girl, her face, hands, and lower arms covered in dirt. "He locks it when we're bad."

Tommy regarded her with pity at first, then looked down to see a small leather-bound diary in her hands. She held it close to her chest. "He doesn't know I have this. Don't let him take this one, too."

"What is going on?!" Tommy demanded. The girl did not react. She simply raised a finger, pointing upward.

"At night, he takes me away from this place. Shows me secrets."

The thudding of footsteps made Tommy turn. The trap door was violently pulled open, and the crazed man from before peered down into the dark.

"Have you repented, yet?"

Tommy threw himself forward up to the trap door, surging with momentum to try and either knock over and run past, or tackle and beat some answers out of the crazy old man. He stumbled up and half-tackled him to the floor. But Tommy didn't land on the scrawny old man, instead, he hit solid hardwood.

The room was empty and quiet again. He looked back at the trap door, and could just see the girl's face there. She smiled, and pointed upwards again. As she did, the trap door crashed down with a slam as loud as thunder. Tommy backed away, towards the stairs. There, he heard something hissing. At first, he feared another snake, but at the top of the stairs was another small child. This one was beckoning him to come up with a motion of his hand. The hissing sound had been him going *"Pssstt"* at Tommy. He was maybe six, with bright eyes and shaggy golden hair.

"Hey," Tommy said quietly, but the child put a finger to his lips and ran off down the upstairs hall. Tommy followed him up the stairs. At the top, he saw the child peek out from the corner of the stairs up to the spire. Tommy followed, but every step made the floorboards creak and groan like he was stepping on the unquiet dead.

At the stairs, Tommy saw no child, just slightly dirty footprints ascending. Tommy climbed the stairs, following the tight corners to the landing. Here, he recognized the door he'd forced open back in the real world.

He turned the knob, and the door swung inwards. The walls were painted bright white, and recently, too. Murals of animals and sunny fields played across the entire span. There were wooden toys and soft pillows everywhere, orbiting the center of the room, where a cradle sat empty. But nearby, a chair was rocking slowly. A woman in dark Victorian dress rocked back and forth, a gentle creak coming from the chair. She had her head down, and her hands in her lap. Soft blonde hair fell around her head. Tommy wanted to say something, maybe apologize for barging in, but he found no words that would make sense. He couldn't even be sure this was real.

"He used to be kind," said the woman, her voice barely over a whisper.

Tommy held still for a moment. The woman turned her head up. She was very pretty, with bright eyes, but long lines in her face from worry.

"I love my children," she said, "But he would make them servants. Even slaves. He is so cruel to them."

"What is this?" Tommy asked, finally having found a voice.

The woman smiled at him, but there was no mirth there, only the weak smile of someone who has been trying to be brave for too long.

"My tomb," she said.

Her eyes suddenly seemed deeper, almost sunken. The smile melted and the long worry lines seemed to take over her face.

"Mary got the worst of it," she said, "Especially after..."

She paused then, looking to the cradle, then looking away. Tommy saw tears forming in her eyes.

"My daughter is beyond saving," she said, "As is my husband. But the others, those who cannot find rest, me, my children, the slaves... We can rest. Please, help us find rest."

Tommy's insides felt like a lead slab had fallen. He realized the woman he was speaking with was dead. Everyone he'd been speaking with was dead, long dead, and this hazy house of shadows was merely some twisted dream from the departed.

"I'm dreaming," Tommy said.

"No," said the woman, "You're dying."

The air grew thick then, like the cold, choking damp New England winters Tommy knew so well. The woman seemed to have some pity in her eyes, maybe even something more, something familial and warm, but it brought no comfort to Tommy.

"Dying? What do you mean, dying?!"

Very close by, a door slammed against a wall. The woman jumped, suddenly surprised. She looked back to Tommy.

"He's coming, you have to go!"

"Who's coming?!"

"My husband!"

Tommy heard the bellow of that old man from before. He turned to the stairwell to try and place the distance of the noise. He was reluctant to leave, but as he looked back to the woman, a vacant skull stared back at him from the neck of her dress.

Tommy took the stairs two-at-a-time, then charged down the hall to the stairs back down to the living room. He heard the heavy thud of boots on hardwood walking after him.

"*Mary?!*" Demanded the voice, "*You have the harlot blood again!*"

Tommy jumped down half of the flight to get to the living room. But now, the house seemed different. The furniture had been upturned, walls splattered with blood, and everywhere signs of struggle and death. Horrible circles had been drawn with gore, insane markings like the ones from Mary's diary were etched into old wood floors, floors he knew were still there, faded, worn, but that meant they were still there under the mess, and under the facade of the newer renovations.

Standing amidst it all, in a circle of bodies, was a young woman. Beside her was the old man, Old Man Worthington, but his body was twisted and warped like Dr. Reid's had been. The young woman bowed before the old man. She was covered in blood, streaked on her hands and face. She held a long, crimson-dripping dagger in her hand. The bodies around here were twisted, torn apart, or cut apart. Mary's mouth was covered in slick wet red, dripping down her chin and staining her dress.

On the floor beneath her was a body, and all over the body were cuts into strange shapes, like some foreign language, arranged in a circular pattern, just like the one on the floor.

Both the old man and young girl looked to Tommy.

"*Another*," she said. The Old man let out a shriek, and took two long strides towards Tommy. Tommy backed away and threw himself out the front door.

Outside was dark, misty night, and Tommy scrambled away as fast as he could. The thing chased him. Tommy staggered along the path towards the back end of the field, passing a massive barn on his right. Horrible screaming noises came from that barn, noises that seemed to cause the thing chasing Tommy to slow, and turn towards the barn. They sounded human, and animal, and wrong. Tommy kept running, all the way down to where the lake was.

But as he descended the steps, he saw no lake, only a deeper valley where many small cabins and homes were built. There were maybe three dozen men, women, and children here, dark skinned and dressed in simple, poor garb. Tommy looked around, unsure of what to even say. He looked back up the hill, and now he could hear shouting, sounds of struggle and pain. Thunder from various rifles thudded off the rocks and trees around him.

People began to cry and run, taking refuge in their cabins. Tommy looked around desperately for some kind of idea what to do, or where to go. The ground shook with a spasm of force that knocked him off his feet, and sent an endless rumble through his bones. Tommy tried to get to his feet, but just as he did, he saw the wall of water breaking through the trees, maybe fifty feet taller than he was, scooping up branches, trees, rocks, and other forest detritus as it reared up over him, ready to crash down and sweep him away into darkness. He instinctively held his breath, and folded in on himself. He felt a crushing pain, and then emptiness.

Tommy awoke on the ground, his body cold, his heart pounding, and a ringing pain in his head as if someone had struck his skull with a hammer like a gong. He rolled over, his whole body aching with the reality of his injuries. Everything burned with pain, and he could feel the slick, wet blood on his back mixed with the damp earth from his gravedigging. He looked up at the house, at the spire, the memories of his dreams overlaying the scene and conjuring terrible histories from the old stones. From the windows in the living room, he could see the long shape of the Reid-thing as it loomed over someone, or something. Tommy climbed to his feet and peered inside. He could see Mary, and Reid, and he was fairly sure they had Tatiana on the floor. He wanted to burst in and do something, but... That thing had thrown him away like he was a rotting banana peel. He literally could do nothing but watch them kill Tatiana.

He shut his eyes. He thought of Maya and almost wretched right there on the grass.

Tommy moved slowly back towards the tree line. In a cold, acidic place in his gut, he was sure the thing had heard him, and could see him in the dark.

His only light came from firefly flickers as he slipped away, his head swimming. All the crazy haunted house rumors really were true, but this was worse than any of them had imagined. People were dead, and Tommy was alone, helpless, wandering in the pines with no idea where he was going or what he would do. The dreams, or maybe memories, or leftover nightmares he'd walked through just left him drained, and alone in the night.

He wanted to flee, to find help. The nearest place was Tatiana's condo complex, just on the other side of the lake. If he could get there, he could get help, but would they even believe him? He could say that it was a home invasion or something, but how long would it take for help to arrive? What if they killed Tatiana? What if they killed everyone Tommy called on for help?

Out of habit and dazed confusion, he found himself along his normal running trail, and there, wreathed in unnatural starlight, was the little graveyard. Here lied the Worthington family, from two centuries ago. The fireflies didn't seem to hover and blink in here. The small collection of faded stones were obsidian shadows in the night. Tommy leaned against one of the still-standing stone pillars, trying to breathe and letting the tears out.

He was helpless. Just as he had been as a child. Just as he had been when his mother would torture him, or one of her boyfriends would smack him around, or his stepmother would pull her passive-aggressive mind games on him, or his natural biological father would smack him hard enough to loosen teeth. He fell to his knees, the tears coming in heavy sobs now. He tried not to make noise, but the wellspring had opened, and the pain was coming out, watering the ground before him.

All his childhood, he'd been helpless. Everything he'd done before he fled that home of madness was a pointless endeavor, and now, in spite of everything he had done to rise above, he was still that helpless child, alone, scared, with no friends or family to call on to save him. The old wound ripped open further, and the horrible memories came flooding back, twisting him up in knots. Memories of agony, of betrayal, of broken promises and love withheld out of spite.

The deep agony made him vomit, his body shuddering, as if trying to expunge his own toxic soul. The time his stepmother tried to get him to sneak into the neighbor's house, just so he could get caught sneaking around. The time his real mother had left him home alone for four days at the age of six, scared, hungry, with no idea when she would return. The man who called himself Patrick that locked Tommy in his room without dinner for the night because he'd been watching the TV too loud. The burns from cigarettes that littered the apartment, never certain if one was still hot unless he could see their embers glowing in the dark, always worried about fire. Every horrific thing came back to him at once, causing new heaves of suffering sobs, pouring the years of pain and hatred, of fear and loneliness out onto the ground.

This is what he'd been running from for years. This is why he buried himself in projects, like the house, like his job, like learning new trades and working overtime hours. This is why he went hunting occasionally, and why he always had to avoid the hard liquor. It was anything to stop this pain from bubbling to the surface, leaving him a weak, blubbering mess when the moment counted. He couldn't do anything to save Tatiana, he couldn't do anything to save himself, he could only suffer in the dark, as he had always done. He was still a child, a weak, small, helpless boy who did not deserve the agony inflicted on him.

In the cool night, he began to realize he could see a little more than before, he could make out the shapes of the roots and fallen stones on the ground. He thought his eyes were adjusting, but as he wiped his tears on his shoulder, he could see a faint luminescence. Tommy looked for the source of the light, and it seemed as if the fireflies all around him had started to swarm. They flitted and danced on the nightly breeze, surrounding him even here in the graveyard.

"We know that pain..." came a voice, one from just behind Tommy. A warm hand landed on his shoulder. Tommy looked, and could see, just barely, a faint outline. It looked like a young boy, his features gently bending the firefly glow into recognizable lines and shapes. Tommy thought he could see something like a smile, and remembered his own little brother, and all the cruelty he passed on to him because he didn't know any better, the hateful words, the mean and painful pranks, and a new wave of shame washed over Tommy. He felt his throat tightening.

Another hand fell on Tommy's other shoulder. He turned, seeing a grown woman in a very old style dress. Her face was soft, kind, and familiar: the mother from Tommy's dream. She stroked his cheek, and Tommy could feel the touch.

That touch spoke to him, it spoke of tenderness and love. It spoke of a real mother's love for her children, of that which Tommy had never known. Kneeling in that morbid dirt, surrounded by the dead, it was the most kind, warm, loving touch Tommy had ever known. He looked up to the woman's face. He thought she was probably smiling at him. He could see other forms now, other children, boys, girls, all just barely visible as vague shapes in the phosphorescent glow of the fireflies. Perhaps they even were the fireflies, his eyes were too muddled by tears and gloom to tell. But the touch was real, solid, and it had pressed against his flesh.

"Help me," Tommy pleaded.

The lights went away. Tommy sat in the darkness, alone once again, abandoned once again. He slumped his shoulders in defeat.

Beneath his knees, he felt the Earth begin to move.

Chapter Fourteen

It was a strange sensation, a jolt of vibration at first, but then a series of rumblings. Tommy tried to get to his feet, but stumbled as the ground shifted beneath him, he fell on his side. With the fireflies gone, he could not see what was happening, until something poked up through the earth near him. The old, packed Earth began to crumble, roots were torn asunder, and the small trees toppled over around him. The little bit of extra light that came in was just enough for Tommy to see a few dark points come up from the ground. Those points resolved into finger bones, then into a full skeletal hand. Soon, the head followed, caked with damp earth, its skull filled with mud and leaking crawling insects as it rose up from the ground. Others followed, maybe a dozen all together, some only the size of small children, others full grown adults. There were more than just the five bodies buried here. The Worthington's must have buried dozens, maybe generations. Tommy tried to get up, his first instinct to run, his heart leaping with confused terror, but the first skeletal figure put a single bony finger to his cheek.

Something moved behind him, and he felt a touch upon the handcuffs in front of him, a subtle pressing. Then, a sharp release of tension and his arms fell freely from their bondage. The steel landed on the loose earth before him, sinking in. He was now acutely aware of the ache in his shoulders from being trapped for so long. He straightened his posture, and the stretching both eased the ache, and spread it out through his back.

The dry, muddy hands helped lift him off his knees. He could feel it now, not so much hear the words, but feel that they were going to help him. It was as if they needed this, needed him, needed his pain, his loneliness, his desperation, his ceaseless and aching lack of love to pull themselves up from the restless grave.

No... No, not quite. It was the longing. One that the restless dead shared. They knew Tommy's pain like no living person did. They ached as he did. They were left, abandoned, to rot, like he was, even during life. This was the body count of Jedediah Worthington, his family, his victims.

He knew who they were, their names, their lives, as if he had always known, as if they'd been his own family. Ethel Worthington had been Jedediah's mother, had come with him from England when he was much younger. When he set up the plantation, she had objected to his harsh treatment of the slaves.

He quoted scripture to her as he smothered her to death, in his eyes, a mercy.

One young man was Jedediah's cousin, Arthur, who helped him plant the seeds, but was injured when Jedediah swung a hoe too fast... possibly intentionally, as he never liked Arthur's sinful drinking.

And the small skeleton... He knew this was Jedediah's youngest child, his son, and though he loved his son, he loved his rage and his zealotry more. The boy had always been reminded that he'd killed his own Mama. But deep down, the way clever children do, he knew it was a lie, and it was his father that had blood on his hands.

Tommy's heart welled with gratitude and fresh tears appeared in his eyes, but the old matriarchal body put a finger to his lips, leaving grave dirt on his mouth. Then she gestured for him to follow, and they stalked off again into the woods. He didn't know what they intended to do, but he knew by the direction they left the graveyard, they were headed for the lake.

The raised dead stood at the edge of the black water, and the matriarchal skeleton, dragging long rotted skirts and shedding wisps of decayed hair, stepped forward, her feet dragging tattered old boots. She put a single finger into the black murk. Tommy could almost hear a tone, as if the distant ringing of a chime, a single note held for a heartbeat, and then gone in the thick black waters while ripples carried the echo off into the black mire.

For a long moment, nothing happened, but then the ripples began to appear. The Waters began to bubble and churn as if boiling. Just as in the graveyard, things slowly broke the surface near the water's edge. Smooth domes slowly rose, exposing muck-filled eye sockets. More bodies began to climb from the depths, soggy and coated with dark slime, some with ancient rotted flesh still clinging to their bones beneath tattered, wet rags that stuck to their gaunt forms. At first, their demeanor seemed angry, even hostile, but Mother Worthington raised her arms, and they paused. Their demeanor changed. They stood tall, and the first one out of the muck nodded to the Matriarch. She turned, looked at Tommy, and made a gesture up the incline. Then she started towards the manor, and the others followed, dozens of them, rising from the muck of the lake bed and following her lead. Tommy walked with them, a strange mad smile on his face. He wasn't alone anymore. He had a family.

Something in the sky crackled, a distant storm beginning to roll in, threatening to tear the sky open. It would be pitch black once the clouds rolled in. Tommy stood among the dead as they walked for the manor. He wondered if the wounds he'd suffered already had killed him, and he was just one of the walking corpses. But as they crossed the field, a dark shape came slinking out of the tall grass. The canine whined and nuzzled Tommy's hand. Tommy knew then that he was still alive. He bent down and embraced Mac, the pup was hurt, but alive, scared, but loyal. He seemed to want to sink back from the walking dead, but Tommy rubbed his fur and smiled, pulling the pup close.

"Don't worry boy," he said, "They're with me."

He embraced Mac good and hard, and this seemed to comfort them both. The shaggy pup licked him, and a few of the smaller skeletons paused to look at Mac. Their skulls did not move, but

Tommy sensed a smile. The tiny hands stroked Mac's fur. Mac seemed still pensive, but allowed it, and soon they resumed their march.

Fat droplets of rain began to fall from an onyx sky that choked out the cold radiance of the stars, replacing it with a hot rain. Lightning crashed somewhere in the deep woods, all blue and purple fire in a fraction of a heartbeat. The peal of thunder made Mac cower, but Tommy wasn't afraid. The silent dead beside him took it as a battle cry, raising their arms and letting out their silent screams. Their bony feet sounded like pebbles on soft earth. Ahead they ran, Tommy among them, Mac trying to keep up with a paw he clearly didn't want to use. The pup was nothing if not loyal, and Tommy was going to spoil this good boy rotten after today.

In the lights from the house, he could see the gangly form of Reid climb out of the Kitchen door into the yard, unfold himself, and cry out a challenge with a voice like grinding metal and glass. The dead swarmed him, tearing at flesh and hair, spreading grisly, bloodless muscle and sinew around in the dark. The smaller, sharper bones of the tiny hands attacked from all around, specifically tearing flesh and trying to pull apart joints. The Reid-thing did not give easily, and though it lost pieces, in handful-sized chunks, the flesh still clung to a strong set of twisted bones.

Tommy broke past them all, dodging a pair of swinging leg bones, and stepping into the house. Like any good carpenter, he knew exactly where his tools were, safely locked away where they belonged. Sitting where he'd left it since the last demolition, he hefted the sledgehammer from its resting place beside a toolbox. Mac stepped beside him, sniffing the air. Tommy heard the cry of pain from the next room, and his stomach churned. He knew that voice, and it terrified him as much as it lit his fury. He peered around the corner, and saw the naked gray girl holding Tatiana on the floor with her foot, her clothing torn, and using a small knife to cut into her back. Next to them was the corpse of corporal Miles. Neither was paying attention. Tommy could take two quick steps and take out at least one of them. He did not hesitate. His foot went forward for the first step, and the floor made its trademark creak. He was too far into his stride to go back, but Miles was turning, with the gun. Tommy started his swing before his foot landed for the second step. Heavy metal connected with wet flesh and bone, slamming Miles's head backwards, causing the skin to tear, and blood to splatter away from the gaping hole. The gun fired, but without aiming, missing Tommy completely and puncturing the drywall. Mac tackled the corpse, biting at the stringy remains of the neck. Tommy hefted the sledge again, and looked to the dead girl. Even in the floodlights, her skin was still gray like cooked meat. Her eyes were black spheres. She had been carving some strange sigils into Tatiana's back. Tatiana's face ran with blood and tears.

Tommy went to swing at the dead girl, but he wasn't fast enough. She opened her mouth, and that vile shrieking noise she'd made in his dream came out, hitting Tommy hard as if the full weight of his blow had been bounced back to him. Tommy went sprawling backwards. He couldn't pull air into his lungs, but he still tried to get back up. She was walking over to him now, and in the light she looked far worse than he could have imagined. Her head was covered in gnarled, stringy hair, flying wildly in the air like millions of writhing worms. Tommy tried to heft the hammer again, but she pointed a finger, and spoke another sound like glass being dragged on granite.

The sledge flew from Tommy's hands as if it had taken flight, and it smashed through the wall next to the chimney, crashing through to the other side and landing somewhere in the darkness outside. He looked at his hands, then back at the grinning monster child.

"You are Thomas?" she said, her voice now sing-song sweet.

"What?" Tommy said, as much because she'd actually spoken as that her voice and tone were dripping innocence from a mouth of blood.

"You freed me," she said, "You took my body from this house, removed the binding. Your kindred pain awakened me. You found my diary and let the Dream Maker free... I thank you. I may allow you to live if you leave now."

Tommy didn't know what to say. His eyes went to Tatiana, who was trying to get off the floor, but some pain or binding was preventing her. In the dark, he could see some of his cables for the electricity had been used to bind her down.

Mary Worthington looked back, following his gaze.

"Oh, she will die. I need a blood sacrifice to be completely whole."

Mary paused, looking back to Tommy with her head tilted a little to the side, like she was listening to some far-off noise.

"You intend to defy me," she said, "Like the others did. The Magistrate and his false-god preacher. They imprisoned me here. They drowned the slaves I had used to revolt against my father. It's just as well. I would have had to slaughter them, too. They knew too much and would have tried to stop me before my work was complete."

Another battle cry shook the house, as outside, the thing that was Dr. Reid fought on against the corpses. The dead woman regarded this with a small smile.

"You raised them, didn't you? How?"

Tommy had no words. He should have had a response, something witty and insulting, but all he could do was shrug. His imagination had often conjured him as a strong, courageous man, but here he was, flapping his mouth to no effect against a teenage girl.

The house shook, something had impacted violently against it. Lightning crashed into the ground outside, causing the lights to flicker. The dead woman looked into Tommy's eyes.

"Such suffering," she said, "I know that pain. Abandoned, tortured by those who are supposed to love you. Do not fear. Your time in that pain is over."

Another shriek, and Tommy fell. The floor beneath him vanished into uncountable splinters, sending him crashing hard onto the stone foundation of the basement. Darkness swallowed him. He could barely hear a growl and some struggling above him. It sounded like Mac. Tommy tried to roll over, get to his feet, but everything on his body screamed in burning, cutting agony.

He could see, through shafts of light from the floor above, another tool box. He knew what was in this box. Maybe it wasn't enough, but it was something. He had the key, somewhere, in his pocket. He reached into the denim, found the keys, but as he pulled, a searing pain screamed at him from his thigh. His keys were stabbed into his flesh, and now stuck there. His hands trembled. He needed to push through. He could cry about this for weeks, for years, he could carry this trauma like he carried others, but he needed to get those keys!

He seized a piece of wood from nearby and put it between his teeth. Then he grabbed the keys by the ring.

He counted. One. Two. Three.

Then he pulled, and the keys came out with some pieces of his flesh. The pain made him cry out in something between a moan and a scream.

He crawled over to the tool box. The key was sticky with blood, but it slid inside and turned. He flipped open the latch. There sat the beautiful gleaming black plastic casing. He lifted the tool up, taking the battery pack and sliding it in like a gun magazine. Up above, he could hear Mac skitter back across the floor, growling still. Tommy watched the sub-flooring move, as weight shifted. He managed to get on his shaky legs, and heft the tool up. He watched as the weight shifted again overhead. He stuck the tool to the sub-flooring and pulled the trigger. A loud thunk sounded, and above him came the dead woman's scream. It wasn't one of those horrible shrieks, but actual pain. Tommy used the nail gun again, several times, ensuring the dead woman's foot would be trapped. He heard the stamp of the other foot, and used the nail gun again, trying to catch the other foot. Three more thunks had the dead woman's feet trapped, screaming and spitting fury.

Tommy felt some small satisfaction, but he had to do something else, soon. He tried to remember what else he had down here. He was fairly certain his circular saw was nearby, but he wouldn't have time to find it, and he had no usable extension cord for power. It could still be dangerous to swing, though. No, he had to move fast, clear his mind. He knew where his tools were. It was like a map in his brain.

He heard Mac growling again, barking, and felt the thuds as the pup made another charge. This time he heard the full weight hit the dead woman, and she seemed to fall back onto the floor, loosing dust down upon him. Tommy didn't waste his chance. More screams of pain and fury followed the thunk of each nail he put through the flooring, drawing an imaginary outline of her body.. A dark black blood was starting to dribble down from the broken flooring, oozing through the woodwork.

Tommy ran out of nails. He put the gun back into the box, then climbed up the cellar steps, feeling more than a little proud of himself. The elation at his own ingenuity lasted only a moment, but he would carry that pride forever.

He returned to the dining room to see the screaming, spitting dead woman on her back, her knees up, and her feet kept flat to the floor, despite her attempts to tear away, which only spread her tar-like blood all over the place. Mac was going after her again, chewing on her neck, keeping her from making any coherent sound. Mac looked positively feral, channeling that wild dog DNA.

Tatiana had crawled over, and was using the cables that bound her as a weapon, slamming her bound hands onto the woman's face over and over. She was sobbing and bleeding, pounding her fists into the dead woman with hateful agony. Tommy let her. Tatiana had earned this. He wouldn't stop her.

Mary Worthington pulled an arm free from the floor, tearing gray skin completely off, and in some cases pulling the nails right through. She caught Tatiana by the hair, twisting and yanking hard, pulling Tatiana off balance. Tommy came forward, but not quickly enough. The dead woman opened her mouth again, and that baleful shriek pierced his skull, sending Tommy to his knees, cradling his head in his hands. Mac fell away, whimpering and bolting out of the room. More of that shrieking filled the air, and Tommy looked up through bloody tears to see the nails that held her down were rising into the air. Tommy forced a foot beneath him to push away, to get some distance. The little glinting shards of metal spun and danced in the light, dripping ink-black blood, before aligning towards him. Like a swarm of bloodied wasps, they flew at Tommy. His stumbling retreat saved him from some, but several nails intruded into his flesh and sent fresh pain-fire through him. He cried out and took a few stumbling steps, falling to his knees again.

The pain of the nails was fleeting compared to the electric pulse in his head, he saw his blood staining the floor in front of him. He was dizzy, bleeding from almost everywhere.

He could feel her approaching, that weight on the floorboards. He knew this time, she would kill him. He could almost feel a strange, pleasant peace come over him at the thought. It was a mere heartbeat, for his next thought was about Mac, Tatiana, and her little girl. He'd brought this suffering upon them. He would die with a heavy soul, one that would weigh him down. He would be trapped in a familiar pattern, one he had already grown used to. He would be just another trapped soul on these grounds, reliving misery.

It was an old ache, a terrible one, but one he had endured before. But the others did not deserve that. If he was going to die and suffer, he would at least do that alone.

Tommy rallied and made one last attempt to lunge at Mary. Mid-turn, her clawed hand raked across his face, drawing jagged parallel lines of crimson, and just barely missing scratching his eyes to the pupil.

Tommy fell back, blood dripping in his eyes and running down eyelashes. He opened his mouth, but no words, no scream, nothing came forth but a simple, resigned sigh.

He had been so focused on Mary, he barely registered the movement behind her. But he did see when the light shifted. Tatiana's figure was in shadow, hefting the floodlights above her head like a mallet. She brought them down on Mary's head, lights-first. Glass exploded and the room went dark but for the flickering of sparks and occasional electric arcs jumping through the dead woman's body. Tatiana ran to Tommy and helped him up off the floor. Mac joined them and seemed to push Tommy with his muzzle towards the door. Tommy took shaky steps to the front door, practically carried, but he didn't let the weakness stop him. He just let his loved ones support what he couldn't. Beyond was dark night, and the storm. In flashes of light from the electric spears striking the Earth, they saw the lanky form of the thing that had been Dr. Reid, flesh scraped nearly bare, down to muscle, dangling chunks of skin and dripping black onto the ground as the rain washed vital fluid away from the gaping wounds.

Its empty sockets looked in their direction, let out a hideous cry, and approached them. Several of the dead still were trying to catch up and harm it, but many had been ripped to jagged pieces, unable to even follow, let alone do harm. Mac growled and held his ground.

Tatiana gripped Tommy so tight that he could feel her fingers dig in almost as badly as the nails did.

The thing was within two long strides of them. Its elongated fingers could seize them within seconds. Tommy turned back to the house, and the lilting front porch with its weight leaning on old supports. He needed to replace those, and the roof... Why not start the demolition now?

Tommy pulled Tatiana hard by the shoulders and threw them both against the support beam, taking the brunt of the contact himself and causing the rotted wood to split. The wood cracked, snapping in half, just as the Reid thing came closer. Timber crashed down between them and it, frightening Mac back into the house. All Tommy could see was dust, but he pulled Tatiana with him back through the door. Mac was bounding up the stairs, and he had no better ideas than to follow. To his left, he could just see the outline of a smoldering form rising from the floor, and even in the darkness, he sensed the seething hatred from those cold, dead eyes.

Tatiana found her feet and ran with him up the stairs behind Mac. At the landing, Tommy turned immediately into the half-finished bathroom. He grabbed the pedestal sink he'd loosened at one point, and hefted the heavy porcelain thing, turning back to the stairs. A shadow was coming up fast.

Tommy threw the sink, and it smashed into something heavy, shattering and sending whatever it was tumbling backwards again. That elation of victory fluttered through his heart once more, and lasted only a moment.

A shriek sounded and the floor beneath Tommy and Tatiana began to quake. He pushed her down the hall, just as the floorboard burst into flames, ignited by Mary's hellish power. Heat licked up the bare wood fast, and smoke began to rise.

Between them and safety were deadly smoke and the desiccated Mary. Tatiana started to the right for the steps to the master bedroom, but Tommy grabbed her and pulled in the other direction. She resisted at first, but fell in behind him going up the stairs to the left. Only now seeing the walking corpses, the shambling family, the siblings and aunts and people lost to time did he finally figure out what had been missing. It was the only thing that made sense to him, the only thing that explained anything. This home hadn't been a tomb for just one body...

Tommy pushed through the door at the top of those stairs. There sat the grisly scene he'd been avoiding, but by instinct or some subconscious plan, here was the room in the spire. Before him was the large hexagonal window that looked out over the property. The room remained exactly as he'd left it, but there in the corner, the huddled mass of rags left on the chair in the corner, the source of that ungodly stench, remained inert in the gloom. He turned back to see the silhouette of Mary standing in the door frame. Lightning from behind them flashed and revealed the gleeful malice in her eyes. Tommy put himself in front of Tatiana and Mac, edging them back towards the window. Mary lifted her lips back from her teeth, like a wolf.

Out of the corner of his eye, Tommy saw something stir. In this ancient nursery, in this room that had no key, the sole occupant stirred. It rose from its place in the chair in the corner, shedding rotted scraps of thread and cloth as it stood on bony legs. The oily mess of her old garb fell to pieces on the floor. Mary froze.

The bones crossed the room, tatters of old cloth, cobwebs, and over two centuries of dust falling to the floor with each step. The lightning shone on the skull of a long dead woman in a rotted old dress. Yet, in the flashes between the lightning, Tommy had an image burned into his retinas, of that kind face that greeted him in the misty dream. It looked at Mary with great sadness. Tommy could see the resemblance in his mind's eye, and felt the warmth extending from her, an intangible, yet unbreakable force. Gossamer strands of intangible silk drifted towards Mary. Mary had frozen, but now a trembling, gray hand caked with blood trembled before her dried lips.

"M-mother..." she said. The madness fled from her eyes, and with halting steps, the charred Mary approached the standing bones. If the dead could shed tears, she would have. She hesitated, almost stepped back into the smoke and flame that slowly ate its way up the stairs. But a single strand of web-like nothingness landed, and Mary seemed to quiver. The death-stained rags closed in on her, enveloping her.

The corpses embraced, and something like a low wail came from deep within the folds of the ancient thread. The empty skull turned to Tommy, and a single pearl of light shone within. The room began getting hazy with smoke. The available air was getting thinner, choked with smoke or consumed by the growing fire. It seemed it was this house's destiny to burn, like Linda had said months ago. Everyone had told him to burn it down. It was a joke then. He didn't smile until now.

Tommy turned to see the big window behind them. The wood holding the old panes of glass was weak, rotted like the rest of the house, exposed to the assault of New England's bipolar weather for centuries, it could crumble with just a little force.

If he broke that glass, the rush of oxygen would cause the fire to surge. He remembered that, some random item he learned from dealing with inspectors or insurance people, or maybe even from his father. He could almost feel the pressure weakening the wooden bonds. He looked back to the dead woman, to Mother Worthington. The skull nodded ever so slightly.

Tommy swallowed hard. Mac was panting desperately and whining at his leg. He bent down to pick up the pup, who almost jumped into his arms, the pain in his body from every cut, bruise, scrape and nail screamed at once. He had to grit his teeth and pull in a long, but shallow breath. He looked at Tatiana, and nodded to the window. Her eyes went wide and she shook her head. There wasn't time to argue. The fire was crawling towards them, and the smoke was starting to envelope the bodies, who seemed to be sobbing against one another in tearless agony, or perhaps bliss. Either way, they were burning together.

Tommy took her hand. She shook her head again, terrified. He gripped her hand tight, tight enough to hurt. The oily garb began to catch licks of flame, and the leathery dry skin of Mary had begun to smolder anew. The heat was blistering. Tommy shut his eyes. He had never taken a leap of faith before. He never had a reason to.

One push.

If the window broke, but they didn't fall through, they'd be dead in an instant anyway.

Dark rivers of smoke rose up into the angled roof of the spire. Tommy swallowed. He threw his aching body back, and for half a second, almost expected to land in cool water.

Glass shattered into a rain of glistening shards, falling around them like a lethal ice storm. Tommy fell with Mac in one arm, Tatiana sailing beside him, their hands clasped. The moment stretched out in front of him, the speed of life slowed to a crawl. He had time to watch the lightning flash off the glass shards, casting electric blue fire into the air around them. He felt Mac scrabble with his feet against Tommy, terrified and instinctively scrambling for purchase. He saw Tatiana's face as she screamed, but the sound was lost in thunder. The storm still raged, peppering them with icy rain, and every drop measured a tick in this stretched time. Tommy was certain this would end him. He pulled Mack and Tatiana close so he could break their fall. He would use his body to cushion the fall. Tatiana had a daughter, Mac was innocent... He shut his eyes and prepared himself for the crunching pain, the last he'd ever feel.

He did land hard, but his weight and momentum crashed into something that slowed his fall. It felt like thin slats of wood catching him, and then he landed on soft muddy ground. Mac bounced off of Tommy's chest, rolling over and away, but scrambling to get back up immediately and kicking up thick mud. It was too dark to see very much until the surge of fire erupted out of the eye of the spire, and Tommy saw dozens of the dead, several smashed to pieces around him. They'd caught him and Tatiana. They knew he was going to jump, and they caught him. He breathed a quiet thank you to Mother Worthington. It wouldn't be until much later that he began to wonder if it had been her plan from the beginning.

Looking down, he saw he was lying on top of their bones, and some of them poked painfully into his back. He pulled himself up and off of them, shedding glass, blood, and shards of bone. Everything hurt, in dull pain, sharp pain, hot and cold pain, too much for him to wrap his head around. He could barely get to his knees, and it hurt to breathe. He could only pull in short, shallow breaths. Was his vision going dark, or was it the contrast after the fire? He couldn't tell. Everything beyond the flames was darkness. When Mac came up to nuzzle him, he almost fell over. The poor pup seemed confused and afraid, but again, loyal and determined to stay by his side.

From around the side of the house, a shadow broke from the gloom, taking long, loping steps as it flung bony shapes off of it. It turned towards the front of the house, where they sat bathed in the light of the burning tower.

It looked directly at him, and its face, already twisted into a painful grin, grimaced and ripped more flesh as something like rage came over its stolen face.

It stalked towards them. The lanky form of the Reid-thing shambled forward, limping, its body ravaged by damage from bony hands. It barely kept its own bones together, stitched only by threads of sinew and cartilage. Its flesh smoldered, caught in the rapidly spreading fire. It screeched at them, reaching forward.

All around Tommy and Tatiana, the bones rose up again, and put themselves between the monster, and the living people.

More skeletal limbs reached out of the darkness and began to seize the arms and legs of the thing. The remaining dead swarmed it from the shadows, ripping the creature limb from twisted limb. It fought back, but each time it swept a body aside, it lost a piece of itself to the fray. The army of the dead took each piece and added it to the burgeoning inferno.

Despite the screams and those shrieks of power that rent the very air and shattered bone, the creature's jaw was taken, then its throat. It could only emit a thin wheezing noise with its dead, ashen lungs. It was like watching ants disassemble a dead beetle, pulling each gruesome piece of gray meat off the twisted bones and adding every last bit to the blaze.

Soon, the house had become a massive pyre, the flames rising high into the night, overshadowing the stars themselves. The power line snapped and fizzled, lashing out from the home like an angry snake. Mac limped back over to Tommy and nudged him. That wet nose spurred Tommy back to his senses. Tatiana still stared in wordless shock at the burning wreckage of the house, the roof beginning a slow collapse inward as the timber below buckled. It looked like the house was swallowing itself. She noticed the standing, grime-covered bones and let out a scream. But no one moved. Even the standing corpses did not react to her fear. They just watched the blaze. Tommy could see black wetness leaking from their sockets. He held Tatiana's hand in the dark. She squeezed his knuckles hard enough to crack them, but the sound was inaudible over the sizzling and snapping of flame.

The bodies around them watched the burning home for several moments, then, all at once, they turned and walked calmly back towards the lake, their pace sedate, their demeanor one of fatigue, and a desire for rest. Tatiana watched them go, her jaw moving without sound until she finally squeaked out something coherent.

"Is... Is it over?"

In answer, heat bloomed from the house, and sent an eruption of sparks high into the air, dancing along the column of smoke and crackling like firecrackers as old pitch and worn timber blackened to ash.

Only a handful of the dead remained, standing statue-still in the firelight, watching the fire above them all with faces incapable of expression. Yet Tommy was sure he could see a twisted mix of relief and loss, of the release of pain, the guilt of their actions and the compounded guilt of their relief. These people had claimed their revenge, and still found themselves empty.

He looked down at his muddy, bloodied hands. He swallowed hard and shed tears, his breath coming in shallow sobs. One of the skulls looked his way, a taller one, he couldn't divine which person it had been. But he looked into the sockets as if they were living eyes, and knew this familial pain was one they shared. This was a Worthington, though what generation or name, he couldn't say. But it gave a slight tilt of its dirt-crusted head, and turned to the rest of the assembled spirits. As if of one mind, they turned away from the inferno.

The bones made their slow trek back to their resting places, some carrying armfuls of their friends and family, returning to the dark earth or darker lake, dividing by family and by victim, to their respective resting places in the ground or the depths. Tommy saw one figure pause, looking back at them. It seemed like it was trying to speak to him, but no words were carried to him on the breeze. He did feel a vague sense that he had their gratitude, that they were now free from Mary's curse. It wasn't language, nor a look in the eyes, for the bones were capable of neither. But Tommy knew, the way any broken child knows, that it was time to let the fire burn out, and find a peaceful place to rest.

The fire consumed everything, and burned so hot that by the time the fire department arrived, all they could do was prevent the whole forest from going up. Tommy and Tatiana had retreated to the street by then, and watched the remaining supports holding the manor aloft crumble down. The trees were too wet to spread the fire very much, but the heat was enormous, and rapidly drying out everything. The windows of Tommy's trailer were bowed inward, and the tail lights of his truck were drooping slightly, the bumper having developed blisters.

But the skies were clearing, and beneath that frosted sky, a silver moon shone once more, and cast a majestic light down on the woods. Tommy could see the reflection of that silver crescent in the ripples of the lake.

There were questions, oh so many questions, but Tommy stuck to his story of being attacked by Dr. Reid, and an unknown assailant, who set fire to his house. He gave his statement while an EMT pulled glass shards and nails from his back. Tatiana had bandages everywhere. She backed up his story, showing them the things Mary had carved in her back.

He never asked what the ultimate outcome of the investigation was. His hospital stay and recuperation brought different police and an insurance adjuster to ask him questions. He answered them again and again, leaving out every shred of truth.

His time in the hospital felt longer than the agonizing time he'd spent at his father's house when he was young. Though instead of his stepmother's cold, manipulative stare, he had to contend with the gaze of judgmental nurses and bland food. Tatiana was a few rooms down, and would often come in to see him. She couldn't sleep for the nightmares, and was desperately afraid to even see her daughter again. She didn't know how she'd hide the scars. Tommy held her as soon as he was physically able, and let her weep into his shoulder. He shed a few of his own tears with her.

Tommy didn't know what to do, either. He'd put everything he had into that house. Even if he went back to work and took ungodly amounts of overtime, he'd be living out of his truck for months. If the insurance paid out to him, it would only be to the value of what was lost, which would leave him, if he generously estimated it, at a net loss.

After half a week, Tommy was released. Tatiana had left sooner, as she needed to get back to her child.

With nothing else to do, Tommy went out to the property, to survey the wreckage.

The house was ash all the way down to the stone foundation, which was still warm to the touch, or perhaps that was just the sun beating down on it all morning. Part of him wanted to believe that the ashes that had buried his tools were only from the house, and not a single charred atom of any Worthington body remained. Tommy looked across the property to the distant lake, and tried not to think of the slime-coated bones that lurked on its bottom. They were there for him, for their own revenge, their own justice, not his. When he realized who they were, what they were, he realized that alone might have soured him on the property in the first place.

His lost nestegg, by comparison, was a minor sleight. He kicked a tiny lump of charcoal, almost vindictively, like he could force it to surrender his money. But a second later, his shoulders slumped. The catharsis was a pointless exercise now.

He went into Ingham, Mac at his side, to get some food. He and Mac sat outside and devoured some cheap cheeseburgers at one of the four plazas with populated stores, his battered body baking in the sun, cooking above the black asphalt. Mac was the smart one, who immediately hopped into his truck bed on the scorching hot day. Tommy followed for fear of the rubber melting off his shoes.

Together they shared some terrible, ketchup-soaked grease piles and over-salted fries. Around him, cars eased into the drive-through lane. Birds chirped and darted around thin trees planted to give the plaza the appearance of something natural.

Tatiana would be ok. Her injuries were slight compared to his. The carvings on her back were shallow, and the scars would fade quickly. He talked to her over the phone a few times, and it was hard not to both break down in tears here and there. He noticed she would start to sound a little slurred by the end of the calls. He didn't begrudge her any of it. But he did make her promise to put the bottles away if Maya was home, just as a personal favor.

She did not react well at first.

"*What the hell, who do you think-*"

"She's smart," he said, "Smarter than I was at that age. She'll know. And no, she's not my kid, but she's a *good kid*. She should feel that way."

That gave her pause. That got her to agree.

His thoughts were chased away when a large bulk with an avocado nose came into view. The man smiled at Tommy and swaggered over.

"Damn, son, I heard about what happened. I'm glad you're okay," said George. He kicked some dirt, seeming a little anxious about something.

Tommy shrugged, "More or less."

"Jesus, I was just pulling your leg about that cursed stuff. I'm real sorry. Truth was, a lot of us was hoping you'd really pull it off. Woulda been a fine house. Get some rich Hollywood lib to move in and then we coulda taxed the shit outta him." He grinned a little too wide for that comment to have been just a joke.

"No, it's fine," Tommy said, "I'm fine."

Here, George's grin faltered a bit. "Well, look, uh... You know, we... I mean, me and the guys, were talking it over. And I was hoping we'd see you again, kid. Well, if you need a place to stay and lick your wounds, I know old Franklin will put you up for a while. He's got a little apartment above his garage ain't nobody using."

"Really?" Tommy asked, surprising even himself at his eagerness and the sudden swell of hope.

"Well, shit, yeah. And if you're looking for work, too, this town needs a good handyman. Old Earl's good, but his hands are getting weak, you know. And only other good handyman around here got the DT's half the time. It's odd jobs, but you know, until you can get your shit together. If you want it."

Tommy smiled. "I'd love that. Yeah, let me give you my number. Just let me get my feet under me, insurance money come in and replace my tools, you know?"

George nodded. He climbed up onto the tailgate to sit with Tommy and Mac. He took off his red cap and wiped his forehead sweat.

"Ya know, when I was your age," he said, and Tommy could feel a really long story coming on. But this time, he didn't mind. George talked, at great length, his rambling stories oddly comforting now. He made crude jokes, he smelled only a little bit like beer, and he put his arm on Tommy's shoulder and offered to let Tommy use his own workshop in his garage for as long as he needed.

They exchanged numbers, on paper because George didn't have a cell phone. Then after the older man walked away, Tommy picked up his garbage, ushered Mac into the cab, and they drove over to visit Tatiana and Maya. He really hoped that Tatiana would still want to be with him. He was preparing himself to be sent away, bracing himself against the real possibility that the trauma and memory would be too much.

Each step going up to that apartment, his legs felt heavier and heavier.

He didn't want to lose her. Heck, he didn't want to lose Maya, either. He could live with the manor reduced to ashes. It had never been the home he wanted to begin with.

His heavy boot-steps brought him to the door. It opened, and a smiling Tatiana, mid-laughter, looked him over. He sucked in a breath.

"Come on in," she said, "We're playing Mario Kart."

"And Mommy's losing!" Maya called from the couch.

Mac trotted inside, and he heard Maya squeal with delight. He followed behind, and left his fears outside.

· · · ·

On a beach of bone-white sand, with shade from the long canopy of palm trees, wide blue waves caressed the shore. The gentle whispers were calming, and under a wide-brimmed straw hat, an older man watched the clouds roll past with happy indifference. He was accomplishing nothing, and it felt better than anything else he'd achieved in his life.

A warm wind rolled over him, and he watched it play with the whitening hair on his arms. This peace shattered at the sound of the buzzing noise. Beside him, on a small wicker table, a flip-phone vibrated. It was probably that damned lawyer again, but when he picked it up, the info said it was a phone number from Rhode Island, US. He was briefly puzzled, but then he wondered if this could be his son. He flipped it open and raised it to his ear.

"Hello," he said.

"Hey, uh... Dad," said Tommy.

It was his son, but not the one he expected. He looked at the number on the little screen again, then raised the phone back to his ear.

"My boy... How the hell did you get this number?"

"Well, it wasn't easy," said Tommy, "But that's not important. Look, I wanted to tell you that, uh... Well, you were right."

The old man wasn't sure whether he should be flattered or not.

"Shit, boy, you on something?" he asked.

"No, Dad, listen."

"Is this about the house I told you not to buy?"

"... Yes, but something else you were right about."

He chuckled and took off his hat. His phone was bumping against it and it was getting in the way.

"Wow, I get a two-fer. What happened with the house?"

"Burned to the ground," said Tommy, "Sold the land to a developer. Again, not important. It's the other thing you were right about. About living life. And, well... God, this is hard."

"Take it one step at a time, boy. Nobody's running a race here. But I am dying of curiosity."

The pause on the other end took a long time, and he could hear his son breathing. He was clearly working his way up to something.

"Well, Dad... You're gonna be a grandpa."

"Hot shit!" he said, "Really? Wait, you get married in the last year?"

"No, no. But I did meet someone, and we're living together."

"Damn, she ain't like Margot, is she?"

"No, Dad! Jesus, let me talk!"

"Sorry, I'm just... just excited. Happy for you."

Tommy took a breath. "Her name's Tatiana, and she's absolutely amazing. She already has a daughter, but, well... Now little Maya is gonna have a half-sibling."

The old man let out a joyous laugh. "Sounds like you finally found what you were looking for, kid. I'm glad. That really makes my day."

"Well, it's a long way off yet, but I wanted you to know."

"You gonna call your Mom?"

"God, no," said Tommy, "If I've learned anything this year, it's you don't hold onto things that hurt you."

He raised an eyebrow at that. "But you're calling me?"

"Don't ruin it, Dad. Anyway, we've got a little house in Warwick now, and would love for you to-"

A high-pitched squeal came on the line, and Tommy laughed. The phone banged. A second later, Tommy's voice came back on.

"Hang on, Precious, I just want to finish my call, okay?"

"Okay, Daddy," said the voice, and he could hear skipping footsteps and a sing-song melody from a happy child.

"Sorry, Dad," said Tommy.

"Don't apologize. Never apologize for that. But, ah... Daddy?"

"It's, uh... Tatiana's daughter, Maya. What can I say? She's been doing that for a couple months now. I guess I'm an improvement over her bio dad."

"Well look at you," he said, his chuckling became a warm laugh that was lost in the sound of crashing waves.

"Yeah," said Tommy. They shared a peaceful silence, the second in their history, but a welcome one.

"Text me your address and let me know when I got a Grandkid. And in the meantime, you go and love the heck out of the people you found."

Tommy was quiet for a long moment. "I will."

"And don't do it because you have to. Do it if it makes you happy."

"... It does. Honestly, I couldn't be happier."

"Good. I'll text you *my* address, and you can send me post cards. I love ya, boy."

Tommy echoed the sentiment, and hung up the phone.

The old man stared out at the white-tipped waves and smiled. Maybe he did something right. He hadn't done much right, but maybe he did one thing right. He put the phone down and stood, stretching in the sun. He threw off his hat and loose shirt, then walked down the hot sands to take another swim. The cool water would feel good on his sun-burned skin. The word 'Grandpa' flicked through his head, and he liked the sound of it. He looked forward to painting a family portrait.

Epilogue

As he stood looking at the huge swath of land he'd just purchased, Bill Wyatt smiled and rubbed his hands together. He could see it now. A perfect little cul-de-sac, he could fit ten, maybe a dozen luxury homes on this property, *and* call it waterfront. Hell, there was already a well and a big oil tank. The land had untapped potential. He strode among the dried weeds and looked at the empty expanse. The one thing marring the property were the ashes of the old house, but that was easy enough to clear. His feet crunched on old, dead grass and weeds, gritty dirt and dry rocks. The wind brushed away some more ashen remains into the air as tiny black wraiths.

Branching out, that's how it was done. With his own people clearing the land, and a guy he knew doing construction, he could keep the costs at a minimum. Why, each home would probably cost only about a hundred thousand dollars to build, and he would recoup more than triple that on each house. He could almost taste the money rolling in. All this empty land would be pure profit waiting to pour into his bank account. He was so glad that friend of his Project Manager clued him in to this place. Talk about a motivated seller! He bought the entire plot for a song.

He kicked something in the grass and frowned. He knelt down and found a small, leather-bound book. It looked old, like it had come from some library a hundred years ago. He opened it and it had the scrawlings and scribblings of a teenage girl.

He laughed. Maybe there was still some trash that needed to get cleared. Well, his people could do that. He just wanted to get a look at the place for himself. Unlike Bramblewood, this land was better suited for homes rather than condos. After all, condos didn't have the resale value that homes did, no matter how many units you crammed together. He could get up to half a million per, if the market held steady. Now *that* was a dream come true! Boom or bust business was always profitable if you bought low and sold high.

For some reason, he slipped the book into his pocket and headed back to his gleaming BMW. He wouldn't even remember doing it, later, when the book appeared on his office desk.

A little piece of paper fluttered down from the trees, something like notebook paper, with a single word scrawled on it in uneven letters. "*Dream*"

He barely noticed it. Ignored it. It was beneath him. He had things to do. More land to acquire, more houses to build, more money to make. Fast cars and loose women didn't buy themselves, and you never slowed down, not if you could make those numbers go up even more. He could have a fleet of new cars with the profits from this project. He could have more. He always needed more. He craved more. He dreamed of more.

Afterword

I do truly hope you enjoyed this book. The haunted house trope is so thoroughly and definitively explored that I wanted to bring something new to the table. This, coinciding with a period in history when housing prices are absolutely and completely bananas, and that house flipping is not only a genuine occupation but a premise for at least a dozen reality shows, opened a door that I don't think anyone had stepped through yet.

If someone has gone through that door before me, I hope at least we wound up doing things differently in this strained metaphor.

I was somewhat limited, initially, by the fact that I don't actually know anything about house flipping, or actually watch any of those house flipping shows. I have looked at a LOT of really amazingly awful houses that were within my price range. There was a shocking amount of material to mine there. The house in this book is completely fictitious, but some parts are based on real things I've seen, which is why it might seem like a disjointed Frankenstein's monster in descriptions.

But the story isn't really about the house, it's about Tommy.

What began as a story about a haunted house became a story about enduring abuse as a child, which was even harder for me to write about because I find that topic utterly abhorrent to my entire being. The true horror in this book is what ordinary people do.

The house is just the backdrop.

That idea alone took me about four years to develop, off an on, as the first chapter sat on my hard drive untouched while I poured myself into writing *Icon*. That's also why it stayed there for a couple of years after.

Icon was a flash-in-the-pan story that appeared in my head almost fully formed.

Good Bones was a labor, a struggle, an uphill battle the likes of which would make Sisyphus cry tears of blood, if he wasn't doing that already. I have written and deleted dozens of pages that just literally went nowhere and added nothing. And then I've sat down and hammered out entire massive sections of intense psychological development that made me cry at the keyboard.

So I sincerely hope you've enjoyed it. And if you didn't, then at least appreciate the effort that went into it, and the cover art, and maybe recommend it to a friend who likes deep psychological and Lovecraftian horror.

But more than anything else, thank you for giving this book a go. And if you yourself have struggled to heal from past trauma, I hope this book helped in some way.

About the Author

Peter J Larrivee is a horror and weird fiction writer from the Land of Lovecraft. He's been published in *Perihelion, Night Terrors Volume 21*, the *Hell is for Children* charity anthology and on *Trembling with Fear*. In addition, he is a long time contributor to Motif Magazine, an arts and entertainment publication.

When not working or crafting nightmares, he can usually be found in bookstores or out with his family.

Read more at https://petelarrivee.wordpress.com/.

CPSIA information can be obtained
at www.ICGtesting.com
Printed in the USA
JSHW081729060723
44214JS00001B/41